Love Finds You™

~ *in* ~

HOPE

—— ❧ ——

K A N S A S

❀ Hope Carlson ❀

Love Finds You™

~ *in* ~

HOPE

KANSAS

BY PAMELA GRIFFIN

summerside
PRESS™

Summerside Press™
Minneapolis 55438
www.summersidepress.com

Cover Design by Lookout Design | www.lookoutdesign.com

Interior Design by Müllerhaus Publishing Group | www.mullerhaus.net

Photos of Hope and surrounding prairieland are public domain.

*Summerside Press™ is an inspirational publisher offering fresh, irresistible
books to uplift the heart and engage the mind.*

Printed in USA.

Dedication

· · · · · · · · · · · · · · · · · ·

First and foremost to my Lord and Savior, the author of all hope,
the One who grants all dreams—I owe You everything.

Also, to my wonderful critique partners, Theo and Mom—
you are the best, and I would be lost without you.

And to my sons, Brandon and Joshua—
thank you for always being there.
Even when times were tough, we
"three musketeers" survived through
the difficulties, and I will never forget how
you have always stood by me.

And to my father—thank you for all your
support through the years.

I love all of you and am grateful that you're in my life.

And now, Lord, what wait I for? my hope is in thee.

PSALM 39:7 KJV

Hope, Kansas

NESTLED BETWEEN LYONS CREEK AND TURKEY CREEK LIES THE TOWN of Hope. It is thought to be named for the son of one of its founders—part of a group of approximately forty Michigan Civil War veterans and craftsmen who planned the town site.

Prominent among Hope's citizens was Wesley Swayze, grandfather of John Cameron Swayze—a famous news commentator, commercial spokesman, and game-show panelist of the 1950s and '60s and distant relation of the late actor Patrick Swayze. David Eisenhower, the father of President Dwight D. Eisenhower, operated a general store in Hope with his partner, Milton Good, in 1885.

The Topeka, Salina & Western Railroad arrived that same year. In 1887 the Santa Fe Railroad followed, which made Chicago's grain and livestock available to Hope. Bustling with new settlers and receiving commodities by train, the town quickly grew.

The settlement stands on high ground amid a rolling prairie of towering grass. Once devoid of trees aside from the hackberries, cottonwoods, ash, and elm along the creeks' bottoms, long inclines now lie rich with mazes of hedgerows, cedar windbreaks, and picturesque farmhouses and silos. The scenic view is one reason Hope is memorable to many.

Pamela Griffin

Chapter One
....

Hope, Kansas
Midsummer 1889

"Don't just stand there with your mouth hangin' open like a fish. Do you want a new ma or don't you?" Andy directed the tense question to their little sister, Maggie, who hovered outside the stable door in clear indecision about whether to join them.

"Yeth," she whistled through the space of her two missing front teeth.

"Where's Baby Lynn?" Sam wanted to know. She hoped their little sister hadn't been left unattended.

"I finally got her to thleep. Thee was awful futhy."

"It's a good thing she's napping and not nosing around." Andy clasped one hand over the wrist hooked around his bent knees. "She's too young to keep secrets. Now get in here, Mags, and shut that door. If Pa sees you lurking outside and gets wind of what we're doing, we're all as good as doomed."

Maggie did as ordered, moving across the barn to join them. The young schemers sat in a semicircle around a glowing lantern, its flame steady enough to cut through the dark interior. Patches of blue sky shone through the cracks of walls and roof. Usually the barn doors remained open during the day so the children could tend to their chores, but now they stood closed in deep secrecy.

"You sure we won't get in a heap o' trouble?" Tucker asked. "Pa's not stupid."

The children cast uneasy glances at each other.

"All I can say is if we do, it'll be worth any licking. Once we have our ma, those who want to can go back to the schoolhouse for lessons. Sam can take up her writing again, and we won't have to worry about no more burnt meals—"

"I can't help it if I forget and the bread always gets burnt."

"And the meat…and the stew…and the pies…," Tucker added. "It's 'cause your nose is always buried in one of Ma's books."

Sam's face went warm, and Andy tousled her hair.

"Aw, that's okay, sis. I imagine Pa likes the idea that one of us Munroes is smart with books." Andy looked at each of his siblings in a grave, straightforward manner. "Sure as shootin', we'll get ourselves a new ma and Pa won't be alone no more."

"But how can he be alone, Andy, if he's got us?" Clarissa's eyes were big, green, and curious.

"There's different kinds of lonely," Andy explained. "Uncle Caleb told me a man like Pa shouldn't keep to himself and stay holed up at the cabin so long—he should marry again. Even the Good Book says so, accordin' to Uncle Caleb. That was back when I wasn't beholden to the idea, before Mrs. Jeffries got married, when she was always nosin' around Pa."

"Are you beholden to the idea now, Andy?"

"I reckon I am, Maggie, or I wouldn't be sitting here."

Tucker shook his head. "I still say Pa ain't gonna like it."

"But if what Uncle Caleb thaid *ith* true," Maggie insisted, "and we're doing God a favor, then it should be all right. He'th a preacher; he oughta know. And we're doing Him a favor, aren't we? By finding uth a ma and a wife for Pa?"

"I suppose," Sam answered, not feeling at all sure.

"Every man sometimes needs a little shove to get him started down the right path," Andy insisted. "Uncle Caleb said so. And with Pa's dilly-dallying around, saying he won't marry again, he sure doesn't seem to be heading down any right path. Doesn't seem to be heading down any path at all, if you ask me."

"Will our new ma sing us to sleep like our real ma did?" Clarissa's soft voice broke the tension.

All five of them grew still and stared at the lantern. Their gazes grew wistful and distant as if they each lived in their own memories.

"We can put 'must sing pretty' on our list," Andy reassured. "Read back what we have so far, Sam."

Sam cleared her throat and lifted the scrap of brown parcel paper closer to the lantern's light. "'Traits for our new ma: Must know how to cook and clean and take care of young'uns. Must like young'uns. Mustn't scold or spank or make us stand in the corner. Mustn't make us eat what we don't like, especially greens. Mustn't be meanhearted or a gossip or a busybody. Mustn't be forgetful.'" Sam's face heated in embarrassment at the memory of her burned meals. "'Mustn't hate animals, especially not pigs, and must be ready and willing to marry Pa.'"

"That's an awful lot of mustn'ts," Andy reasoned. "Maybe we should hone the list some. Ain't no woman alive could be all that, I reckon." He rested the back of his head against the wood siding of the barn. "What about Widow Abercrombie?"

Aghast, Sam stared at Andy as if he'd broken all Ten Commandments in one fell swoop. "She must be fifty if she's a day! You cannot seriously believe Pa would ever agree to marry a woman so old, Andy." Frowning, she jotted down, *Must be younger than Pa,* and then tilted her head, further studying the paper. *Or leastways, not ancient.*

"If he agrees at all," Tucker added, their usual voice of gloom.

"How old is Pa?" Clarissa asked.

"He's got to be really old by now," Tucker said with a slow, emphatic nod. "'Round thirty, I expect."

"He's still much too young for Widow Abercrombie," Sam insisted. "All in favor of crossing off her name as a potential ma?"

Three heads of tousled hair in shades of wheat, corn, and carrot nodded, and Andy gave in. "I suppose you're right."

"Of course I'm right." Sam looked over the list again. "What about Miss Proctor?"

Maggie and Tucker scrunched their noses in distaste at the thought of Pa marrying the town's schoolmarm.

"Aw, she'll make us read all the time!" Tucker complained. "And do our letters."

"And numbers," Maggie added with a groan.

"And just what's wrong with book-learning? Ma liked to read too," Sam reminded them with a superior sniff. "You children need to go back to learning lessons at the schoolhouse, instead of what little I can teach you. Ma was steadfast that all of us get a proper education. And Pa agreed."

"But Miss Proctor'll make us learn all the blessed day and night long," Tucker insisted, "and she smells funny."

"Like mothballth and chalk dutht," Maggie added.

Andy sniggered. "Yeah, well, we can't have a ma that don't smell nice."

The sun's rays soon glimmered through cracks in the western wall as the Munroe brood continued to select and dismiss every unmarried or widowed woman in the county. After yet one more prospective ma had been considered and crossed off, Andy kicked at the hay in disgust.

"Aw, this is gettin' us nowhere! We're gonna hafta be less picky, and that's all there is to it. Tucker, you need to learn to eat all your greens anyhow. And asking for a ma that won't use discipline when you misbehave is a mite far-fetched. Not to mention, Pa won't like it."

Tucker sighed. "Oh, all right. I'll sacker-fice."

"You won't have to sacrifice much, because I still believe that kindness and gentleness are important in a ma and we should keep those traits on our list." Sam smiled. "Say! Why didn't I think of it before? What about Aunt Alison?"

"From way back East?" Andy gaped in surprise.

"Sure. Who better to understand what we're feeling than someone who lost her own ma when she was little?"

"I remember Ma talking about Auntie Alithun. Didn't she ride an orphan train?"

Sam nodded in answer to Maggie's question. "That's what Ma said. Her folks adopted Aunt Alison when she was even younger than you, Clarissa. She and Ma became sisters and bosom friends till Ma came out West with Pa. Ma said two sisters bonded by blood couldn't have been closer."

Andy didn't look convinced. "A woman all the way from Boston? What would she know about living on the prairie? Would she know how to cook? Or clean? Or how to ride a horse?"

"Well, how would I know? Ma spoke highly of her, and that's good enough for me. Her address is on Ma's letters. I could write her, pretending Pa's doing the writing, and then take the letter to the postal clerk when I go into town." She smiled, gaining more enthusiasm with her idea. "When I sell eggs to Mrs. Merriweather, I could do it then. Pa would never be the wiser."

"If you recall, Ma said they had a maid who even dressed her, while they were growing up!" Andy argued. "She never did any work since her pa was an important doctor, 'cept for sewin' up them little doily things. I'll bet that's all Aunt Alison knows how to do."

"And if you'll also recall, Ma said *she* didn't know how to do much of anything till she came to Kansas with Pa on the wagon train. It's a gamble, sure, but if Aunt Alison is anything like Ma, she can learn too."

"What's a gamble?" Clarissa wanted to know.

Andy shared a stubborn look with Sam then regarded their littler sister. "Well, now, 'Rissa, I reckon that's what the lot of us are doing. 'Cause if Pa ever found out what we're planning, there'll be hell to pay for sure!"

"I don't wanna go to hell." Tears welled in Clarissa's eyes.

"Hush, sweetie." Sam held her close. "Andy didn't mean it like that. He's just exaggerating. Aren't you, Andy?"

"Sam's right." He gentled his voice and smiled at their little sister. "You know me; sometimes I talk a little wild."

"And use words Ma wouldn't approve of," Sam chided beneath her breath.

Andy took another look at the list, ignoring her. "Well, then, as the oldest Munroe here and captain of our group, I say this is what we ought to do. There sure isn't another soul in all of Dickinson County that'll come halfway near suitable to what we're hopin' for. Everybody agreed on Sam writing the letter for Aunt Alison to come and be our new ma?"

"Agreed!"

Footsteps crunched outside in approach. All five children stared at one another for the span of a startled breath and then jumped up and scattered like barn mice. Each Munroe took up whatever chore they could lay their hands on as the door suddenly creaked open, swinging wide.

Their pa's tall and sturdy silhouette filled the small space.

* * * * *

Rafe crossed his arms over his chest and stared with suspicion at his offspring, all of whom were busy at work in a barn dark as soot, with only a lantern's feeble glow to guide them. With little regard for aim, Andy forked hay into the stall for one of the two horses. Sprinklings of dried grass landed on Maggie, who was kneeling over a box of recently acquired, twittering chicks. Sam carried a pail, heading for the water trough, while Tucker clumsily swept droppings and Clarissa chased the barn cat in the shadows—likely to smother him in one of her exuberant hugs.

"What are you children up to?" Rafe kept his tone casual, feeling that something was afoot.

He was convinced when Sam said, "Nothing, Pa. Just doing our chores." She gave him one of her bright, false smiles—what Andy called her "hatching trouble" smiles. Maggie didn't look at him, and Clarissa stopped chasing the cat, her face puckered up in a sad, guilty way.

"You could see better to do them if you left the doors open to give light." Leaning casually against one of them, blocking any possible escape, he regarded his nervous brood. "Are any of you going to tell me what mischief you've been plotting for the past hour? Andy?"

His fourteen-year-old son stood mute.

"*Hmph.*" Rafe directed his attention to his eight-year-old, knowing she never could tell a lie well; her fair, freckled skin flushed as rosy as a ripe peach if she tried. "Maggie, maybe you'd care to answer?"

"You shouldn't be asking such things, Pa," Sam quickly said. "You might spoil the surprise."

Andy darted her a look of shock mixed with warning. The others stared with anxious eyes, clearly afraid of what she might say. Only Clarissa seemed unaffected, as a golden tabby came slinking around her legs. A gleeful smile replaced her worried frown as she scooped up the animal. The yellow ball of fur gasped a hoarse "Mew!" as she smothered its face against her chest.

"Surprise?" He redirected his attention to Sam. "What surprise?"

"If we tell, it won't be a surprise."

Rafe puzzled over Sam's vague words; then it hit him. He would be thirty-two in September. Still some time away—but Amy had always made such a big hullabaloo out of his birthday, cooking him a grand meal, presenting him with something she'd painstakingly knitted or sewn, and, later, playing the pianoforte he'd ordered for her through the Montgomery Ward Wish Book. It had come from Chicago by train…two Christmases before he lost her.

Since then, the pianoforte sat quietly near the hearth, untouched and dusty from disuse. But he couldn't bear to stow it in the barn or even give it to his brother's church. He hadn't visited the latter in quite a while.

Rafe eyed each of his brood, noting their shifty behavior. If they *were* planning something special for his birthday, he didn't want to dampen their excitement by insisting they reveal their secret. This past year and a half had been hard on them too. Amy always took such pleasure with her surprises, involving the children in her well-thought-out schemes. In that respect, they were like their mother.

Rafe uncrossed his arms and moved from the door. "Sam, it's nearing suppertime."

His eldest daughter dropped the empty pail. "I clean forgot! Sorry, Pa."

She hurried from the barn, her exit seeming more like an escape.

"Clarissa, Maggie, go help your sister."

"Yeth, Pa." Maggie put the chick back in its box with the other chirping birds and covered the box with its wooden lid. Clarissa approached, carrying the captured tabby.

"Cat stays in the barn."

His golden-haired daughter let out an unhappy little sigh, set the sleek tomcat down, then scampered after her two sisters. The cat raced up into the loft as if a hound were chasing it.

"Will you be going into town soon, Pa?" Andy leaned on the handle of the rake. "Sam mentioned we're low on flour and sugar."

"I expect I will, son. I need supplies to get that chicken coop built." The money from the sale of the piglets would dwindle fast, and he hoped for a good crop this year. His children appeared to be growing as fast as cornstalks.

"Can I come too, Pa?" Tucker asked.

"Maybe we should make it a family outing," Andy said quickly. "All of us can ride into Hope like we used to. Would that be all right, Pa? Sam said something about selling more eggs."

Rafe narrowed his eyes in guarded consideration. Andy had never before asked for his sisters to tag along; his idea of a trip into town was men's business. Likely it had to do with whatever surprise they had planned for his birthday. Rafe supposed a little fun wouldn't hurt, though, as long as his children didn't cause trouble. Let them keep their secret, this once.

A new pair of wool socks or a shirt with all its buttons would come in mighty handy.

Chapter Two

....

Boston, Massachusetts
Three weeks later

Alison Stripling couldn't believe what she was hearing, although she could believe that Mr. Hawthorne had said it. But that he would take her to task in front of a customer stung what little remained of Alison's pride.

"I honestly don't believe the hat makes you look the least bit manly, Mrs. Price." With difficulty, Alison kept her tone well modulated. For both the shop owner and the mayor's wife to call the perfect little hat, over which she had toiled hours to make, "inferior" and "monstrous" felt comparable to how a mother might feel whose baby had just been insulted.

The skin above Mr. Hawthorne's heavy, bewhiskered jowls darkened a deeper shade of red. "If Mrs. Price thinks the plume inappropriate, then off it goes. It's not your place to quibble with the customer, Miss Stripling."

Mrs. Price lifted her double chins a victorious notch.

Alison stared in horror as the shop owner mercilessly pulled at the soft wisp of a curling, black feather she'd centered amid a cluster of burgundy flowers in a dashing, spirited way. With a sickening crackle, it came loose from the tapered crown.

Mrs. Price sniffed. "You certainly cannot expect me to wear that hat in such deplorable condition! Really, Mr. Hawthorne, I expected better from your millinery shop, though being one of the newest shops in Boston, I did have my reservations. I must say, I'm quite displeased."

"Only tell me what you desire, madam, and I shall see that your every wish is accomplished to the letter."

Alison watched in disgust as her stodgy manager bowed and scraped before the haughty mayor's wife. The soft feather would have helped to draw attention from Mrs. Price's hooked nose, but of course, anything Alison said now would be dismissed or ignored.

And after this latest insult, her endurance had reached its limit.

With a gentle hand, she lifted the poor, damaged hat from the counter where Mr. Hawthorne had carelessly tossed it and took the forsaken feather with the other. Setting the ruined version atop her own head, she used the hat pin from the one she'd worn to the shop. Taking that hat in hand, she then looked Mr. Hawthorne in the eyes.

"If you'll excuse me, I'm going home." Alison noted how their mouths dropped open in surprise but moved toward the door.

"Miss Stripling, you can't just leave. And in the early afternoon! That's store merchandise you're absconding with. Don't think I won't deduct it from your wages. Miss Stripling—did you hear? If you walk out, you needn't bother coming back!"

She opened the door and looked over her shoulder. "I'm sorry you misunderstood, Mr. Hawthorne. Please allow me to elaborate. *I am hereby terminating my services for your shop.*" And with a flourish she left Hawthorne's Milliners, the bell hanging above the door tinkling a gleeful hurrah. She'd finally gained some grit and refused to take any more of his verbal slurs, which had gone on almost since the afternoon she'd shown him her first creation.

Her exhilaration lasted four blocks, from the congested business district to the path leading to her aunt and uncle's palatial home where she kept residence.

The overhanging branches of stately elms and oaks kept her cool in the shade while the sun dappled coins of golden light on the stone walkway. The breeze cooled her face and cleared her head. But it didn't give her the answers she desired.

She had no need to work for her keep. Yet she sought more from life than tea parties and socials. Still, even if she *were* the toast of the town, she doubted the prospect would please her. She wanted her contributions to matter, to be worthy of more than impressing society.

She thought of Amy's mother, Aunt Eliza's sister, who'd become Alison's mother as well. The dear woman had given her a chance, adopting her from an orphan train when Alison had no one, and had treated her as a beloved daughter. She owed it to her mother's memory to show the same consideration and help to those in need with whatever aid she could lend. She *did* have a talent for making hats, or the persnickety Mr. Hawthorne never would have kept her in his employ. But surely God must have something of true merit in mind for a twenty-four-year-old spinster recently jilted.

Stephen had been a pompous liar who cared more about society's conventions of "family and bloodlines" than what Alison could give him as a prospective wife. She couldn't help it if she didn't know where she came from or even *who* she came from. But that shouldn't matter if her alleged sweetheart truly loved her, as he had endlessly vowed. What a little fool she'd been for blindly giving away a year of her life to the shipbuilder's son.

Once inside her uncle's manor, Alison frowned into the looking glass in the foyer as she removed her hat. It was a perfectly *lovely* hat.

Furthermore, Mrs. Price *had* stipulated that she wanted a plume in it, no matter that the woman claimed she had no recollection of such an order.

Was it so much to ask that her work be appreciated? That she herself be valued as an individual with creative skill rather than just an ornamental showpiece—and a flawed one at that?

She'd been fortunate that Aunt Eliza and Uncle Bernard, both childless, had taken her into their home nine years ago. The Honorable Bernard Graystone employed servants that awaited and fulfilled their every wish. But neither the judge nor his wife appeared to need Alison's presence as a companion, what with their many charitable committees and social expectations. So what did she have to offer anyone, truly?

Just a heart that understood compassion, a word of encouragement when asked, and a bit of ribbons, flowers, and feathers sewn to straw and scraps of shiny cloth.

She sighed in dissatisfaction. What kind of trade required those qualities other than a milliner's shop?

Absorbed in her musings, Alison suddenly noticed a letter on the entry table. Her name was scrawled across the front in bold, black handwriting.

How odd. No one ever wrote to her, not anymore. Amy used to, but Amy had passed on to a better life, joining their dear parents in the Great Beyond. A twinge of sadness tugged at Alison's heart. She missed Amy, the hollow ache in her chest made worse since Alison knew she would never see her sister's honeyed smile again. Not in this life.

Picking up the envelope from the sterling salver and setting down her hat, she noticed that the sender of the letter resided in the same town where Amy lived. A jolt of amazement that she'd just been thinking of Amy made her blink and stare. She tore into the letter and read its brief contents with a mixture of surprise, curiosity...and dread.

"Alison," her aunt's voice came from the adjoining parlor, "is that you, dear?"

"Yes, Aunt Eliza." Alison's mind spun with the words that jumped out at her from the heavy parcel paper.

"Please come into the parlor, child. We desire a word with you."

Alison wished for more time to dwell on the astounding written request. Yet she folded the missive, tacked on a bright smile of greeting—false though it felt—and entered the parlor.

Aunt Eliza sat across from Uncle Bernard by the hearth. He sat in his wingback chair, immersed in a book, with blue rings of smoke drifting in the air above his pipe. He nodded a greeting to Alison and promptly returned to his pages. Her uncle appeared ill at ease—as did Aunt Eliza, whose green eyes were troubled. She sat forward in her chair as Alison came near.

"You look exhausted, dear. Did you walk home? You should have waited until Frederick arrived with the carriage, though I suppose it's early in the day for that, isn't it? Do tell us what has happened. I'll have Jenna bring you tea."

She rang a little bell in her usual flurried way and gave instructions to the maid who had seemed to magically appear at her elbow. "Jenna? There you are. Do fetch Alison a cup, please."

Once Jenna departed, Aunt Eliza turned her full attention to Alison.

"Did Mr. Hathaway send you home early, dear?"

Telling the news was inevitable. They would soon discover the truth of Alison's scandalous behavior, or so the gossipmongers would spin the yarn. She took a seat on the sofa next to her aunt.

"Actually, I've decided to end my employment there."

"Really? Well, I must say I'm not entirely displeased. You have a lovely flair for fashion, but a woman's place is near hearth and home, not taking a man's job in the workplace beyond. Isn't that right, Your Honor?"

"Hmm?" he huffed over the stem of his pipe, as if just coming into the conversation. He cleared his throat in a brusque manner. "Yes, yes. Of course, dear."

Alison smiled. She thought it sweet how her aunt addressed her uncle by his title and how he always seemed to agree with whatever Aunt Eliza had to say.

"I scarcely can conceive that a man has the knowledge to know what a woman wants in a hat," Alison speculated in amusement.

"Well, yes, you may be correct in that assumption. Although they do make good tailors."

Alison declined to ask what tailors had to do with milliners.

"All that aside, there's something we thought you should hear from us before you hear it elsewhere."

Uncle Bernard drew his book closer to his face. Alison knew he hated confrontations in his home of any sort, perhaps because he faced so much of it in his decades-long career as a judge. Jenna came in with tea, and Aunt Eliza waited to speak until Alison had been served and Jenna left. That she waited at all made Alison suspect the worst.

"There is no delicate way to approach this, except to come out and say it." Her aunt's eyes shone sympathetically. "I learned this morning that Stephen Sumpter has become betrothed to Mrs. Fairaday's daughter. I'm sorry, dear. I wish I had never introduced you to such a callous scoundrel. If I felt a morsel of kindness toward the woman and her brazen daughter—who hasn't an ounce of good sense in her primped head—I might sympathize with her for gaining such a delinquent for a son-in-law."

"Eliza!" the judge exclaimed in shocked amusement.

"Yes, yes, I know. Forgive me if I sound uncharitable or verge on gossip, but it really is quite shocking how Gwendolyn threw herself at that man during the Cromwells' ball...."

Alison barely acknowledged the remainder of her aunt's diatribe. Not even three weeks. Stephen had waited *less than a month* to become engaged to another woman. A woman of means, with a bloodline of illustrious ancestors dating back to the original colonists.

She blinked, feeling like she had as a small child when she'd missed a ball thrown to her and caught it hard in the stomach. It had knocked the wind from her lungs. She felt breathless now, a painful sort of breathless. Somehow she retained enough presence of mind to speak. "I don't blame you. I know you've always had my best interests at heart. My unfortunate alliance with Stephen wasn't the first time my lack of history has been the object of my disgrace."

"Now, then, I'll hear no more foolish talk from you either, young miss." Her uncle lowered his book, his expression grave, much to Alison's surprise. "There's not a blessed thing wrong with you. My courtroom is filled with felons who bear the true mark of disgrace, and you are nothing but a delight. It's not your fault that current Bostonian society is brimming over with pretentious snobs whose sole aim is to entertain themselves in tittle-tattle and make others feel deficient."

Aunt Eliza smiled widely and clapped her hands together. "Hear, hear, Your Honor! I couldn't have expressed such sentiments better myself."

Alison's face warmed at their loving praise and attempts to

console. "While that may be true—and thank you, Uncle, for expressing such faith in me—my future here is uncertain. Please don't misunderstand. You both have been wonderful and kind, taking me in as part of your family. Yet others in the circles we gravitate toward don't feel that same kindness. To mothers with marriageable sons, I'm a risk to their family line, since I have no knowledge of my parents' identity. Don't forget the awful rumor started recently that my father was insane, killed a man, and was put in an asylum, never mind that no one would have any way of knowing such a thing. True or not, the damage was done. No member of the Boston elite wants even the barest hint of insanity marring their perfect bloodlines. And lately I've noticed a few neighbors watching me as if they think I might snap at any moment and start baying at the moon."

Her aunt tsked and her uncle grumbled.

Alison shook her head. "I think I shall never marry, not after this failed engagement. Instead, I shall content myself with spinsterhood. Yet I am *not* content to whittle away my hours with vain amusements in a society that merely tolerates my presence because I'm your ward. I want my life to have purpose. For my accomplishments to have meaning. I want to be like Mama and Papa, who traveled to Ohio for one reason and ended up taking a three-year-old child from an orphan train to raise as their own." Alison would forever be grateful they'd spotted her and taken interest. If circumstances had been different, her future might have been quite bleak indeed.

Aunt Eliza drew her brows together. "What exactly are you saying, dear?"

Alison drew a deep breath in sudden comprehension, her eyes lowering to the crude letter with its heartfelt plea. Her aunt's gaze also dropped to the brown paper.

"Whatever is that you're holding?"

"Perhaps the answer I've been praying for."

A thrill of excitement winged through Alison. She'd had no real time to mull over her decision…and yet the timing couldn't have been more ideal.

"The chance I'm looking for to start over, where no one knows my past to judge me without cause, and the chance to make my life mean something. I believe it lies here, in Hope, Kansas."

"Hope, Kansas!" Her aunt's voice hoarsened with shock. "Where Amy's family lives?"

"Precisely." Even the name of the town buoyed Alison's expectations.

"But—why would you wish to travel to the middle of nowhere? It's little more than grass and wilderness and savage Indians, according to all I've heard."

"They need me, and that's what I want—to be needed." She reached over and covered her aunt's tightly clasped hands with her own. "You and Uncle Bernard have been a blessing to me, but you don't really *need* me. And you mustn't worry. Amy once wrote that the Indians aren't the threat they were, since many have moved onto reservations."

"Nonsense, of course we need you."

"Your aunt is correct, Alison; you always shall have a home with us as long as you wish it." Her uncle's eyes then narrowed in thought as a slow smile curved his thin lips. "And yet…ever since you were a child, with those eager brown eyes that took in the world around you, you've had that great thirst for adventure, always seeking more. You and Amy were two peas in a pod in that regard. Yet, unlike Amy, you possess a spirit some would call obstinate, one that would make a weaker man concede to anything. It's that stubborn spark that keeps you fighting, Alison." He nodded once with emphasis. "You need a strong man; settle for nothing less. That pallid excuse for a mama's boy is as weak as they come. You might not see it well enough now, but he did you a good turn in breaking the engagement."

Alison didn't know whether to feel commended or chastised. But she didn't point out a second time that she had decided to remain a spinster.

"Regardless, you simply cannot travel all the way to Kansas without a chaperone." Her aunt brought the conversation back to what clearly troubled her.

"I don't see why not. According to local society, my reputation is in ill standing because of my lack of heritage. What should it matter if I break one of their silly conventions when most of our acquaintances already consider me deficient in bearing and familial ties? I no longer give a fig what they think about me. I tried to fit in with their high expectations and failed. And I'm sick up to my eyeballs with trying."

Uncle Bernard chuckled, and Aunt Eliza shot him a quelling look.

"You shouldn't speak so, Alison," she reprimanded gently. "They regrettably may be misguided souls, but they are still our friends."

"Why shouldn't the girl say what's on her mind?" her uncle answered before Alison could respond. "I've been wanting to say something on that order for years. Leave her be, Eliza. She has a good head on her shoulders. She won't do anything foolish. If she has her heart set on going to the Midwest and making a difference there, let the girl live out her dream."

What started out as a possibility became conviction.

"Thank you, Uncle." Alison moved toward him and kissed his temple before turning back to her aunt, sinking to the rug before her. "I'll send a telegram the moment I arrive in Hope. And I'll write as often as I'm able. You needn't worry."

"Well, I don't like this one bit." Her aunt gave a faint smile. "Still, I haven't seen your eyes shine so since…well, since I don't know when. This is really that important to you?"

"Yes. Amy's husband pleaded for my help with his children. While I don't know much about little ones, surely he thinks I could be of good use or he wouldn't have asked. He wrote that it's been very difficult since Amy died. He's coped the best he could, raising both crops and children, but is at his wits' end with both."

"But, Alison, *six* children?"

The thought made her stomach a bit queasy. Still, they were Amy's children, likely as sweet and gentle as their mother. Besides, if her sister had been able to learn to take care of little ones, so could Alison. As young girls, they'd dreamed of motherhood and shared with each other their aspirations of having a family. With her recent avowal of spinsterhood, this would be the closest Alison would ever come to that dream.

"Where will you stay? Surely you won't sleep under the same roof with him! I've heard that those cabins are little more than the size of a glorified barn."

She hadn't thought of that—hadn't had much time to think of any of the particulars, really.

"He must have somewhere respectable for me to lodge. Amy did write that he's an honorable, God-fearing man, and his brother is the preacher of a church there."

Her aunt didn't look convinced. "This is truly what you want, my dear? You do have a habit of acting before you think. Why, you only received the letter today!"

"It won't be forever, Aunt Eliza. I'll stay only until they no longer need my help. But if it will reassure you"—she gave a reluctant smile—"I'll give the matter more thought."

"That would be wise." Aunt Eliza sat back with relief. "Do drink your tea, dear, before it goes cold."

Alison did as encouraged. Though her promise to wait mollified her aunt, Alison had already decided. The seed of her conviction to fulfill her dream had sprouted into a root of determination. Her decision might have been reached quickly, perhaps could be considered somewhat reckless, but acting on impulse didn't *always* get her in trouble. Besides, this time was different. She didn't know what to expect, but she felt assured that those living in Hope, Kansas, would welcome her as much as she welcomed this opportunity for a new start with them.

Chapter Three

....

Alison could barely sit still. The bench beneath her skirts felt hard and uncomfortable, the diminutive bustle making little difference. The passenger beside her snored enough to set her nerves on edge, but neither discomfort proved powerful enough to douse her anticipation.

So, this was Kansas. She had never seen anything so utterly wild, so delightfully untamed, so vastly impressive, as these infinite lands of the Midwest.

The grass grew so high that if she were to stand amid their thin blades, they would soar far overhead and she would be lost from view to the world around her. Barely a tree stood in sight, except for those gathered near the streams passing by. In Boston, trees grew without number wherever she looked; where they didn't stand, buildings did. But here she could look up and see miles and miles of unfettered blue sky laced with frothy white clouds. Beneath, where the grass didn't grow wild on the rolling plains, lay seas of shimmering gold, and she wondered if these were the wheat crops about which Amy had written. She had never seen so much land and sky. And a train wall impeded what she could see from the small window!

An innate sense to be one with this land made the discomforts of train travel—the soot, the smoke, the stuffiness—somehow tolerable, even forgettable. She couldn't wait to reach Hope, and, like a small, eager child, she wondered how long it would be before the train pulled into the station.

She hoped Mr. Munroe had received her letter. She had written her acceptance early, though she had waited seven days before informing her aunt of her decision. It would be terribly awkward if she arrived before her announcement giving the time of her arrival, with no one to greet her. But at least she had an idea of what to expect, from Amy's correspondence.

Hope apparently boasted over seven hundred people, seven dry good stores, three drug stores, two restaurants, and an assorted number of butchers, bankers, clothiers, and other myriad businesses. Somewhere in all that, if the need presented itself, she could surely find a citizen willing to take her to the Munroe cabin.

At long last the train slowed. Alison felt its shrill whistle invade her from the soles of her shoes and upward, resounding within her being. It whisked through her in a strange tingle, like the experience before an impending storm.

She hoped the thought wasn't a bad omen and then shook her head at the silly notion.

Fluttering with nervous excitement, she could barely take in a breath. She grabbed her parasol and carpetbag packed with the remainder of lunch, a book of poetry by Keats, and a recent issue of *Godey's Lady's Book* then hailed a burly porter to bring her Saratoga trunk filled with all else she'd brought with her.

A hot wind blew, different from Boston's cool sea breezes. Under her tailored jacket, her shirtwaist clung to her body, and trickles of perspiration ran along her skin. Surely the days weren't always so sultry!

Wiping sweat from his brow, the porter straightened. She thanked him, giving him a dime for his trouble. Her practical aunt might have criticized her for such a tip, but her benevolent uncle likely would have nodded his approval. Buying the trunk along with the train fare had taken a generous chunk of her earnings, but she still had some tucked away, sewn inside the interior of her carpetbag.

With her belongings at her feet and her open parasol over one shoulder, she searched the groups of passengers and those who welcomed them, hoping to find a pair of eyes searching for her. The oddest sensation tickled down her spine as she realized she had no inkling of what Amy's husband looked like! Only a hazy recollection of the man and quite biased at that, as subjective as an unhappy nine-year-old could imagine him. In her letters, her sister had described him as attractive, strong, and kind but had given no details about his actual appearance. However, Amy's vague description could apply to any number of men at the depot, though Alison had no way of seeing what was inside their hearts.

A slender boy with straw-colored hair poking from beneath a battered cap caught her eye. He wore a pair of denim overalls that hit a few inches above the ankles, clearly outgrown. He studied her from her newly refurbished hat to the toes of her button-up shoes, a look of pained acknowledgment clouding his thin features. His sky-blue eyes, the same color and shape as her sister's eyes, never left her as he approached, and she reasoned that he must be the eldest of Amy's children.

"Hello." She gave a nervous smile. "Are you Andrew?"

He winced. "Andy's just fine, Ma'a—er, that is, Aunt Alison," he rectified. "That is your name?"

"Yes, I'm your aunt." She looked beyond him, expecting his father to join them. When no man did, she returned her attention to Andy. "It's just you?" Realizing how rude that sounded, she hurriedly said, "I'm afraid my trunk is rather heavy."

He cast her luggage another of his pained glances. "I reckon I can handle it."

As skinny as he looked, she didn't think he could drag, much less carry, it; he surprised her when he grabbed the handle and managed to hoist it onto his back and shoulders. She had no inkling of how he could carry it in such a manner. With as red as he grew in the face, she felt both guilty and relieved when they approached a crude wagon and he let the trunk fall in the back.

He untied the horse and jumped up on the driver's side, taking the reins and waiting for her to take a seat. Awkwardly, she managed to step up without crushing her skirts. Frederick had always given her a hand entering and exiting a buggy, and when Stephen courted her, he had done likewise. She got the uneasy feeling that Andy wasn't thrilled with her presence and felt annoyed because he'd been the one designated to receive her.

Just where was his father? Before she could ask, Andy pointed ahead to the left.

"See that there? That's our newest dry goods store—that one belongs to Mr. Eisenhower and Mr. Good, and it's where we do our trading. I expect you'll grow accustomed to it quick enough."

Trading?

"And way out over yonder, if you squint real hard, you can see the schoolhouse. That's where Uncle Caleb preaches. It's right pretty, sitting near Turkey Creek. Pa and me and my brother Tucker like to fish there with Uncle Caleb."

"Is that where your pa is now? With your uncle Caleb?" She wondered what manner of business would keep Andy's father from meeting her train when he'd sounded so desperate for her arrival in his letter.

"Er, no." A flush of red crawled up the boy's neck and washed his face in color. "He's out and about town, I reckon."

He *reckoned*? He didn't *know*? "Then I'm to meet him here?" Looking for a man who resembled Andy, she studied the boardwalks along the storefronts and the townspeople walking there. A few waved to the boy, calling out a greeting. Their eyes studied her with curious regard. She wondered if anyone in Hope knew that Rafe Munroe had sent for his wife's sister.

"I was told to take you to the cabin," Andy said. "I expect you'll meet him later. Sam—that's my sister—told me I was to 'acquaint' you with the town. She uses them fancy words like Ma did. I don't cotton to them none, though a few sneak up on me now and then. From listening to Ma and Sam, I expect." He sighed, treating the prospect of good grammar like a curse, and glanced her way. "You need anything before we head to the cabin? We don't go into town much, 'ceptin' when the little ones would walk to school and to church on Sundays. We don't live far. Takes little more'n two parts of an hour to reach our homestead by wagon."

"I should like to visit the telegraph office so I can let my family know I arrived safely."

"Sure thing."

Alison studied the wooden buildings along the street they traveled. Her eyes widened then narrowed to peer closely. "Is that sign on that building up ahead correct? Is that an *opera* house?" She couldn't recall Amy writing of one.

"Yes'm. Built three years ago. I don't cotton to that type of entertaining, all them high-pitched, loud operas like Ma preferred, though I liked to hear *her* sing. Pa said she had the voice of an angel." Andy looked her way suddenly. "Can you sing?"

Not like Amy. "I manage."

"That's good. Clarissa and Baby Lynn like to be sung to, especially during a storm." He abruptly changed topic again. "The

Cyclone Minstrels—that's what they call themselves—opened the opera house with their show. They were all right, I reckon. A good deal of the town turned out, though we Munroes mostly keep to ourselves. Don't get into town much anymore."

Alison hid a smile at his roving conversation, wondering if he felt half as nervous to welcome a stranger into his father's household as she was to be there.

He pulled up before the telegraph office. "I'll wait here."

"This won't take long." Sensing his desire to return home, she managed to take the long step down without falling and quickly walked into the dim interior of the small building smelling of fresh sawdust and sweet ink. A thin reed of a man welcomed her to Hope and jotted the message to her aunt. She paid the nickel asked of her, thanked him, and hurried back to the wagon. Moving her reticule from her hand to her wrist, she then gathered her skirt to take the wide step up.

"May I give you a hand, miss?"

Shocked to hear a man's voice so close, she turned to look. A dark-haired gentleman with dancing blue eyes lifted his hat in greeting and then looked up at Andy in question.

"Uncle Caleb," Andy squeaked. "Didn't know you'd be here."

"Why shouldn't I be here? I live here."

"Uh, yeah." The boy's face flushed darker. "Pa around?"

"I haven't seen him since this morning. I think introductions are in order, Andy?"

"Right—sorry. Uh…this is Ma's sister, Aunt Alison. She's come from the East for a visit. This is my uncle Caleb, Pa's brother."

Alison didn't add that Rafe sent for her, though Andy's uncle did look puzzled. She smiled warmly and took the hand he offered in greeting.

"Welcome to Hope. I trust you had a pleasant journey?"

"It was an experience, especially when changing trains. I almost missed the last one." She laughed at the memory. "But I managed to arrive on time and in one piece, so I'm thankful for that."

He smiled. "My wife, Ivy, and I live by the creek east of here. You must come and visit during your stay."

"Thank you for the invitation. I accept." She received his hand up into the wagon.

"Hate to leave so sudden-like, but we gotta get goin'," Andy explained in a spiel of words. He cast an anxious glance around as if looking for someone—or evading someone. Alison got the strangest notion that was exactly what he was doing.

Caleb narrowed his eyes at Andy in curious speculation then smiled at Alison. "It's a pleasure meeting you, Miss Stripling. I hope to see you at the church meeting."

"Since we're almost family, I'm certain you will."

Andy choked in a sudden coughing spell. Her polite rejoinder had barely left her lips and her backside scarcely touched the boards before the wagon jerked to a swift advance along the rutted road, leaving Andy's uncle gaping after them. Keeping hold of her parasol with one hand and grabbing the seat with the other, just managing to keep her balance, Alison cast Andy a surprised glance.

"Sorry 'bout that," he offered sheepishly. "We need to get home before Pa. I still have chores that need tending."

She let the matter of his discourtesy drop, though his anxious behavior made her wonder just what kind of man his pa was. Did his children fear him? Amy hadn't implied that he was anything but kind, though grief could change a person. For the first time, Alison worried that she might have made a mistake in coming to Hope.

The ride to the Munroe cabin grew quiet. Beneath the shade

offered by the parasol, Alison took the opportunity to soak in the ruggedly beautiful surroundings, hoping to ease her qualms. More of the stately tall grasses she'd viewed from the train swayed in the whispering wind and filled the plain in all directions. Huge flowers with yellow petals and brown middles spotted the land. She noticed a long line of trees with low, twisted branches, evidently planted with purpose and not growing wild, and decided to ask Andy about them.

"Osage orange and hedge seed—used for fences to make boundaries," he explained. "They make good windbreaks and fireguards too."

Windbreaks? Fireguards?

The land must be as wild as she'd heard.

A flock of dark birds came into sight and soared across the expanse of azure blue. Would she ever grow weary of gazing at such a remarkable sky?

Whatever had plagued Andy soon passed. He relaxed, filling her in on the legend and lore of the area. She listened avidly to his riveting if somewhat ghostly account of an old prospector who'd been lost in a nearby cave in the days of the 49ers: a man who went missing but, in the years following, was often spotted roaming the plains, carrying his axe and a rusty shotgun. Engrossed in the account and the thought of rock caves that could swallow a person whole, Alison didn't pay attention to the change in surroundings.

"There it is," Andy said proudly. "Home."

Alison looked past a boundary line of trees to where he pointed. At first she didn't see the cabin, as it was set away in a clearing beyond a tall hedge of brown grass. Short, spindly trees stood by a narrow stream. As they drew closer, the smallest house she'd ever seen came into view. Green vegetation in the form of leaves and stalks rose above a large square of earth to the far right.

"There's my family." Andy brought her attention back to the humble dwelling. "Looks as if they're coming to greet you."

Alison watched five children leave a log cabin and assume a stairstep line of age and height before the wagon stopped before them. From the youngest, an adorable child who shyly peered up with eyes the same delft blue as Amy's, to the eldest girl, whose russet hair blew around her face, each of the Munroe children curiously regarded her. All were neatly dressed with their faces washed, except for the freckle-faced boy with hair as brown as a walnut. Streaks of dirt smeared his cheeks and coveralls.

"Hello." Alison again managed the step down from the wagon and gave what she hoped would pass for a confident smile. "I'm your aunt Alison, newly arrived from Boston. I do hope we'll have a lovely time together."

All the girls smiled, two of them exchanging glances. The youngest giggled and clapped a hand over her mouth. Alison's attention dropped to the little tot with the big blue eyes and red-gold hair that shone like ballroom silk.

"You must be Lynn," she greeted softly.

The girl shook her head.

"No? But I thought…?"

"*Baby* Lynn," the child corrected and giggled again.

"It's what we call her, though she's three," the eldest girl explained. "I'm Samantha, but everyone calls me Sam. I turned twelve a couple of weeks ago," she said proudly. "Next to Baby Lynn is Clarissa. She's six.…"

At the introduction, the fair-haired child gave a sweet curtsy, pinching the skirt of her gray dress between her fingertips, an action Alison felt sure the girl had learned by mimicking Amy.

"She wants to be a dancer someday."

"Like them Russian ballerinas Ma spoke of," Clarissa added in awe. "She said they danced in Boston."

"Yes, I remember," Alison confirmed, which earned her a smile. "Next to her is Maggie. She's eight."

With straight, braided hair a shade somewhere between Samantha's bright russet and Baby Lynn's red-gold, Maggie nodded shyly and dropped her attention to her bare feet.

"And this is Tucker—"

"Wanna see my pet frog?" The boy reached for his coveralls and Alison drew back in shock. "I got a pet snake too—*umph*." Sam had stepped behind him and clapped a hand over his mouth.

"He's nine. He just came from playing by the creek; that's why he's so dirty. Don't mind what he said. The snake isn't big. Pa wouldn't let him keep it if it was. It's just a little grass snake."

Alison wondered just how "little" a grass snake was and where he kept it. Surely the reptile wouldn't have a home in the cabin!

"Come on inside." Sam's tone conveyed her nervousness. "Tucker," she addressed the boy, "help Andy with Aunt Alison's trunk. Clarissa, fetch her a dipper of water. I'm sure she's parched. And this heat doesn't help."

The children took off running to their assigned duties and Alison relaxed. They seemed to mind well—one concern marked off her list of worries in this new, unfamiliar task of caring for them.

She closed her parasol and stepped into the cabin after Sam. The place looked cozier than her first glance suggested. A rock hearth took up the middle of one wall; a brightly colored rug and rocking chair sat before it, and a table with two long benches sat a short distance away. The kitchen and parlor were one room. A door closed off what she assumed must be a bedroom, and a narrow set of stairs against the wall led upward.

"Pa built onto the place after Clarissa was born. That's why it's bigger than most cabins."

Accustomed to a manor home with more than thirty rooms, Alison tried not to show her astonishment. This was *bigger*? It would take time to accustom herself to such a rudimentary lifestyle, but she'd faced more difficult challenges. Certainly she could learn how to be a pioneer, as Amy had done.

She looked around the entire room, noticing her sister's little touches. A hand-stitched sampler on the wall. A crocheted doily on the table beneath a glass containing wildflowers. A pianoforte, dusty from disuse.

"Where—do you want us—to put this?" Andy huffed the question as he and Tucker, both red in the face, carried Alison's trunk inside.

Sam now looked uncertain, even anxious, her mouth dropping open a little as if she'd forgotten something. She recovered quickly and nodded to the closed door nearby. "In there."

The boys grunted as they awkwardly lumbered past. Alison frowned with a twinge of conscience. Had she packed too much? She had left a goodly amount of her possessions behind, but since she had no idea of how long her stay might last or what the weather in Kansas held, she'd felt it necessary to pack for all four seasons.

Alison's attention wandered to the instrument, looking so forlorn without its loving owner. She rested her parasol against the wall and moved toward the pianoforte, as though drawn by its silence. Alison put wistful fingers on the faded ivory keys, felt a tug at her skirt, and looked down.

"Do you play?" Baby Lynn asked.

"Not like your mother could."

"Sam plays."

"Lynn—hush!" Sam grew agitated. "I don't, not really."

"Yes, you do." The tot nodded. "I heard you when I was sleeping."

Clarissa walked inside holding a dipper.

Alison drank the cool water, grateful it refreshed her dry throat.

A mangy cur suddenly shot through the door, yipping and making a beeline straight for Alison. She choked on the water, coughing, as a pair of paws planted themselves squarely on the silk skirt of her black-and-burgundy traveling suit.

"Brutus, no! Down!" Sam hurried forward, pulling the dog away. "He gets excitable when there's company. Tucker, take him outside." She addressed the boy who stood in the doorway, watching.

"Don't she like dogs?"

"Tucker!"

At Sam's demand, Tucker led the animal out by the scruff of his neck, and Andy followed.

Attempting to gather her wits, Alison handed Clarissa the empty dipper and then noticed with dismay that she'd managed to spill water on her bodice with Brutus's enthusiastic greeting. "Thank you," she told her niece, doing her best to blot the material with her gloved hand.

Clarissa smiled nervously before speeding back outside. Sam looked at the youngest. "Baby Lynn, bein' as how you brought up nap time…"

"Aw, do I hafta?"

"Yes."

Sullen, the child moved toward the staircase and then turned back to face Alison. "I like you, Auntie Al–son. I hope you stay a long time." She whirled around and scampered up the stairs.

"I have to start the meal. I'll be outside." Sam exited the cabin in a rush, leaving Alison alone in the room.

She shook her head in a slight daze, unaccustomed to such flurry. Home in Boston had been quiet, with little to upset the usual routine. Here at the Munroe cabin, life seemed to run in an ordered sort of chaos, making her somewhat breathless and dizzy. As a child, she supposed she'd been just as lively. But *six* of them! What had she gotten herself into?

Her gaze fell to the instrument's keys and her thoughts revisited days of her childhood when Amy would play the grand piano and urge Alison to take part in a duet. Unskilled, Alison would giggle as Amy patiently taught her which keys to strike, until both girls were doubled over with laughter at their combined efforts. Reminiscing, Alison found her fingers trailing the same pattern of keys. A flat pitch made her wince.

"Get away from there!"

Alison jumped at the deep masculine voice bellowing the order and snatched her hand from the keys.

"Who are you?" the man snapped, moving inside the cabin. "What are you doing here?"

She stared in wide-eyed shock as a stranger a good deal taller than herself, his solid form lean and muscular, seemed to fill the place. The room, which appeared to be small before, now felt claustrophobic once he moved even closer and his storm-blue eyes swept over her form. A dusty black hat covered his brown hair, which grew to his shoulders in an unkempt manner. Her heart thundered out a plea. Surely this wild, untamed ruffian couldn't be their...

"Pa!" Sam's voice rang out behind him, confirming Alison's worst fears.

Chapter Four

....

Rafe glared in irritation at the fancy-dressed intruder with the huge brown eyes growing bigger by the second and then swung his attention to his eldest daughter. She had that "hatching trouble" look on her face again.

"What's going on here?" His question allowed no excuses.

"Um, this is Aunt Alison. Ma's sister. She's come for a visit to help, right? Aunt Alison, this is my pa. I need to see to dinner now."

"Saman–tha!"

The girl stopped in her tracks. With a guilty look, she inched her gaze upward until her eyes met his.

"Did you know about this?"

"Maybe a little?" She gave him an uneasy smile.

A little. He would guess she planned the whole thing. Recalling the woman who still gaped at him like a fish eyeing a hook, he managed to control his temper. "We'll talk later." Pulling in a deep, steadying breath, he turned back to their unexpected visitor once Sam left.

The sight of who he thought had been a stranger touching Amy's most prized possession had kindled a flame of fiery resentment. He'd only seen his wife's sister twice, and that had been years ago. The girl had grown up; he couldn't be blamed for not recognizing her.

"My apologies." He attempted to make things right. "You took me by surprise."

She continued to regard him as if he might throw her over his shoulder and run outdoors with her. He lifted his hand to explain, and she took a step back.

He tried again. "Out here on the prairie we tend to forget our manners. Kansas is a long way from Boston. Simpler. Nothing like the high society you're accustomed to."

"That's right, you're from Boston, aren't you?" Her voice sounded tight.

"Not an area you'd be familiar with. It was happenstance Amy and I met. But you wouldn't remember me. You were just a young'un when Amy and I moved west. And quite the little spitfire." He chuckled, though it came tense, and worked to get his irritation in check. He still didn't know the extent of the damage his children had caused but was sure to find out.

Amy's sister continued to stare, as if trying hard to picture him. His smile came forced. Life had changed him since those ignorant days of his youth.

She shook her head as if to clear it and then pulled an envelope from her reticule, handing it to him. "Did you send this?"

He took the letter. His stomach dropped when he recognized Sam's pretty, bold handwriting. With a grimace, he lifted it. "May I?"

She blinked, as if surprised he would ask, and nodded.

He read the letter, anger chasing disbelief, both fighting for control of his reaction. "I see." He kept his tone quiet and grim as he stuffed the page back into the envelope. "It appears, Miss Stripling, that my children have seen fit to try and pair us off."

"*What?*" She sank heavily to the bench at the pianoforte.

"They want a new ma. They want me to marry again." He delivered the words in a dead tone. "I didn't send the letter."

"Oh! B–but I didn't come here for anything like—like *that*!" She sounded horrified.

"Of course you didn't. I'm not saying you're at fault. You're the victim they chose. They've been hankering after me to find me a wife and them a mother." He shook his head in wry disbelief. "Caleb warned me that they were asking him a lot of questions, but I didn't expect any trouble. I should have known better."

"Your brother?"

He glanced at her in surprise. "You two have met?"

She nodded, still looking lost. "In town. When Andy came to collect me."

Andy. Of course. Now his odd excuses for the trips to town made sense, as well as his telling Rafe earlier that he had errands to run for his "surprise." The Munroe children were in for a little surprise of their own, one of Rafe's choosing and not at all to their liking.

"I–I'm sorry to impose. I really had no idea…."

At her subdued tone and clear mortification, Rafe reassured her. "*None* of this is your fault. Though I imagine you'll want to return to Boston soon?" He tried not to sound too hopeful.

She blinked slowly at his question. "Y–yes, of course."

He let out a grateful breath. "You can have my room; I'll sleep in the barn. I can take you back into town at sunup tomorrow so you'll be sure to catch the next train. Now if you'll excuse me, I need to have a talk with my brood." Without waiting for her reply Rafe left the cabin, ill at ease to be forced into such an awkward position.

Outside, all remained quiet, with not a mischief-maker in sight. His steely gaze went to the barn, which he realized must have been the meeting point to hatch their scheme.

Rafe approached the building, his stride long and determined. The door stood slightly ajar. He stopped upon hearing a number of loud whispers fall over one another. He assumed their quiet racket kept them unaware of his approach.

"I told you Pa wouldn't like it!"

"But what did he *say*?"

"He wasn't pleased to see her. Not at all."

"You think he'll make her leave?"

"I hope not. She's the best of the lot, from what I can tell. Kind. Pretty too. Except she must have rocks in her trunk. I never carried a trunk so heavy in all my born days."

"Who cares about that silly old trunk, Andy, when we've got more important problems to work out?"

"Did he seem really, *really* mad, Sam?"

"Yes, 'Rissa, but don't worry. If anyone takes the blame, it'll be me."

"And me, since I'm the oldest."

"But what'll we do if he sends her away?"

"I reckon we'll have to start from scratch."

"Now that Pa knows what we done, you think he won't catch on a second time?"

"You could be right, Tucker. But Uncle Caleb's on our side. He'll help."

"How can you be sure?"

"Because of what the Good Book says about it not being good for a man to be alone. And you know he believes everything in that book."

"Do you?"

"Well, Ma did. She sure loved reading them stories from it. And she prayed an awful lot."

"Maybe that's what we should do. Pray to God to make it work out right?"

"I think that's a good idea, Maggie."

The sudden gentle cadence of his eldest daughter whispering a prayer for help from above stopped Rafe from entering the barn, as though his boots had suddenly grown roots into the ground.

Shortly after losing his sweet wife and stillborn son, he'd fallen away from God and the faith his brother preached about. No matter his personal convictions, Rafe found he couldn't invade such an earnest gathering to give a severe reprimand and decided that his own private meeting with the children would have to wait.

Then Rafe realized something else. They weren't going to give up the ridiculous notion of ordering a ma, like one would send for an item from the Wish List. Once their minds were fixed on something, his children became obstinate, a trait they regrettably got from him.

His eyes went to the cabin, and he stared in deep thought until, at last resigned, he reached a decision.

* * * * *

Alison sat motionless on the bench, barely taking note of what she saw. She replayed the humiliating experience a second time. He hadn't written the letter, and he didn't want her here. His relief that she'd agreed to take the next train had been palpable, almost insulting.

The last place Alison wanted to be was where she wasn't wanted. She certainly had no intention of remaining under the terms his children sought. She had thought them so well-behaved! That they had stooped to such trickery astonished her. Why would they do such a hurtful thing?

With a disillusioned sigh, she tried to collect her chaotic thoughts into a semblance of order. Rafe had said they wanted a mother. She thought of Amy, with her sweet and gentle ways, and slowly began to understand. The children wanted a woman not only to take Amy's place but also to be the very image of the mother they dearly missed. In their childlike manner, they had sought a way to meet that need.

Her initial anger faded to compassion, and she ached for their pain.

But their *father*! He was a different story altogether.

Alison closed her eyes at the recollection of his first words to her. He'd been so angry! In retrospect, she couldn't blame him; he'd thought her an intruder touching Amy's things. He'd been a victim in this plot as much as she and taken by surprise just as she'd been. Once they conversed, the turbulent, dark storm in his eyes had faded to a calmer blue gray, though his wild, unkempt disposition never waned. Conceivably, her impression of the man was due in part to his chiseled jaw with its faint shadow of a beard and the piercing color of his eyes that seemed to look through her, into her very soul. Was it any wonder she thought him a wild man at the commencement of their meeting? Or an outlaw, such as those she'd heard roamed the West and preyed on the unsuspecting? True, this was the *Midwest*, not as dangerous and wild as she'd heard the far West could be, with Hope being a civilized settlement—but still untamed territory compared to Boston.

Suddenly, she realized something else. He had called her a little spitfire.

He remembered her.

A flush of embarrassment warmed her face at the memory of what an irrational child she'd been. She tried to reconcile the bitter man she'd just seen with the happy youth who'd taken Amy from

Boston, but she couldn't recall that boy's face. The past fifteen years had erased many memories. That had been the worst day of her childhood, an upsetting event she'd pushed to a shadowed corner of her mind and almost forgotten as she'd grown older.

Now she struggled to remember that long-ago spring morning. Bits and pieces came back to taunt her. Petulant, she'd refused to speak to Amy's beau the first time she saw him, in her childishness blaming him for taking her big sister away. She found him alone before their wedding and, among other things, yelled that he was mean and that she would always hate him.

Over the years she'd matured, gaining the understanding of an adult—but how ironic that Alison should now come to him, when *he* didn't want *her* there! When she decided to accept the request of the letter, to come to Kansas, her heart had only been caught up in the children's needs, not those of their father.

But the need they secretly sought—to be *his wife*—she would never agree to that!

A heavy step at the door made her stiffen; Andy's tread hadn't been so powerful, while everything about his father evoked power. She knew he could be the only person standing there, since she'd heard no wagon or horses to announce a visitor. Alison held in a breath. Turning to look at him, she awaited her fate.

His eyes regarded her with a tinge of remorse she hadn't expected to see. "No need to look so worried. I'm really not an ogre."

She blinked at his low words, which were calmer than before, and gave an uncertain nod.

He strode to the hearth, a few feet from where she sat. His broad shoulders grew rigid as he stared into the unlit chamber. He removed his dusty hat, slapping it against his denim-clad leg, and she sensed that whatever else he wished to say wasn't coming easy.

"I find myself in an awkward position." His admission came as wooden as his stance. "I've come to realize that my brood isn't going to quit their foolishness of finding themselves a ma. And this one experience has created enough problems. I don't want them causing others strife too."

His shoulders rose and fell on a deep sigh, and he turned to look at her.

"Fact is, Miss Stripling, I could use your help. Though if you refuse, I certainly wouldn't blame you. Not after the harsh welcome I gave."

"What sort of help did you have in mind?" Her question came wary.

"I'd like you to stay—just long enough to help me convince them that their plan, if it were to come to pass, would never work out like they're expecting. It'll mean we'll have to come up with our own plan, but knowing my brood, this is the only way to stop them from making more trouble. It'll get the message across a good deal better than a few well-deserved swats to their backsides." His features relaxed. "So, what do you say? Will you help me?"

Alison drew in a swift breath. She had always wished to offer aid to someone who needed it, to give back as she'd been given to all her life. It had been her dream in coming here.

But *this*...!

"I'll sleep in the barn. You can have my bed and as much privacy as can be managed with a houseful of seven. If you'd rather not involve yourself, and I can see by your shock that's more than likely—"

"Yes."

His brows lifted at her reply.

Had she really just agreed?

"You'll help me?" He looked as stunned as she felt to hear her answer.

Here was the chance to rectify her mistake. To say the journey had wearied her and she meant no, she could never do such an outlandish thing and would be on the next train to Boston. He would understand....

And the children—her little nieces and nephews—would go on as they had before.

She sighed at the prospect. "Yes, I'll help you. The children must learn that they cannot manipulate people. But to take part in anything dishonest, I'm not at all comfortable with that."

"Nothing dishonest. Just a good dose of truth. We'll meet after dinner and come up with a plan. With you being a stranger to a life on the plains, it shouldn't be difficult."

Noting the crafty gleam in his eyes, Alison didn't ask what he meant. She was almost afraid to know.

Chapter Five

....

Rafe sat at the head of the table and eyed each of his brood as they gathered around for the evening meal. The children avoided his gaze. Once seated, each of them immediately reached for the food.

"Ahem!" From the opposite end of the table, Alison cleared her throat, looking at them in surprise. "Aren't we forgetting something?"

"The bread," Sam chimed in. "The bottom is burnt, sorry, but I'll fetch it from the stove."

"It wasn't the bread I was referring to, Sam."

"Then what?" Clarissa looked puzzled.

"Why, to thank the Lord above for our bounty, of course." Alison looked at Rafe in confusion that his children would need to ask. He inclined his head for her to proceed. Her eyes narrowed a bit in shock when he didn't offer the prayer, but at his directive she bowed her head, looking to see if her actions were being followed. The children glanced at one another, uncertain, then at Rafe, who nodded to them, and they followed her example. "Dear heavenly Father, we ask You to bless this food. For what we are about to receive we are truly thankful. Amen."

Each of the children looked her way once she lifted her head. She smiled. "Please, resume what you were doing. Eat," she clarified, when they continued to stare.

Rafe watched the proceedings with mixed feelings of wry

amusement and grim purpose. His brood was on their best behavior, acting quite unsure of themselves, by the frequent and stealthy glances they cast his way. Likely they were speculating on how much he knew. He decided to remain silent about all of it. If they realized their plot had been uncovered and he then carried out his scheme with Alison, anything they might come up with wouldn't have much impact on the children. He should pretend ignorance and appear to carry through with their plan.

He could be a schemer too....

He smiled at his eldest daughter. "Good meal, Sam." Besides the burnt bread, it was some of the best food Sam had dished up. "I hope our guest finds our humble fare to her liking?"

"Oh, yes." Alison smiled. "This meat is very good. We've never had any like it at my uncle's home. What is it, exactly?"

"Salted pork."

Sam fidgeted, clearly ill at ease, as if waiting for more to follow. When nothing did, she offered them both wary glances. "Thank you. I'm glad you like it."

Rafe reached for a bowl of mashed corn. "Wasn't it kind of Miss Stripling to come all the way from Boston to pay us a visit? And so unexpected?"

Maggie choked on her food. Sam sat as still as a mouse with a cat who watched its every move. Clarissa looked up, her eyes as big as saucers. Tucker bowed his head as if continuing the earlier prayer. Even Andy looked peaked. Only Baby Lynn smiled and clapped, sticking her fingers in her corn before scooping more into her mouth. Rafe gave her a tender smile, putting the spoon in her hand. "Use this, not these." He patted her fingers.

"I felt it was high time I came to see Amy's dear children," Alison explained. Rafe looked her way, catching her conspiratorial glance. "Your mother wrote about each of you, how well-behaved you are, never causing a moment's heartache. Always doing what you're told. I just had to see such paragons of virtue for myself."

"What's a paragon?" Tucker asked.

Sam pushed her plate away.

Clarissa began to sniffle. "Excuse me. I have to go to the necessary," she blurted and ran for the door.

"Maggie, aren't you hungry?" Rafe pretended ignorance, noticing she hadn't taken another bite.

"No, Pa. I—I don't feel tho good either." She lowered her head, evading his steady gaze.

"What's a paragon?" Tucker asked again.

"A paragon of virtue is another way of saying that you're all good and honest children," Alison explained.

"Oh."

"Tucker, don't you want your pork? I know how much you like it."

"I ain't so hungry no more, Pa."

"Now that's a real shame, all of you without appetites. And such good food it is too." He took another bite, smiling wickedly. "Mmm-mm!"

At his exaggerated response, Alison placed her napkin over her mouth to cover the laugh she quickly disguised as a cough.

Softly, she cleared her throat. "Pardon me. I must still have some of that trail dust tickling my throat. I've never traveled so far. It was quite the experience, and I've never felt so weary. I imagine with a good night's sleep I'll be fully recovered by morning."

"I imagine so." Rafe nodded, still faintly grinning with their conspiracy. "You'll have the entire house, along with the girls. The boys and I will take the barn. Isn't that right, boys?"

Andy blinked. "The barn?"

Tucker looked at his brother and then at Rafe.

"Where else? Wouldn't be proper for us menfolk to stay inside the cabin with a lady present."

"Why not? You stayed here when Ma was alive, and she was a lady."

"A good deal different, Tucker. Your ma and I were married."

"But I thought you and Aunt Alison was going to—*OW*!" Tucker's words came to a swift halt as the sound of a shoe made a thump beneath the table. Rafe assumed from Tucker's reaction that Sam had kicked him in the shin. Tucker shot her a glare and both of them scowled at each other.

Rafe pretended not to notice. "You thought what, son?"

"Nothing," the boy mumbled.

"It wouldn't be right for us to sleep in the cabin. A woman like your aunt needs her privacy. All women do. It's up to us men to give it to her."

"We can give her privacy. Bein' as how me and Andy sleep on the other side of the loft, beyond the quilt, she wouldn't even know we was there."

"No, son. That won't work."

"Does that mean we have to live in the barn all the time?"

Rafe pretended to consider. "We can come in for meals, I reckon."

The boy frowned, clearly not happy with his answer.

"Now, who wants some pie?" Rafe clapped his hands together in enthusiasm. "Sam? Bring it on over here. It smells absolutely di–vine!"

Woodenly, she moved to do as asked. "I–it's not very good. The crust got a little burnt around the edges."

"I'm sure the peaches inside are fine." He cut out a hunk and lifted it. "Maggie?"

She shook her head, still not looking at him.

"Andy?"

"No, thanks. Supper did me in." His plate had barely been touched.

"Tucker?"

"No, Pa."

"I thought peaches were your favorite. You're not feeling ill too, are you? I sure hope there's no sickness going around."

"No, I'm fine."

"Hm. I'll bet you'd like a piece wouldn't you, Baby Lynn?"

She nodded with a grin, and he dropped a chunk oozing with glazed golden fruit to her plate.

"Sam?"

"I'm not very hungry either."

"Well, then, I guess that just leaves more for you and me, Miss Stripling." He reached for her plate. She handed it to Tucker, who handed it on down the line until it reached Rafe. He plopped half of what remained onto her plate, then handed it back to Maggie, who quickly passed it to Tucker, who wistfully eyed it for a moment before handing it back to Alison.

Rafe ate two-thirds of his pie before speaking. "Since you children aren't wanting dessert, you boys can go tend to your evening chores. Sam, leave the dishes till later. I want you to check on 'Rissa and make sure she's all right. Andy, Tucker, clear out a section of the barn for us to sleep in. Maggie, take Baby Lynn and clean her up." Mashed corn and gooey peaches not only covered her fingers, but also her face, hair, and dress.

"Yes, Pa." A chorus of subdued voices answered as the youngest Munroes left the table. Once the door shut, leaving the two adults alone, Alison shook her head in amusement.

"Do you honestly believe they don't suspect that you know they sent for me, what with that act you just performed? That is what you were doing, wasn't it? Pretending ignorance?"

His smile came positively devilish. "Oh, they'll wonder, all right. And it'll nag them something fierce, even make them a mite jumpy, trying to figure it all out. No less than they deserve, and they deserve a good deal more." His tone became grim. "For the time being, this is the best way to go about it, because then they won't suspect what *I* have planned." He pushed his plate aside and settled his forearms on the table, clasping his hands in a no-nonsense manner. "Now, onto my idea before my pride and joys return. Can you cook?"

"When I haunted the kitchen in my childhood, after Amy left, the cook took pity on my boredom and let me watch her. She showed me a few things, but I never caught on well."

"That's exactly what we want. Starting tomorrow, you'll be relieving Sam of her kitchen duties. And, Miss Stripling, I'm sure I don't need to add that you won't be giving it your best?"

She grinned. "Yes, Mr. Munroe. I think in this matter I understand you perfectly."

* * * * *

Alison woke before dawn, which astonished her. She'd always been an early riser but had not exaggerated about the train travel being exhausting. Then, too, the pack of dogs howling in the distance long into the night provided little means for relaxation.

Where to locate water to wash with presented her first problem; surely they didn't use the stream! It had looked muddy from afar. Or perhaps they used that large barrel of water she'd noticed outside the cabin?

Deciding she would need to dispense with her morning ritual for the time being, she said her morning prayers, sure to include a plea for guidance with regard to Rafe and his family. She then dressed in one of her eight day dresses, pinned up her hair, and swept into the main room. Recalling breakfast with her aunt and uncle, she tallied what she would need for eggs, sausages, biscuits, slices of pork, pancakes, fresh fruit, butter with marmalade, and coffee with cream.

First, came the eggs…or not.

Hens and chickens would be kept in the barn, surely, and she couldn't risk going inside with Rafe and his boys sleeping there! That is, if Rafe was still asleep…

She bit her lip in contemplation. No, she'd better not take the risk of introducing yet another awkward situation. Yesterday had been difficult enough.

That left sausages. And pork. Was all of it salted? Where would the meat be kept? Somewhere cool, surely. Along with butter… if there was butter… How did one churn butter?

She investigated a surprisingly large cupboard, looking at all the items and behind cloth sacks containing flour, cornmeal, sugar, and salt. Locating a bottle of cider, a treat she had always loved, she decided that would do for another day. Shouldn't it be chilled? How did they chill anything during such hot weather?

Remembering her need for water, she stepped outside the cabin into the gray dawn. A glance inside the uncovered barrel showed tiny insects floating on top. She certainly couldn't wash with that! Returning to the cabin, she pondered what to do next.

Her gaze went to the black cookstove in curiosity. How did one bake bread in that? The stove at her aunt's had been bigger and wider, though the cook never let her near it after Alison accidentally set fire to a dishcloth she'd used to pull out a sheet of burnt rolls. In baking, she could empathize with Sam and wouldn't have to engage in pretense to damage any meal.

Pancakes, however, she could manage. She had watched the cook make them often enough. After a short hunt, she found an apron, rolled up her sleeves, and set to work.

Sam entered the room to find Alison elbow-deep in a huge bowl of batter. The girl's widened gaze took in the spattered table and floor and the thick dusting of flour that covered both.

"Good morning," Alison cheerfully greeted.

Her niece gave her a doubtful smile. "You're cooking breakfast?"

"I should lend a hand as long as I'm here. I'm making pancakes. I hope you like them."

Sam moved closer, curiously peering into the bowl. "Pancakes?" She seemed a little worried. "What did you use?"

"Flour, butter I found on a plate in the cupboard, and salt. I couldn't locate fresh water, which is why it's lumpy. I thought I might flatten them out with a spoon as they cook."

Sam again looked at her oddly then studied the concoction Alison was stirring.

"It's Tucker's job to fetch water. He should be here soon. Every morning he fills the barrel with water from the stream—what we use for cooking, drinking, and cleaning."

"Oh?" Alison felt a little queasy. "I noticed the bugs inside."

"Likely gnats or 'skeeters. There's a cover, to keep most of 'em out, but someone probably forgot to put it on."

"You don't have a well for drinking?"

"No, we do. Ma insisted on it. But we usually just drink from the barrel. It's easier."

Good for Amy, but Alison felt appalled at Sam's last words. She couldn't drink water with dead bugs in it—nor should the children.

Her father had been a physician, and she knew all about cholera and how it could strike from drinking tainted water. The children appeared to be in good health, so thankfully they'd been spared thus far.

"I couldn't find eggs. I presume they're kept with the chickens in the barn?" She remembered how her uncle's cook had always sent her young assistant there and Geneva reappeared with a basket of eggs.

Sam studied Alison as if she'd grown another head. "Chickens are in the henhouse. We don't have eggs at breakfast, not anymore, but I'll get them for you if you like."

No eggs? Alison couldn't imagine a breakfast without poached eggs.

"Thank you, Sam. Or do you prefer Samantha? It's such a lovely name."

"Sam's fine. It's what everyone calls me. Everyone except…"

At her sudden glum look, Alison guessed. "Your mother?"

Sam nodded. "I'll just go get those eggs."

She whirled around for the door and stopped. Another Munroe now stood on the threshold of the cabin, and Alison swiftly inhaled.

"Pa! I didn't hear you come in."

Neither had Alison. Had they been talking so loudly that they hadn't noticed the hinges creaking when the door swung open?

Rafe looked weary, as if he hadn't slept well. His bleary eyes took in the appearance of his home, and Alison saw him cringe.

"You two are up and about early." His words were congenial; only his manner seemed grim.

"I'll go get the eggs," Sam said for the third time and dashed around him and out the open door.

"I take it you didn't pass a pleasant night?" Alison broached the subject carefully, since her presence in his home was the cause of him losing his bed.

"I've slept in worse places than a stack of hay."

Then why did he seem so grouchy? She didn't have long to find out.

He closed the door and approached her. Alison's stomach gave a funny little somersault when he stopped less than a foot away. He had a sweet, musky smell about him, of hay and the outdoors and a scent she felt must be his alone. He stood so tall she had to tilt her head back to look into his somber eyes.

"Being as how we're trying to get the children to *not* want you here," he dropped his tone to a confidential and disapproving whisper, "it's probably not a good idea to befriend them."

"Befriend them?" She blinked in confusion at his absurd statement. "I was simply making conversation and asking the location of things I need, since I haven't a clue."

"Seemed rather cozy, you bringing up Amy and sympathizing with Sam."

"*That's* why you're being such an unmitigated boor this time? Sam is my niece, and Amy was my sister. *Of course* I speak of her!" Alison stiffened her spine, lifting the batter-soaked spoon and shaking it at him. His eyes widened in surprise at her aggressive response, and he leaned back to avoid getting hit with splatters of dough. Her initial nervousness in his presence had set with the sun. She wouldn't be bullied or shirk from him again. "I loved her just as much, and I'm sorry for your loss. However, *not* talking about her won't make the emptiness go away. My agreement to stay and help you with your bizarre plan stemmed from my belief that I wouldn't be forced into deception."

"I'm not asking you to lie. Just don't be so all-fired nice to them."

"You would prefer I behave like a shrew?"

"If it gets the job done."

She let out a disbelieving huff. "Which, to my knowledge, would involve acting out a lie since being shrewlike is simply *not* in my disposition."

The absurdity of her claim suddenly came clear, as she stood toe-to-toe with him, facing him down and shaking a batter-soaked spoon in his face.

"Is that so?" He lifted his brow in wry amusement and wiped a doughy splotch from his shirt, giving his hand an emphatic shake to let the batter drop to the floor. "It seems your current behavior is much as I remembered it in Boston, Miss Stripling. You've never lost that waspish tongue of yours."

His effrontery almost astounded her, until she remembered with whom she spoke. Rafe Munroe, the man who'd stolen her sister away. The man who'd nearly bitten off her head upon their second meeting, when she hadn't done a blessed thing wrong. He was one to speak of dispositions!

"You're the exception to the rule, Mr. Munroe. Shrewlike is the only manner in which I can engage with you without showing any form of deceit."

"I don't give a fig how you act as long as you stick to our arrangement."

"Trust me, I've no intention of doing otherwise. The sooner I'm gone from your cheerless cabin and your pathetic life, the sooner I can return to Boston!"

"Pa?"

At the sound of Baby Lynn's voice trembling with tears, Alison and Rafe turned as one toward the child. She stood at the foot of the stairs, her bare toes peeking from beneath her nightgown. In one hand she clutched the hand of a doll made up of scraps and rags.

"Good morning, Sweet Pea." Rafe's manner changed drastically as he moved toward his youngest, scooped her up, and held her against his chest with one arm. His other hand traced her lashes. "What's this? Tears?"

"Don' make Auntie Al–son go away—please, Pa!" She wrapped her chubby arms around his neck and squeezed him hard. He cradled his hand at the back of her head and smoothed her tousled hair gently.

Alison stood in dumbfounded amazement, watching the interaction between father and daughter. He glanced in her direction, and she remembered to close her mouth.

"No one's making your aunt Alison do anything she doesn't want to, honey." His words to the child were tender, his somber gaze on Alison falling somewhere between remorseful and resigned. "What your aunt does is her choice. She's welcome to stay. My home is hers."

If she didn't know benevolence was part of his plan, she might have been touched. She must be touched—in the head, for thinking his character could change. She looked away from him and approached her niece.

Baby Lynn turned her head on his shoulder and looked at Alison, her big blue eyes shimmering with tears. "Will you stay?" she whispered. "Please?"

"I won't be leaving soon," Alison hedged.

"But I don't want you to go. Not eveh." Baby Lynn sniffled.

Alison felt helpless. She knew little about how to reassure a child so young, especially since she couldn't offer the comfort of the promise her niece sought.

Rafe kissed his daughter's head and set her down. "No use talking about things that haven't happened. You go upstairs and get dressed now."

"Can't." Her voice still wobbled. "Can't make the buttons go in the holes."

"Where are Maggie and Clarissa?"

The child shrugged her small shoulders.

Rafe sighed. "All right. I'll help you this time." He held out his large hand for her tiny one, but she shook her head of springy curls.

"Carry me!" she begged, a big smile chasing the misery from her face.

"Carry you?" Rafe teased in mock horror. *"Carry you?* You're such a big girl now, *I can't carry you!"*

She giggled. "Please, Pa!"

"Carry you, huh? *Hmph."* His mood changed like quicksilver as he suddenly grinned and scooped her up, planting her atop his shoulders. She squealed, grabbing him around the neck. Alison couldn't see how he didn't choke from Lynn's effusive affection.

"Giddap, horsey, go!"

He laughed and obeyed, stampeding up the stairs with his small rider and ducking so neither of their heads would hit the overhang leading into the loft.

Alison stood transfixed, still holding the spoon in her hand, her gaze on the spot she'd last seen them. Rafe might be a horrible excuse for a host, but apparently he was a doting father. This was a side to him she hadn't expected, and the shock of her discovery unsettled her, making her feel sorry for her rash of spiteful words. The cabin wasn't really that cheerless, and perhaps his life wasn't so pathetic. She really must learn to curb her impulsive tongue.

Turning back to her task, she set her mind wholly to preparing the meal, blocking out further thoughts of the man in the loft above her and the thumps, rustles, and giggles she heard as he helped his youngest child to dress.

The boys trudged into the cabin, looking better rested than their father and bellowing about being hungry. They took one look at the room and stopped in their tracks. Andy glanced at his brother. "Fetch Aunt Alison some water, Tucker."

"Sure thing, Andy." The boy grabbed the pail of old water sitting near the cookstove, raised his brows when he saw that flour had gotten in there too, and left the cabin. Andy, obviously realizing that Alison wouldn't know how to light the stove, set to work doing so.

Clarissa and Maggie appeared, followed by Sam, who carried eggs she'd gathered in her skirt. Carefully, she set the cradle of it on the table and the brown eggs, one by one, into a bowl.

"What's the eggs for?" Clarissa asked.

Alison stopped scooping the dough into the pan and stared at her in utter shock. "You've *never* eaten eggs for breakfast?"

"Unh-uh."

"Sure you have," Sam said. "You just don't remember. Ma used to make them."

"Oh." Clarissa studied the eggs and then looked at Alison. "Sam makes cornmeal mush or porridge."

"Yeah, lumpy, rocky, so-thick-it'll-choke-you porridge," Tucker joined in, returning with the water.

"If you don't like it, you make it!" Sam glared at him.

Alison peeked inside the pail, expecting brown silty liquid, and felt surprised to see it so clear.

"This is from the stream?"

"Nah, it's from the well. Too far to walk to the stream every cotton-pickin' time we want a drink. Besides, Ma insisted it wasn't fit for human consum–consum—"

"Consumption," Sam filled in.

"Yeah, that."

Alison felt relieved to know they didn't always drink from the outside barrel. "What do I use to clean this mess? The water in the barrel is hardly suitable either."

Tucker eyed the flour-spotted area. "You wanna clean? *Now?*"

Alison almost laughed at the pained look in his eyes.

"Of course. We can't sit in such filth while we eat."

"Like the pig?" Maggie wanted to know.

"You like pigs, Aunt Alison?" Tucker grabbed another bucket from beneath the table.

"I wouldn't know. There were no pigs at my uncle's home. At least I don't think there were. The cook usually sent one of the help to the butcher for fresh meat."

"No pigs?" Tucker looked aghast. "You had chickens, though?"

"I imagine we must have, since we ate eggs every morning. I stayed inside the manor most of the time, or strolled through the gardens, when I wasn't at the milliner's shop."

"We've got a yellow cat," Clarissa piped up. "Only Pa don't let him in the house no more, ever since he jumped on Ma's pianoforte. And Pa had to make a coop so he wouldn't eat the baby chicks."

"I use ta have a snake."

"Used to?" Alison looked at Tucker in alarm, recalling Sam's startling announcement of Tucker's odd pet.

"It got away," he said sadly. "If you see it, tell me before Pa gets wind it's gone."

She wouldn't have to. They would hear her scream clear to the next county.

"Maybe your frog ate it," Maggie suggested.

Tucker scowled. "Frogs don't eat snakes, silly!"

"You like to ride horses, Aunt Alison?" Clarissa asked.

"I can sit a saddle well." Barely able to follow the rapid back-and-forth, Alison swiftly clapped her hands together. "The morning isn't stopping for anyone. Tucker, please collect water for washing. Girls, I'll need you to tidy up while I finish breakfast."

She felt bad, appointing them to clean her mess, but she reasoned that wouldn't gain her any favor, which was the purpose of Rafe's plan. However, the girls exchanged glances, shrugged, and set to work with no complaint.

"I'll tend to the milking," Andy said.

"You have a cow?"

"Sure do," Sam answered. "Maggie, fetch cream from the springhouse. We'll have to churn more butter today too. That was the last of it."

Industriously, they set about their chores while Alison prepared the meal.

Breakfast was a complete success—in that it was a total disaster.

Chapter Six

....

Rafe went out to the porch, his stomach growling from lack of food. He'd eaten what he could stand of all three meals. What hadn't been burnt almost to a crisp tasted soggy or bland.

With a subdued laugh, he remembered the looks on his children's faces, from shock to disgust. The pig would have plenty of scraps.

The door opened and Alison appeared. "Mind if I join you?"

He shook his head, not really caring either way. She closed the door, coming to stand beside him. "Congratulations. I think your plan worked."

He grinned. "No offense, Miss Stripling, but that was some of the worst food I've had in all my born days."

She laughed. "No offense taken. I told you I couldn't cook. I think your children have learned that by now."

"Yes," he mused. "Did you see those pained looks they kept giving each other? Maybe tomorrow morning wouldn't be too soon to tell them you're leaving."

In the last glow of sunset, he noticed her stricken expression and how her dark eyes flinched. "That might be too soon. What about Baby Lynn? She won't take it well."

"Baby Lynn is three. She'll get over it."

"I'm not so sure...."

"I thought we agreed that the whole idea was to get them to see you're not ma material so we could resume our lives."

"Oh, I'm not shirking our deal, Mr. Munroe. Far from it." Her chin lifted a notch. "I'm merely suggesting that we should take this slowly, a step at a time, instead of jumping right to the conclusion. How believable would it seem that one minute you're welcoming me into your home and the next you're announcing my departure?"

"I doubt that after their empty bellies have been complaining all the day long they'll care one way or the other when you leave, just that you do."

"I'm not so sure they're convinced."

"You think you know my children better than me?" Why did he feel so defensive all of a sudden?

"Of course not. But from what I understand, you've been… absent most of the time."

"Now you're saying I neglect my kids?"

"What I'm saying"—she turned to face him full-on—"is that with Amy's death, you were under a great deal of strain, and it's understandable. But as a result, you distanced yourself from your children, with the exception of Baby Lynn."

"How can you claim to know so much about me or my kids after being here for little more than a day?"

"I listen to what they tell me, and I sense what they don't." Her soft-spoken yet firm words stymied him, and he stared at her openmouthed. "As you have stated," she continued, "they *are* your children. So if you've decided to end this ruse, then you have only to say the word. Once you take me back to town, I'll rent a room at a hotel until I can obtain passage for my return home. Good night, Mr. Munroe."

He watched her turn and enter his cabin, her stride as regal as a queen.

Irritation with her insolence fought with admiration for her pluck. But confusion won over them both.

He couldn't figure out Amy's sister. One minute she seemed the timid mouse, and the next she glared into his eyes and shook a spoon in his face. A reluctant grin tugged at the corners of his mouth when he remembered the sight of her, covered head to toe in sprinklings of flour, while she chastised him as if she were his mother. He didn't recall much about his mother. She'd died when he'd been too young to remember. But the queer, unsettled feelings he had for Alison when he'd stood near her didn't come close to anything he felt for kin.

Since Amy died, he'd experienced the occasional physical yearnings of a man when he caught sight of a pretty woman, but he'd evaded the temptations, usually by leaving the area. Alison had grown into an attractive lady, with thick, dark hair, heavily lashed brown eyes, and a womanly form. He'd felt those same stirrings with her but had nowhere to run.

He certainly hadn't slipped so far from his faith that he was willing to bed a town prostitute for a few forbidden hours of questionable pleasure, which would undoubtedly only lead to months of guilt. Nor would he ever consider wooing Alison and eventually taking her to his bed without the sanctity of a lifetime commitment. She may be a little tempest at times, but she was also a virtuous lady, and he would never do her such a grave dishonor.

He wanted no commitments—sanctimonious or otherwise.

Caleb often said it wasn't good for a man like Rafe to be alone, that grieving was necessary to heal but the time must come to release the past and resume living. In other words, take a second wife. But Rafe wanted nothing to do with revisiting the rituals of courtship and marriage; no one could fill Amy's place. And so he managed his days in his own bottled frustration, working hard in the fields with his sons and focusing his attention on raising his crops.

Yet Alison was right about one thing—he hadn't been a real father to his children. He had curtly asked if she accused him of neglecting them—maybe because he knew that's exactly what he'd done, to all but Baby Lynn. His youngest reminded him of Amy; perhaps that was why he coddled her so.

"Blast the woman," he muttered, uncomfortable with the self-appraisal that she had stirred up with her parting words. "The quicker she's gone, the better."

He woke the next morning the same time as always, according to the ash-gray sky. After pulling on his boots, he headed for the cabin, eager to relate the news of Alison's departure to the children, who surely would be relieved to hear it.

Rafe opened the door and stopped dead in his tracks.

All of his brood, except for Baby Lynn and the boys, both of whom he'd left back in the barn, gathered around Alison and the cookstove.

"Like 'Rissa said, porridge or cornmeal mush is what we usually eat of a morning," Sam explained as she stirred the contents of the black pot. "I'll teach you how to make both. Everyone has to learn to cook. Ma did too."

"Don't feel bad, Auntie Alison." Clarissa moved to stand on the other side of her. "Everybody makes bad meals sometimes."

Maggie finished setting the table. "Yeth. We'll all help you learn."

"How are *you* gonna help?" Sam wanted to know, shooting a pointed look at her sister. "You don't know how to cook."

"Maybe we can all learn and teach each other? That's what Ma would have thaid. That we all work together to get the job done well."

"No more eggs." Clarissa wrinkled her nose.

Alison laughed. "Eggs are actually very good. I'm just terrible at making them. Who knew that poached eggs would be so difficult to achieve?"

Rafe cleared his throat. They turned as one. Alison's expression grew wary.

"Morning, Pa!" his girls chirruped gleefully.

"We're teaching Aunt Alithun to cook!" Maggie chimed in.

"*Who's* teaching her?" Sam asked with a huff.

The boys ambled in, knocking into Rafe, who stepped aside.

"'Scuse us, Pa."

Tucker carried a bucket of water. "Brought this for you, Aunt Alison, from the well. So you wouldn't have to fetch it. I can show you how to get it yourself, in case I'm not around. And if you want more water for the barrel, just say so. I scooped out the dead bugs, though."

"I see you got the stove lit," Andy said. "Sorry I didn't get here sooner."

"I lit it," Sam corrected.

"G'morning!" A bright voice came from the top of the stairs followed by a bubbling of giggles as his youngest flounced down the short flight of steps in her bed gown.

"I'll help you dress, Baby Lynn." Maggie moved toward her.

"Unh-uh." She shook her head of red-gold curls. "Want Auntie Al–son to do it! Dress me," she pleaded in her sweet, cajoling way, holding her hands as though clasped in prayer at her throat.

Alison exchanged a look with Rafe over the children's heads. She raised her brows in helplessness and shrugged then moved toward Baby Lynn, who grabbed at Alison's hand as if worried she might get away. Rafe sighed, at last remembering to close the door behind him.

The porridge turned out smooth, not lumpy, the biscuits not so hard, the coffee strong and black. But Rafe barely offered a word and Alison remained quiet, except when the children asked her a question. Once the meal ended, Rafe stood up from the table.

"Maggie, 'Rissa, help Sam with the dishes and keep an eye on your baby sister. Boys, tend to your chores. Miss Stripling, I'd like a word with you outside."

With those grim instructions, he walked out the door.

* * * * *

Taking a deep breath for fortitude, Alison walked outside to join the master of the house. His scowl throughout breakfast didn't bode well about the upcoming confrontation being an easy one to bear.

He stood with his back to her, looking out over the fields. At her step he turned and she shut the door.

"Relax, Miss Stripling, I'm not going to bite. I'm not angry with you."

She released the breath she didn't realize she'd been holding.

"You're right. This is going to take more work—"

The door swung open, both boys ambling outside. They curiously looked back and forth between the adults.

"Go tend to the animals," Rafe spoke to them. "I'll be along shortly."

"Yes, Pa," Andy said.

Tucker made no reply as he looked at them.

"Skedaddle."

At Rafe's order, both boys ran in the direction of the barn.

"Perhaps we should continue this discussion later, when there's less chance of being interrupted?" Alison suggested hopefully. His bad attitude had a habit of setting hers off, like a flame to tinder, and she didn't want another argument.

"We need a second plan…since the first one clearly didn't work." He ran a hand through his hair in frustration. "I was so sure it would. No child wants a ma who can't even boil water without bungling things. I'd hoped this would make them realize how ridiculous their idea was to—"

The door swung open. Sam stepped out with an empty basket hanging over one arm. She had tied on a ragged calico bonnet, the blue ribbon securing it under her chin also frayed. Alison winced at the sad condition of the hat.

"I thought I'd walk into town and sell eggs to Mrs. Merriweather, if that's okay. Maggie and Clarissa are taking care of the dishes."

"Don't dawdle. And be back before noon."

"Sure thing, Pa." She took a few steps away then stopped and turned. "Would it be all right if I bought another slate with some of the money from the eggs? My old one's cracked, and I–I'd like to go back to school again, if that's okay."

Rafe drew his brows together in indecision. "We'll discuss it later. Buy what you need."

"Thanks, Pa!" Her face beaming, she ran past a pigpen and to the other side of the barn, where Alison assumed the henhouse stood.

Rafe eyed the door, as if expecting it to open again, before turning back to Alison.

"Something just occurred to me that might work—"

The door swung open a third time. Alison squelched a laugh at the pained expression that crossed Rafe's eyes before he briefly closed them and shook his head in disbelief.

Maggie stepped outside, the other pail hanging over her arm. She looked at them, uncertain, the tip of her tongue playing with the gap in the middle of her top row of teeth.

"I need to get water," she explained. "Tucker hathn't refilled the barrel."

"Go, then." Rafe gave a sideways nod toward the stream.

She smiled and took off running, her copper braids bouncing.

Rafe turned back to Alison. She honestly tried to keep from grinning, but she couldn't help herself. She pressed her lips together to curb it from spreading.

He lifted one brow. "You find this amusing?"

She shrugged, shaking her head in a helpless effort not to laugh. "You don't?"

"Not particularly." He tugged the brim of his hat firm over his brow. "We'll resume our talk after supper tonight. Once the children are in bed."

"Yes." She gave a wise little nod as if it had been his idea all along. "I do think that would be the best course to take."

Narrowing his eyes, he peered at her closely. His lips abruptly edged into a wry, amused grin, revealing little hollows in his cheeks that could pass for dimples. "Yeah, I thought you just might."

Her heart gave a sudden thump at the pronounced change such a simple expression made in the man—from glowering and forbidding to fetching and youthful. Oddly flustered, she averted her gaze to the rows of green stalks swaying in the wind beyond him.

"Till tonight then, Miss Stripling."

He tipped his hat in a careless manner and strode away. She watched him move toward the barn, his gait strong and sure and decidedly masculine.

Alison pressed a hand to her quickened heart. Whatever was the matter with her?

Tearing her gaze from his retreating form, she hurried back inside the cabin.

Chapter Seven

....

"The way I see it," Rafe speculated as he and Alison sat outside that evening, him on the lid of the barrel and her on a bench, "is that you need to start complaining more."

"Complaining?"

The night insects made whispery, whirring noises as Alison studied Rafe in the light of the lone lantern he'd hung on the cabin wall between them. The children had gone to their respective beds, and a spray of twinkling stars spread across a vast sky as black as ink.

"You don't do enough of it. Maybe if you weren't so agreeable, it might help."

"So, let me see if I understand this correctly: you want me to behave like a whining shrew."

He grinned at her reminder of their previous morning. "It might get the job done. You wouldn't have to lie either. You can't tell me it's been easy for you."

"It wasn't all bad." She'd done rather well, except for a few minor mishaps—all easily rectified. Especially with the girls showing her how. And Tucker had found his missing pet before it slithered across her path. Her admonition that he must keep it in the barn and never again in the house had been received rather well, to her relief. All of the children had behaved like angels today.

Rafe's eyes narrowed as if he could read her thoughts. "I'm just saying—"

She sighed. "I know. You want the children to despise me."

"'Despise' is too strong a word. I don't want them to feel badly toward you, being as how you're their aunt and all."

"Thank you for that, at least."

He ignored her dry rejoinder. "I just don't want them to develop the need to keep you around." He rubbed his jaw in deep thought. "I assume it's safe to say you've never washed laundry?"

"The servants took care of that."

"Hmm. Wash day is the day after tomorrow. Let's make that plan two. And I'll bet my Winchester rifle that you'll be bad-tempered enough to complain by the time you've scrubbed the third shirt."

"And I would have to reply to your presumptuous remark of my character that perhaps it's time I learned to shoot."

He looked full at her. "Don't go making this harder than it is."

"Right. Sorry. Fine. On wash day, attempt to do laundry and complain the entire time." She ticked the activities off with two fingers as she spoke. "Anything else?"

"That should do it."

He looked out at the tall grasses, a sea of rapier-thin silhouettes that danced and swayed in the ever-present wind that had grown stronger with nightfall.

"Why did you come to Kansas?" She posed the question that had plagued her for years.

For a moment, she didn't think he would answer.

"I wanted to own a piece of the land. When my father died of consumption, I'd had enough of living in the city and wanted away from the constant ruckus. I reckon I had that thirst for adventure that grabs hold of many. Caleb settled here before me. When he wrote, describing plains so wide you couldn't see end to end and a sky so big and blue with no buildings or trees to block it, well, it sounded like the answer to prayer. I talked it over with Amy, and she agreed."

Alison could understand his fascination for the wilds, since she'd experienced a similar feeling upon her first sighting of the plains. "Do you ever regret leaving Boston?"

"I can't say it's always been easy. Many that came here went back East after foul weather hit—cyclones that ripped the land apart, blizzards worse than in Boston, because in the city we weren't snowed in without aid. No neighbors live close by—the closest one is a few miles away—but the year the grasshoppers struck was the worst. A swarm so thick, the sky turned black. They must've been five inches high off the ground. If I hadn't had skills as a carpenter's apprentice in Boston, I don't know how I would have fed my family. That year was one of the worst. I lost all my crops to them blasted insects. And then there's the simoons—dust storms that whip up out of nowhere and turn the sky to silt. Flying sand stings your skin like it's biting you, and you can't see a thing—not the sky above or the earth below. It's as if the earth is no longer still but flies in a crazed dance all around you."

His words made her shiver, and she wondered if he exaggerated in a desire to frighten her away from any prospect of staying. She looked up at the clear sky. "Does that happen often?"

"Often enough."

She shook her head. "Hazardous cyclones, dangerous blizzards, swarms of pests eating your crops...again, why do you stay?"

"This is my home. I wouldn't expect you to understand, but living and working the land, it gets in your blood and becomes a part of you. The freedom you can only find in wild, open, untamed country like this, the sense of belonging to your surroundings instead of them belonging to you...it's hard to describe."

He did a fairly decent job of it. She could begin to understand the pull, as some deep yearning she never knew existed rose up within and made her wish—made her wish—

Made her wish what?

She blinked, attempting to break the mesmeric spell he'd woven over her with his words. "What about Indians? When you staked your claim, they were still here, weren't they? Before they were sent to the reservations?"

He nodded. "We never had any attack us. Actually made friends and traded with several of the Kaw, who visited the creek on the way to their hunting grounds. There are those who've made war on the settlers, but there are also the peace-loving tribes who want no conflict."

She looked at him in surprise. "That isn't the general viewpoint I've heard."

He shrugged. "I just wish we could have all found a way to get along. But it doesn't matter what I think. What's done is done." He offered her a sad, twisted sort of smile.

Alison regarded him in frank amazement. This side of Rafe was new to her. She searched for something to say. "That's quite a unique stance on the subject. I've always heard that the Indians were the ones at fault."

He gave her another crooked smile. "My father taught me when I was a boy still in britches that with any conflict, each side is usually right *and* wrong. No one is entirely without blame."

Alison mulled over his words. That could even be said for their own awkward alliance as reluctant cohorts. Both she and Rafe seemed prone to jump immediately into accusations and arguments, and both were to blame for the outcomes of such squabbles.

Oddly enough, she found herself wanting to befriend this man she'd once thought her enemy. She could scarcely believe they were speaking civilly to one another. This break from their discussions of how to succeed in getting rid of her so that the children would agree to Rafe's wishes to remain unattached was…refreshing—even enjoyable?

Wishing to divert from the peculiar and unsettling trek her mind had taken, she changed the subject. "I understand that your brother's church is on the opposite side of town?"

Rafe nodded.

"Out of curiosity, why didn't you stake a claim there?"

"When Amy and I arrived in Hope, it didn't have a name yet. It sure wasn't as built up as it is now, and most of the good land was taken. We were fortunate to find this place, so close to a stream. An older couple lived here but they died, leaving no kin behind. It's a wonder no one spotted it before we did. Amy said the Lord was holding it for us, keeping it hidden from others' eyes. I don't know…." His words came melancholic with a trace of bitterness. "But the soil's rich and the land's produced well, when the weather has a mind to cooperate."

"Those tall green stalks are corn, correct?"

She saw the twitch at his mouth and smiled first. "Don't laugh. I'm no farmer's daughter."

He nodded. "Yes, the corn is the green stalks. Shortly before you came, the boys and I harvested the wheat."

"I read about that in the Scriptures," she said, glad to contribute something. "You thresh the wheat by hand to refine it? To get rid of the chaff?"

"Yes. Only now, I share a threshing machine with a few other farmers. It gets the job done quicker. The girls tend the vegetable garden—the patch growing nearest the cabin."

Again, that most peculiar desire rose up, to learn this land. But to what benefit? In Boston she wouldn't need such knowledge.

The thought didn't settle well with her.

"I should turn in for the evening. I do hope those dogs don't again howl all night." Oddly enough, she didn't want to go, but she needed to rise before dawn. Sam would be showing her how to manage breakfast...and churn butter.

"Dogs?" He chuckled grimly. "Those were no dogs, Miss Stripling. Those were wolves."

"Wolves?" She fought a cold shiver of apprehension and looked at him in shock. She had heard of wild animals roaming the plains, especially at night. But at the same time, the steady, burning look in Rafe's eyes supported her theory that he might be trying to frighten her away from any notion of staying longer than it took their plan to succeed. He needn't worry; she couldn't leave soon enough.

She lifted her chin, refusing to be intimidated. "I probably should have mentioned it, but the girls are teaching me to cook."

"So I heard." A frown puckered his brow.

"Yes, well...I simply cannot continue serving such—tripe—as today's fare. Nor do I feel comfortable about wasting good food. If I allow matters to persist in this vein, we'll all be scarecrows by month's end. Besides, since Sam expressed a desire to return to the schoolhouse"—she watched his mouth open in protest and forged ahead in an effort to help her niece—"I think it would be a wonderful opportunity for her, while I'm here, to get what education she can from a certified teacher. She hopes to be a writer, so she said, and her studies are imperative to excel in that profession."

"A writer? Used to be a teacher. Though, thinking on it, with her bashfulness, she's smart to choose writing instead."

"Sam is shy?" Alison wondered if they were talking about the same Sam.

"Only with strangers. She doesn't like to speak at public gatherings. Three years back, when she attended school, she was required to recite a poem in front of all the parents attending. She became tongue-tied and ran out of the schoolhouse. I found her crying by the stream."

"Oh, how awful! I understand how she must have felt."

His expression altered into amused disbelief. "I find it hard to believe you were ever shy or tongue-tied. You lit into me like a torch to a haystack on our first meeting."

"Hmm, yes, how kind of you to remind me." She quirked her mouth in a wry grimace and he let out a short laugh. At his unexpected levity, some of her tension melted away, and she leaned her shoulder against the door. "Amy told you that her parents took me from an orphan train, I presume?"

"Yes." His tone implied the desire to know more.

"Amy's parents—and her mother's sister and husband—were wonderful to me. I never felt anything less than family." She pondered her early childhood, the moments hazy and likely brought on by all she'd been told. "It was quite by happenstance that they arrived at the station that morning. They'd come to New York to visit her sister at the same time the orphan train prepared to leave the station. Had fate not intervened and my adoptive parents never seen me in that line of children waiting to board, I very well could have ended up here in Kansas. The orphan trains delivered children throughout the Midwest, finding homes for them," she explained.

He nodded as if he knew that, and she wondered what, if anything, Amy had told him about her. Perhaps he already knew her life story; she continued regardless.

"Amy told me years later that I reminded our mother of her baby sister who'd died from scarlet fever. Mother considered coming to the station that day a divine appointment." Alison shrugged delicately. "Whatever the reason, while my new parents were most benevolent toward an orphan with questionable lineage, the townspeople were not. They treated me as one might treat a leper. I was the focus of gossip and had no true friends besides Amy. I withdrew from those who weren't family—not out of shyness, but out of disgust and hatred. Perhaps if my parents hadn't been the wonderful example they were, I might have grown bitter with reproach. But with their help, I learned to offer absolution. I faced my troubles instead of running from them, and I learned to be strong.

"Once they died in that awful coach accident, my mother's sister extended the same kindness toward me. I was fifteen years of age when I moved into the Honorable Judge Graystone's home. They live in an even more pretentious neighborhood than the one I'd known before."

Rafe drew his brows together at her grim words. "The people there treated you badly too?"

She nodded. "I was a foundling, you see. A child without a name. A rumor began that my father was an insane killer residing in the Boston Lunatic Asylum, and you can imagine what havoc that created." She shook her head in weary disbelief, recalling how many chose to believe such an absurd tale. "But I'm drifting from the point I wish to make. If you give Sam permission to attend school—at least while I'm visiting—she won't be able to take over the meals. It's time I learned the rudimentary basics every woman should know, such as how to cook. I won't always live with the Graystones, I daresay, and the likelihood is slim that I'll employ servants in the future."

"If you don't stay with your aunt and uncle, where will you go?"

"I plan to find work as a governess, in a place where no one knows me or my past. I've found I enjoy being with children—well, the little experience I've had with yours—and I'm well-educated, so it seems like a good prospect."

He looked at her for a long time before responding. "When you speak like that, it makes it difficult to refuse. But, Miss Stripling…"

She tensed at the mild warning in his voice. "Yes?"

"Just don't forget why you're here."

"Right. To make the children realize I'd be no good to them as a mother and to aid you in changing their attitude to see me boarded on the next available train. I haven't forgotten, Mr. Munroe. We share the same goal."

She went back inside the cabin, trying not to let his constant mantra needle her. Why had she poured her heart out to the man? She doubted he harbored any true desire to hear her story, if Amy hadn't told him already. But in the peaceful evening, she'd felt an ease previously not experienced in his presence and found herself saying more than she'd intended.

Another thing she resolved to learn was to curb her wandering tongue!

Chapter Eight

....

"You *what*?"

Rafe stoically eyed his brother, who looked as if he might burst into laughter again at any second. "You heard me."

"Indeed I did. I just didn't really believe you'd resort to such measures." Caleb's eyes danced in amusement. "You don't actually think this plan of yours could work?"

"And why not?"

At times his older brother could be a persistent thorn in Rafe's side. Newly married, having finally found the perfect woman, with a baby on the way, Caleb thought he had all the answers when it came to family issues, while Rafe had been a family man for fifteen years.

It could be downright irritating sometimes.

After greeting Rafe minutes ago, Caleb had asked about Alison and why Rafe hadn't let him know she was coming to Hope. When Rafe told him the particulars, his brother at first appeared stunned and then let out a belly laugh that could have been heard clear across Dickinson County. He'd finally managed to pull himself together, apologized, admitted that Rafe's brood had been wrong to employ such methods—and then burst out laughing again.

Yes, indeed. Downright irritating.

"Not that I don't think a few swats on the backside serve their purpose when needed," Rafe explained, "but this plan will teach them a lesson not to interfere."

"Oh, no doubt. A lesson will be taught," Caleb remarked with a smirk. "I'm just not sure who will get the benefit of the discovery."

Rafe narrowed his eyes. "Just what's that supposed to mean?"

"Ah, you know me, little brother. I'm only funnin' with you. So the kids don't know you discovered their scheme, and you're keeping it a secret from them. Hmm."

Rafe sighed, recognizing Caleb's little humming sound of disapproval. He waited for the inevitable censure.

"Deception in any form can bring all sorts of misery, Rafe. Even the best-laid plans falter when trickery is their source. I only hope you know what you're doing by trying to teach the children and using their own game to do it."

"I have it under control."

"You sure about that?"

"Of course. I just dropped by to let you in on what's happening. Since Andy mentioned he saw you the day Miss Stripling arrived, I felt you ought to know. But I need to get home."

"Ivy will be upset to have missed you. She's visiting one of our sick parishioners but should be home soon. She wanted to extend an invitation to a picnic next week, after Sunday service, so she can meet this amazing young woman whom the children have set their sights on to be their new ma."

Caleb's light farewell didn't amuse Rafe one bit. He mumbled, "I'll have to think about it," and headed for his horse.

"You do that, Rafe," Caleb's words followed him. "You think mighty hard…."

As Rafe rode home, he pondered his brother's words.

He *did* know what he was doing, and with Alison's cooperation they would succeed. The woman was intelligent; she caught on fast and could even see what Rafe couldn't about his own children. That had rankled, but her warning that they needed more time to win the children over to Rafe's way of thinking had proven true.

Talking to her two nights prior had been pleasant. He hadn't really conversed with a woman since Amy died, and doing so with Alison hadn't galled him as he had felt it might. He'd been relieved that she appeared to be just as eager to leave Kansas, and he wondered how their second plan was progressing.

As he drew near the cabin, small billows of white smoke rising into the sky caught his attention. He reasoned that Andy had set a fire beneath the big kettle to heat the water for laundry. He smiled, thinking of his children's probable reactions to Alison's ignorance regarding a second chore, the chief one each of his brood despised.

Laughter carried to him on the wind—his children's laughter— and he frowned. His glower deepened as he moved through the boundary of trees and his cabin came in sight.

All of his girls gathered around Alison, who, to her credit, wasn't smiling. The steam from the heated water caused the long tendrils of dark hair that had escaped her bun to damply curl about her flushed face.

"I think you're getting the hang of it, Aunt Alithun," Maggie remarked cheerfully, as, with Clarissa's help, she used the end of a long wooden board to pull from the steaming kettle a sopping piece of clothing. Together, the girls transferred it to a huge pail, near where Alison crouched and rubbed at another piece of clothing on the washboard. Baby Lynn, skipping in circles around the group, looked his way. "There's Pa!"

Everyone looked up, and Clarissa waved. Alison quit scrubbing and straightened her spine, putting a hand to her back, as if preparing for a verbal onslaught. He came to several feet from where they worked. She looked at him a moment, then lifted her reddened hands and lowered her gaze to them.

"They'll never be the same," she fretted. "Just look—are those chilblains?" She met Rafe's gaze, her eyes seeking his approval. "I abhor such tiresome work. Had I known it would be so grueling, I might never have taken the train to come out to this godforsaken wilderness."

He gave her a slight nod, but she winced and he sensed complaints didn't come easy for her. Strange, that with her pampered lifestyle and ignorance in hard labor she would find it difficult to voice her opinions without a plan to prompt them.

"Aw, you'll get used to it," Clarissa encouraged. "None of us likes doing the wash. It's a good thing it comes only once a week, 'stead of every day."

For a desperate moment, Rafe wondered if making it a rule that wash day came every day might help the plan along; then he dismissed the idea. The task *took* an entire day. Buckets of water had to be fetched from the stream for the huge kettle and heated, the task repeated every time the lye water got too dirty. The boys usually took care of fetching the water, and he looked around the area, wondering where they were.

"Being your firtht time to do the wash, it mutht be harder on you than uth. We've been doing it for years and hate it jutht as much. Don't we, 'Ritha?"

Clarissa nodded. "Ma's got a bottle of oil she put on her hands. It's the lye that makes them so red."

Alison pulled a pair of long johns from the rinse water. As she wrung out the clothing, her look upward to Rafe seemed to say, "I tried."

Rafe heaved a mighty sigh as he dismounted. "Where are the

boys and Sam?" Baby Lynn ran to him and he caught her up in his arms, holding her to his side.

Clarissa giggled and Maggie's grin could have split her cheeks.

"Aunt Alithun thaid they had to have their long johns washed too, though Tucker put up a huge ruckuth!"

Clarissa nodded. "She said their clothes were in hor–hor—"

"Horrenduth," Maggie supplied.

"Hor–nendous shape and that they had to strip down to the skin and give her their clothes."

"Really?" He shot another approving look at Alison. "So who carried the water?"

"Aunt Alison said we had to."

"You?" He looked with amazement at his two small, rail-thin daughters.

"We didn't mind. Tucker and Andy couldn't 'cause they haven't got a stitch on." Clarissa giggled again.

"Better run fatht, Pa, before Aunt Alithun makes you thrip down too."

"Actually," Alison spoke, her gaze level, "that's not a bad idea."

"Sam inside?" He ignored the suggestion that sounded more like a command.

"She's seeing to dinner," Maggie answered.

He walked to the cabin.

"You can have Sam bring out your things," Alison's voice followed. "Your clothes could do with a good washing as well, Mr. Munroe."

He stopped and looked at her over his shoulder. Surely she wasn't serious. The sparkle in her dark eyes made clear her amusement, and the manner in which she crossed her arms over her chest made obvious her determination.

"Sam can collect a blanket for you while you wait," she added sweetly.

He sensed that she derived entirely too much pleasure from this second plan—either that or she was trying to unsettle him. "Good thing for me, then, that I have a spare. I'll just go and change."

"Yes, you do that."

Her honeyed words followed him into the cabin, and he managed to curb the smile that teased his lips at her banter. But when he caught sight of his two boys huddled at the table, ferociously clutching blankets around their lean forms, he couldn't help but chuckle.

"Look what she made us do, Pa!" Tucker clutched the blanket even tighter around himself. "She made us strip down to our skin!"

"Good thing, too," Sam said as she stirred what smelled like beans on the stove. He noticed a pot of coffee there as well. "Any longer without a wash and those long johns of yours might have taken leave of your body and walked off by themselves. At least she didn't put up with any of your nonsense, Tucker. Not like we foolishly did."

"Aw, whose side are you on?" Tucker complained. "She made you cook dinner by yourself."

Sam shrugged. "It's not like I haven't done *that* before."

Rafe addressed his daughter. "I'll take a cup of that coffee. But first, I need to go and change."

Tucker's eyes widened in horror. "She got you too, Pa?"

"Yes, son, she got me too."

"Did she threaten if you didn't, she'd tie you up and strip them off herself?"

The image in his mind that the description evoked made Rafe go hot in the face. "No, that she didn't do." The very thought of the petite and pampered Alison Stripling from Boston tackling anyone to tie them down made Rafe chuckle again. Sam gave him a curious smile and he moved into his bedroom to change, the first time he'd entered it since Alison had moved in.

Her trunk stood open, displaying her fineries amid shimmering dresses. A Bible lay on the made-up bed. The hat she'd worn upon her arrival, with its feathery black plume that swayed and bobbed every time she moved, sat propped on the bedpost. Her personal items placed hither and yon made it feel less like his room and more like hers.

Quickly he moved to collect his things from the wooden armoire he'd built for Amy. Her dresses still hung neatly there, and his fingers drifted to the soft blue sleeve of one before he snapped from his reverie and grabbed his spare clothing. The stabbing pain that usually throbbed through his heart at the sight of her things didn't feel as sharp. Maybe Caleb was right about time healing even the deepest wounds. He still missed his sweet wife but was experiencing a measure of peace and acceptance he'd never felt. Maybe concentrating on their children and becoming less focused on his own pain had helped to push him past the edge of restlessness into this new calm.

Whatever the reason for the change, he welcomed the difference.

Hurriedly he undressed and then dressed again, not wishing to risk Alison coming to look for him—not that he believed she would, as well-bred as she was. But sometimes she surprised him, and he wasn't about to take any chances.

* * * * *

Alison hesitated on the threshold. Rafe sat in the same spot as two nights prior, staring up at the stars. She hoped she wasn't invading his solitude but thought he might want to talk since plan two had also been an unmitigated failure.

At the creak of the door he turned to look at her. Silence stretched between them for tense seconds that felt like minutes.

Alison lost her nerve. "I'm intruding. I'll go back inside."

"No. Stay." He shook his head as if remembering her presence. "Have a seat. We need to come up with another plan."

The little thrill she experienced at his cordial invitation dissipated when he added the last. She wondered why it should matter if he wanted her there for the pleasure of her company or the necessity of devising yet another phase to his scheme.

But it did.

She refused to dwell on such silliness and took a seat on the bench.

"Caleb and Ivy invited us to the picnic they're planning next week. After Sunday service."

"Oh?" Surprised that he'd taken a different track in the conversation from what she expected, she gawked at him.

"Don't look so surprised. Caleb said he issued you an invitation to supper the day you arrived in Hope."

"Yes, he was most congenial." She straightened her skirts and winced when she noticed her pink hands. They still hadn't returned to their creamy-white color, and she wondered if something in the lye caused a reaction that made her want to continuously scratch them. "I look forward to hearing him preach."

Rafe remained quiet a moment. "Maybe that should be plan three."

"I beg your pardon?"

"Plan three. The girls wouldn't want a ma who doesn't follow what the Good Book teaches. Maybe if you refuse to attend, they would be more inclined to—"

"No." She cut him off, appalled at such an idea. "I will not sacrifice my faith or obedience to God to fellowship with other believers on the altar of any *plan* you might conceive." She said the last with a wry twist of her mouth.

"All right." He raised a placating hand. "Forget I mentioned it."

"I certainly will."

She gave a little huff of annoyance and twisted her hands in her lap in agitation, running her short nails along the inflamed skin. The very idea! Maybe *he* had chosen to forsake the assembly, but she would have no part of it.

"Will you be going to service on Sunday?" she asked. He rewarded her with a sharp glance. "Sam mentioned you haven't attended in a while, but with the picnic following and it being your brother's invitation, it would be rude to decline. Wouldn't you agree?"

His gaze had dropped to her hands and his eyebrows pulled together in a frown. She forced her agitated fingers to remain still. His solemn eyes lifted to hers.

"Sam shouldn't have told you that."

"I suppose not, but I can better understand why you should be so quick to suggest such a reprehensible plan since you, yourself, have turned your back on God."

"I haven't forsaken God."

"You've forsaken His principles. Don't you think it's time to put an end to your dissolute ways and set a good example for your children?"

In the lantern light she watched his stormy eyes, now the color of iron, spark in irritation. "I'm no heathen, Miss Stripling."

"I never said you were, Mr. Munroe. Yet by refusing to attend worship services every Sunday for well over a year, you're causing an ill effect on the children. I heard Tucker say that if you didn't have to go, why should he? That kind of attitude, the attitude you have fostered, can injure whatever seedlings of faith Amy implanted in their young hearts. Is that what you wish to do?"

He straightened to his feet so suddenly he made the cover of the barrel skid back a fraction. "I don't need your chastisements of my behavior. I get enough of that from my brother!"

Likewise, she stood, and just as quickly. "Then perhaps you should listen to him."

Instantly realizing she had interfered where she didn't have the right to speak and knowing that her tongue had gotten ahead of her again, she hesitated to say more. Yet thoughts of her little nieces and nephews persisted, and she found she couldn't remain silent.

"Think of your children. You love them, anyone can see that. Perhaps you were once distant, but it's clear you're trying to make amends. Think not only of their lives on this earth but also the destiny of their souls. It's by a parent's actions that children learn their true lessons, which will take them through life and become the foundation in every decision they make. I don't have to be a mother to realize that! I experienced that truth growing up in my parents' home."

His face was a rigid mask, and she felt her words did as little good as water dripping on stone, sliding away uselessly. Time and water eventually weathered stone, making it soft, but she had very little time left on his farm, and she lacked when it came to patience.

"I feel that we should discuss your new plan another time, Mr. Munroe. The day has been beyond what I'm accustomed to bearing, and I would like to retire now. Good night."

Without waiting for his reply, she moved to the door. She felt no surprise when he didn't stop her.

Inside, Alison had the cabin to herself. The girls were asleep in the loft upstairs, and the boys were in the barn. Her gaze went to the pianoforte, and her fingers lovingly caressed the smooth wood she'd recently polished. A small gold plate had been mounted near the keyboard with the inscription: *For Amy, the love of my life ~Rafe*

"How did you ever get through to him?" she whispered, the question foolish. Everyone had loved Amy, her sweetness mixed with a strength that stemmed from her solid faith. If anyone could have gotten through to the boor outside, she could. "But you're not here. And I feel so helpless in this role into which I've been thrust. I agreed to help with his plan, but maybe I'm here for a higher purpose— to help resurrect his faith? If that's true, how...*how* can I proceed and not fail, as I've failed at so much in my life?"

No, she would not pity her state of circumstances; they could be so much worse.

Wiping a feckless tear away, Alison turned down the lantern and moved into the bedroom. She had done no more than unpin her hair when a soft knock sounded at the door.

Startled, she spun around and stared at it before gathering her wits about her. Perhaps one of the children needed something or had experienced a nightmare. Alison had suffered many of those in her early childhood and remembered how horrid they could be.

She opened the door and froze in shock at the sight of Rafe. She stood fully dressed but felt flustered even so, and she raised her hand to her heart and clutched the frills on her bodice.

"Yes?" she managed to choke out.

He didn't answer. His eyes opened wider, appearing a bit stunned, as he slowly took in the length of her hair acting as a thick silken cape covering her shoulders and arms, down to the ends that touched her waist and curled gently by nature. Alison tightened her hold on her blouse, not out of fear—she no longer feared this man as she had her first day in his formidable presence. But some strange new emotion made it difficult to breathe as his eyes again lifted to hers.

"Forgive the intrusion, Miss Stripling." His voice, in tone and volume, came lower than she'd ever heard it. "I came to give you this. Amy had the same problem."

He offered her a bottle, which she curiously took. Without another word, he left.

She watched him go until the outside door closed behind him then dropped her gaze to the small green bottle. A tonic for her hands.

How long she stared at the bottle before applying the soothing, fragrant oil to her reddened, blotched skin, she didn't know. But when she finally lay down, her thoughts then dreams were filled with the unfathomable master of the house.

Chapter Nine

....

The days passed sluggishly, one into another. Rafe spent them hard at work, going to the cabin only for meals. During those three times each day, he remained quiet and left the table once he'd wiped his mouth with one of the fancy cloth napkins Alison had retrieved from Amy's wooden chest.

As he lay on a stack of hay one night, trying to sleep, images of the woman living inside his cabin relentlessly penetrated his mind, and he could think of little else.

It had started with her poor little hands, red and chafed, much like Amy's had looked when she first washed laundry and her skin reacted to the harsh soap. But Amy had chosen the life of a farmer's wife, though Rafe had done what he could by purchasing the healing oil he'd obtained from a druggist. Alison never asked for this rugged life, and her stay in it was temporary. She shouldn't have to suffer so just to help him fulfill his plan.

That decision led him to search out the bottle of oil in the cupboard and take it to Alison. What he hadn't expected was the sight of her unadorned hair tumbling over her shoulders in a shining fall, the lantern's glow behind her softly outlining her form and making her look like an angel. No, not an angel. The strong feelings that swept through him upon the sight of her, men didn't have for angels. Feelings he shouldn't have. Feelings that betrayed his love for Amy.

Gritting his teeth, he attempted to block out his mind's image of her silhouette in the doorway. He had long recognized she was pretty but had tried to bury that fact into a dark corner of his mind. What he'd failed to notice was what a true beauty she was. And intelligent. And considerate. And helpful… No! He couldn't do this. To himself, to Amy. The sooner Alison left his home, the better.

Yet on one issue, her words to him persisted, even into his dreams. So it was with a grave manner he rose, groomed, and dressed the following morning, thankful he'd filled a carpetbag with his personal items on wash day and brought it to the barn.

Rafe opened the cabin door minutes later. Dead silence rewarded him as the children and Alison, dressed for Sunday service, stared at him in openmouthed shock.

"If we're going to go, we'd best go," he muttered, as he uncomfortably tugged at the tight neckline of his muslin shirt.

"Aren't you gonna eat something first, Pa?" Tucker asked, sounding almost hopeful.

"Not hungry. Andy, help me hitch up the wagon."

His eldest blinked as if coming out of a stupor. "Sure thing, Pa."

The ride into town was more silent than on former occasions when he'd taken his brood with him, and he wondered if the change in their behavior resulted from Alison's appearance or his choice to accompany them. Likely both novel events had spawned such quiet, well-behaved children. Well, he sure had no cause to complain about that!

He glanced in Alison's direction and noted her approving smile. Oddly, her support encouraged him and some of his nervousness about reentering the fold left. They arrived at the schoolhouse with the seats filled and the service about to start.

His brother didn't look the least bit shocked to see him but clapped Rafe on the shoulder. "I knew you'd come back one day. I've been praying for it."

Rafe grunted in reply. Caleb smiled then moved toward the pulpit as Rafe herded his children to a long bench at the back. He sat on one end, Alison the other, and couldn't help noticing the frequent glances turned their way by parishioners who'd spotted them. He reckoned his presence with Alison would stir up the busybodies to wagging their tongues where they had no right, but he managed to block out the curious congregation to sing the hymn Caleb led and then listen to what his brother had to say. He'd forgotten what a good preacher Caleb was—and if he didn't know how his brother spent hours toiling over each message he prepared, he might accuse him of planning it, spur of the moment, upon sight of Rafe.

Unlike Job, however, Rafe hadn't had *everything* stolen from him. It only felt like he had. Caleb stressed that God blessed Job after his ordeal and better than before, giving him another wife and more children, along with making his way prosperous. That he looked directly at Rafe made him want to squirm, but he kept his body rigid, refusing to flinch.

* * * * *

Seeing Caleb's fixed gaze on his brother, Alison cast a surreptitious glance down the line of children to get a glimpse of Rafe. His mouth was drawn tight, his pose severe and unyielding.

Hearing how God blessed Job with a second wife made the strangest prickles tingle down Alison's spine, aided by the glances directed to her in curiosity. Everyone in town would soon know that Amy's sister had come to visit. She wondered if these people compared her to her perfect sister and found her wanting.

She had asked Andy to take her to the church meeting her first Sunday in Kansas, but the boy had told her he had too many chores, leaving her speechless with shock that he didn't consider fellowshipping with other believers a priority. Her determination bolstered, this morning she had declared that not only would she attend, but the children would be dressed to go before *anyone* ate breakfast. It wasn't her fault they had dragged their feet to comply and missed a meal. Feeling a twinge of remorse, she reassured herself that the picnic to follow would satisfy their empty stomachs. Certainly her refusal to cook would aid Rafe's plan.

After the service, she followed Rafe and his children to the door, where Caleb and his wife now stood, exchanging farewells with each member as they exited the building. A short, plump woman, appearing around the same age as Alison, Caleb's wife had eyes that exuded friendliness and warmth, as did her husband's. Where Rafe's eyes were stormy, their color a steely blue-gray, Caleb's appeared as calm as a clear summer sky.

"I'm so pleased to finally make your acquaintance." Ivy warmly clasped Alison's hand with both of hers. "Amy spoke highly of you."

Alison smiled. "It's a pleasure to meet her friends."

"I echo my wife's sentiments," Caleb added. "Anyone who can get my brother to come to church again is a godsend to the community."

"Oh, I didn't have anything to do with that." She nervously glanced at Rafe, who stood several feet away talking with another parishioner, and felt grateful he couldn't hear their conversation.

"I wouldn't be so sure." Caleb smiled mysteriously. "Are you coming to our little picnic?"

"Yes. I believe that's the true reason for Rafe's presence here today. He didn't want to disappoint you and refuse."

Caleb let out a deep, hearty laugh, drawing the attention of those lingering nearby, including Rafe. "I'm sorry, but I disagree. This isn't the first picnic I've invited him to attend on a Sunday. He's turned down many an invitation, Miss Stripling. Until you came along."

Rafe moved their way, coming to stand beside Alison. "Is my brother being a nuisance?" He looked back and forth between them, his tone glib, his eyes serious.

Still reeling from Caleb's admission and wondering if what she'd said could really have had an effect on Rafe, Alison shook her head. "No. He's most hospitable."

"Really," Rafe drawled, his manner suspicious.

Caleb smiled. "Shall we go find a spot near the stream?" He moved off with his wife.

"Mr. Munroe!" A slender, well-dressed woman glided into view, her smile wide. "It is indeed a pleasure to see you with us again. And this must be Miss Stripling," she gushed. "I've heard so much about you from Samantha. I'm Miss Proctor, Samantha's teacher. I cannot tell you what a privilege it is to have such a remarkable student as our dear Samantha return to the schoolhouse."

Rafe's decision to allow Sam to resume her studies had been a pleasant surprise. Alison now glanced at the girl, who turned beet red after hearing her teacher's effusive praise.

"Samantha is an exceptional student and, as I've mentioned to her, I would greatly appreciate it if she could give a speech at the upcoming harvest celebration."

The look in Sam's eyes reminded Alison of a small creature trapped by a predatory hunter.

"Samantha has a remarkable grasp of the written language, and I'm hoping to gain your support in this matter. She mentioned she was needed at home so cannot comply with my wishes, but surely some arrangement could be made?"

Rafe looked confused. Alison, seeing an opportunity to construct her own plan, spoke up. "I think that's a marvelous idea. There's no reason why Sam can't take the necessary time to prepare a speech."

Sam looked both betrayed and horror-struck. Rafe still looked baffled.

Miss Proctor stared at Alison oddly, as if wondering what right she had to make decisions with regard to Rafe's children. A slight lift of her eyebrows in Rafe's direction appeared to get through to him. His expression cleared and he smiled at the schoolmarm.

"I agree. Sam has a gift and should use it. You have my full support, Miss Proctor."

Sam, who'd gone pale, mumbled, "Excuse me," clapped a hand over her mouth, and ran toward a patch of trees. Maggie looked at both Alison and her pa and then followed Sam, and Clarissa, holding Baby Lynn, did the same.

"Boys, look after your sisters," Rafe urged Andy and Tucker.

Once they took off, Miss Proctor, who looked a bit stunned by the sudden commotion, blinked a few times. "Well, I must take my leave. I'm grateful for your support. It's been a pleasure meeting you, Miss Stripling." Her farewell sounded a bit uncertain, as if the teacher couldn't quite figure Alison out.

Alison also wondered.

Perhaps she'd been cruel to force Sam into a situation that unsettled her. Yet her motives didn't stem from pure selfishness with regard to "the plan." Alison knew that sometimes the only way to dispense with fear was to face it, and this prod might turn into a hidden blessing for her niece.

Nonetheless concerned, she proceeded to look for the girls. Rafe came alongside her and touched her elbow as they walked, pulling her toward him a fraction in confidence so she could hear his low words.

"That was a stroke of genius."

"I hope I haven't overly distressed her. She looked as if she might be ill."

"Sam's tough. She'll be all right. But while your manipulations might have removed you from her favor, we still have the other children to deal with."

"You've thought of something else?"

"Remember your complaints the other day? About the laundry?"

How could she forget? She'd felt uneasy the moment she began them.

"Being as it was a mundane chore the children don't like, they probably felt you had reason to complain. But what kind of person would carry on during an event that's considered fun?"

She darted a glance his way. "I'm not sure I understand."

"The picnic. If you complain over what they find pleasurable, they'll see what a curmudgeon you can be. No offense meant."

She didn't so quickly assure him none was taken. He wanted her dull as dirt, to show no appreciation for an enjoyable afternoon?

She frowned. "I'll have you know that I'm hardly the lackluster spinster you think me, Mr. Munroe."

"Calm down, Miss Stripling." He huffed. "I'm only asking you to pretend."

"Which is a glorified word for deceive."

"Did you never play a childhood game in your life?"

"Of course, but I'm hardly a child."

"No, but surely you can find *something* to complain about, if you set your mind to it."

She realized then that they were standing in the middle of

the street, arguing almost nose to nose, and drawing the interest of parishioners nearby. Though they'd kept their words to a low growl that no one could have overheard, they were creating quite a spectacle.

"Fine," she muttered, retreating a step. "Just dandy."

"Glad we're clear on it," he remarked, just as irritated.

He walked away, and she compressed her lips in frustration. She could think of a great deal to complain about, make no mistake. But it had nothing to do with a picnic.

* * * * *

Honestly, that woman could get under his skin like no woman ever did. After feeling dead inside for so long, it was unusual to *feel* so often—as if he was sparking to life in response to her glib tongue, which could be both sharp and gentle.

Was ever a woman created that could be so exasperating!

"I'm glad I'm not on the receiving end of those glares you're giving," Caleb said cordially, coming up beside Rafe. He looked to see what Rafe stared at.

"Ah, Miss Stripling. I take it there's some difficulty?"

"She's impossible," Rafe quietly fumed, watching her grasp Clarissa and Baby Lynn's hands and skip about in a circle with them. "One minute she's helping me with my plan. The next she's fighting me on it."

"Really?" Caleb's tone made his interest clear.

Rafe glanced at him. "You don't think she's changed her mind?"

"After her ambush of Sam?"

Rafe jerked an irritated hand in her direction. "Just look at her! Her behavior is hardly making the children dislike her."

"Is that what you want? For them to despise their aunt?"

Rafe snorted. "That word again. I don't want them to *despise* her. But I'd rather they learn not to depend on her or want her around. It would sure make life easier."

"On who?"

"What?" Rafe again looked at him sharply.

"If Alison were to leave tomorrow, do you really believe that the children's lives would be made easier, in going back to the way things were before? You think they were happy then?"

"I've changed. I'm not the reclusive father I was."

"Well, thank God for that!"

"Things will be better now."

Caleb nodded. "So you plan to be both a mother and a father to them?"

Rafe grimaced. "If I have to."

"That's just the thing, little brother. You don't." He smiled as if he knew a secret. "Go easy on her. She's doing her best to please, it's plain to tell, but I think she's also trying hard not to lose herself in the process of your little plan. And you know how I feel about *that*."

Rafe briefly closed his eyes on a frustrated sigh, and Caleb moved to join his wife. For a moment he watched them: Caleb's gentle touch on Ivy's arm; her answering smile as she turned and greeted him with a chaste kiss to his cheek; her hand going to his other, sweetly stroking it; their love for each other apparent.

Dear God, how I miss that. How I wish…

Rafe blinked as his mind formed the words.

What was he *thinking*? What did he wish?

His gaze drifted to Alison, now seated on the ground, with her fancy green beribboned skirts puffed out around her and his little girls still in the ring, where they'd apparently "all fallen down" in their silly game. Grimacing, he moved toward them. Alison caught sight of his approach and her eyes sparked the barest glimmer of what looked like delight before wariness masked the gleam. She lifted her chin in a manner suggesting reluctant defiance.

"Oh, dear. I've gone and soiled one of my best dresses," she mourned when Rafe came within earshot. "I simply cannot believe I allowed myself to participate in a game so...so...dirty."

He didn't miss the confused looks his girls exchanged with one another.

"It'll wash," Maggie soothed. "Won't it?"

"That horrid lye will destroy such fine linen. My dresses aren't made to be washed with harsh soap. What I wouldn't give for one of my servants right now! They knew how to make my soiled dresses fresh, without using something so horrendous as that awful home-made soap you people use. Help me up." Her tone went curt. Clarissa and Maggie tried, but the ballooning skirts acted as weights, making a graceful rise impossible, if she could rise at all.

Resigned that she needed his aid, Rafe stepped forward and offered his hands. She looked up a moment before placing her fingers against his palms. The strangest jolt, like the air before a bad storm, went through his arms. He jerked back a little, releasing her hands quickly—and her eyes flared as if she felt it too.

Realizing that his children watched in curiosity, he slipped his hands back under hers and made quick work of pulling her to her feet while trying to ignore the soft warmth of her skin. She stumbled into him while trying to regain her balance, causing a further series of shocks. Abruptly he put her from him, releasing her the moment she stood upright.

"Th–thank you." Her voice came breathy, her eyes still wide.

"I couldn't leave you sitting in the grass."

She gave a dismissive nod, averting her attention to Baby Lynn, and helped the child to her feet, though his youngest appeared as if she would rather roll in the grass. Alison made quick work of swiping the backs of both their dresses free of dirt.

"I suppose playing Ring Around the Rosy wasn't the best idea I had." Alison adjusted her hat, and Rafe wondered how the feather stayed put in such a stiff breeze instead of flying off into the stream.

"Ivy's motioning us over."

"Mm-hmm." She smoothed the front of her skirts, adjusting one of the shiny ribbons.

"I think it's time to eat."

"Splendid."

Alison continued to avoid his gaze.

"I realize you're attempting to do what I asked, but maybe don't lay it on so thick."

Her head snapped up, her brown eyes simmering.

"Make up your mind, Mr. Munroe. Do you want me to complain, or don't you?"

"Only if you make it believable. The girls didn't look like they were going for your act." He glanced at his children, who'd run over to the checkered cloth Ivy laid out. "One second you were laughing like Father Christmas paid you a visit; the next you were moaning as if someone had pulled all your teeth!"

"You have my most profound apology," she bit out, not sounding sorry at all. "I haven't received any training in conniving and trickery. Perhaps you should rethink your plan and hire a stage actress!" She whirled to go, but he grabbed her arm before she could leave. The same tingle moved through his hand as before, but this time he kept his grip.

"All I'm saying is tone it down some."

"Point taken, Mr. Munroe." She whipped her arm from his hold. "Now if you'll excuse me, I need to go find something to complain about!"

Rafe watched her flounce off, half of him wanting to throttle her, the other half wanting to—

He broke the thought off fast, before it could settle in his mind, and wondered where it had come from.

Chapter Ten

....

Alison didn't smile. A sourpuss certainly would score marks with Mr. Insufferable with regard to his infernal plan. Even her former manager at the millinery shop hadn't infuriated her so much that she would forsake her ladylike training to spar with words, which she'd done on an almost daily basis since she arrived at his cabin. Rafe Munroe was the only man east or west who'd been able to produce such a peculiar...fieriness from her.

That led her to think about the spark that shot through her flesh when Rafe took her small hands in his large ones. She'd felt the same jolt earlier, before the church meeting, when he helped her down from the wagon. Rather than take her hand, he had grabbed her around the waist and hauled her down swiftly, making Alison go a little breathless before he just as quickly turned away.

Perhaps if they weren't both under such duress due to his everlasting desire for the plan to reap fruit. Perhaps if he would release his pain of the past and resolve to make a new future.

What was she thinking? Certainly *not* to become anything other than Rafe's collaborator! Not only did he detest the idea, she also shied from the prospect of marrying a man with a passel of children. To have Rafe for a husband would invite trouble and discontent and excitement and...

Excitement?

The drumstick she'd been holding fell to her lap, making her jump and bringing everyone's attention her way.

"S–sorry." She refused to look at Rafe. If she did, she would turn five shades of crimson—if there were five shades of crimson to turn. "Oh, dear. This food is greasy, isn't it?" She snatched up the drumstick, noticing the faintest spot on her skirt. "I fear I've completely ruined my dress now. And were there ever so many bugs?" She swatted the air around her head. "I declare, I've never seen so many bugs in one place...."

And so the complaints continued for the remainder of the meal, until *she* couldn't stand herself. She felt grateful that the few families gathered near the stream for their own afternoon picnics were too far distant to hear the petty vexations of Amy's Bostonian sister.

Tears threatened and she took a bite of the most delicious bread she'd ever tasted to try and stem the tide. "It's somewhat dry, isn't it?" She sniffled lightly, horrified when she tasted salt and realized a stray tear had wet the crust.

Baby Lynn crawled into her lap and wrapped chubby little arms around Alison's middle, resting her head of strawberry-golden curls against her bosom. "It'll be all right, Auntie Al–son." And with a wide yawn, the child closed her eyes as if to settle down for a nap.

That became the last straw for Alison. The plans, one, two, and three—blast every one of them—could go fly away in a cyclone or simoon or whatever other foul weather Rafe said Kansas held.

She wrapped her arms around the warm bundle in her lap, cooing to the tot softly and kissing her hair. For the first time since she arrived in Kansas she felt a true sense of peace and well-being, making her want to cry again, making her wish that Baby Lynn had the right to call her Mama—though, of course, she wanted nothing to do with her bear of a papa. Clenching her jaw to stem her tears, Alison lifted defiant, watery eyes across the blanket and met Rafe's gaze.

He didn't look condemning, but neither did he look approving.

They stared at one another for endless seconds until Ivy mildly cleared her throat, dislodging whatever bond locked their fixed attention, and Rafe looked away. His had been no gaze of understanding or friendliness, though Alison had difficulty pinning down exactly what had glimmered in his eyes.

Baby Lynn fell asleep and Alison continued to hold her, now and then gently swaying, all complaints for the day concluded. The older children ran off to pitch horseshoes with their father and Uncle Caleb, leaving Alison alone with Ivy and the child still on her lap. Once the Munroes were out of earshot, Alison turned to her hostess.

"I apologize for what I said earlier. None of it was true, and I'm sorry I told those silly fibs. You are a wonderful cook, and I would be pleased if I had half the skill you possess."

"Caleb told me about Rafe's plan. I know you meant no harm by what you said."

Alison felt relieved that she hadn't injured Ivy's feelings. "Was my attempt as thespian and pathetic as it sounded?"

Ivy nodded with a sympathetic smile. "It was clear you were ill at ease in saying those things, and no, it didn't really come across as sincere. But don't fret. The children are too young to tell sincerity from pretense, I would think. In all likelihood, they took your complaints as you intended them."

Alison nodded, the relief she should feel markedly absent.

"Forgive me for intruding, but I think you should tell him you don't wish to take part in his little ploys anymore."

"What?" Alison looked at Ivy in surprise.

"Rafe. Tell him how you really feel."

Flustered, Alison tried to form her jumbled thoughts into words. "You mean about the children?"

"I mean about Rafe."

Alison gaped at Ivy for several seconds before she had the good sense to close her mouth. "You're quite mistaken." In her agitation, she smoothed her hand down Baby Lynn's back a little more firmly, causing the child to stir. Instantly Alison stilled. "I have no feelings for Mr. Munroe. Well, perhaps I do feel *something*, but it is quite the opposite from what you presume."

"Oh?" Ivy lifted her brows in clear disbelief.

"I despised the man when he took Amy away from Boston. Did he tell you?"

"I see…. You were, what? Ten?"

Alison felt her face warm. "Nine, actually. At least the best we could determine my age. I never knew the date of my birth, so my adoptive parents allowed me to choose a day once I grew old enough to know what it meant. I picked a beautiful day in the spring. May Day." She was rambling and knew it.

"How unique!" Ivy smiled. "So you were nine when Rafe and Amy left?"

"Well, no, almost nine because of the day I chose." Alison coughed to clear her throat, feeling ridiculous. "I don't understand why my age should matter?"

"I'm just surprised you still harbor the grudge you carried as a child."

"Oh, but I don't! I understand so much more than I did then. As well as that yearning for adventure that drove Amy to move west."

"Really?" Ivy looked at her oddly. "When you brought up your untoward feelings about Rafe, you mentioned your anger, so naturally I thought you referred to your past."

Which would be the conclusion anyone might reach, Alison realized. She felt so addle-brained, she didn't know what she'd said. Or perhaps it was best to bring up past grievances as a defense, to ward off anyone's idea that she might be feeling more than…

"Since that clearly isn't what you meant, perhaps you'd care to enlighten me?"

No, she wouldn't. Not at all.

Alison struggled to remain composed. "Oh, there are so many things that aggravate me about the man, where could I *possibly* begin?" She desperately scrambled for one and brightened when she came up with a sure reason that would satisfy Ivy. "He was most uncivil toward me when I first arrived. Why, he nearly snapped my head off for touching Amy's pianoforte—can you imagine? I've never seen anyone fly into such a rage!"

"Oh, dear." Sorrow touched Ivy's eyes. "The poor man. It was his last gift to her, you see. He was so pleased that winter when he made arrangements for it. Rafe had saved up for it for some time and checked in town every day for its arrival. He was like a little boy, so excited and eager to see her face when he presented her with the gift at Christmas. He wanted to give Amy something she would treasure for a lifetime."

Alison's heartstrings were pulled as tears again pricked the back of her eyes. Ivy made it difficult to remain politely hostile to Rafe.

"Well, there is this plan of his, to curb the children's desire in wanting a mother."

"Yes, and what a foolhardy idea that is! Oh, I don't blame you. I know it's all Rafe's doing. He just doesn't see how much the children need a mother."

On that issue, Alison wholeheartedly agreed.

"Which brings up another question. I hope you don't mind?"

Alison managed a consenting nod and cordial smile, her grip on Baby Lynn tightening as she tensed in preparation to hear Ivy's query.

"Just why *did* you agree to Rafe's plan?"

"Pardon?"

Ivy shrugged. "You could have refused. You didn't know the children well enough to form an opinion, to know if it would be in their best interest to pursue Rafe's course of action or if it would be contrary to helping them."

"Rafe seemed so sure. And he is their father."

"But since you had such a frightening encounter with him that first day in his cabin, it would seem you would have run the other direction, as far away as possible."

It did seem that way....

Alison fidgeted again. "You seem quite knowledgeable."

Ivy laughed. "A polite way of saying I'm nosy? I'm a professor's daughter, and my father taught me to rationalize and reason things out to find the root of the problem. I'm only trying to understand. Rafe is like a brother, so naturally I have his best interests at heart."

Alison smiled. "Well, I had only just arrived that day and didn't want to turn around and go directly back to Boston. I yearned to see the land Amy wrote so fondly of, though she certainly didn't exaggerate about the wind. I don't think the weather has been calm a day since I've been here! Still, it's very beautiful."

"And maybe a bit of Amy's yearning has rubbed off on you? To stay in Kansas?"

"Only until Rafe no longer needs my help."

"Really?" Ivy looked surprised again. "With the way you were talking, I thought you'd decided to stay."

"No. But I do agree with you, especially after getting to know them, that the children need a mother. I don't think it right to put them off the idea completely."

Ivy again got that confused expression with the sparkle in her eyes that warned Alison she wouldn't like what was coming.

"Then, if you don't approve of his plan and have no tolerant feelings toward Rafe and you never intended to make Hope your home as I'd erroneously thought, why do you remain? You've had reason to leave long before now. So what holds you in Hope?"

Alison grew weary of beating around the bush. "By the manner in which you asked, you seem to know more than I. So tell me what *you* believe."

"I think you love him."

Her heart beat so fast it made her dizzy. Or perhaps the lack of oxygen came from holding her breath. She gulped in a huge amount of air.

"That's pre–preposterous! I—I hardly know the man. I told you how he behaved when I arrived." She began rocking Lynn again. "He can be so muleheaded. He is most certainly *not* the reason I agreed to stay."

"Maybe not then, but what about now?" Ivy urged gently.

She wished she could offer an answer, any answer, but felt strangely...defeated. If Ivy weren't so sweet with her queries, Alison might have taken offense in her meddling.

As if she heard her thoughts, Ivy quietly explained, "You must think me an awful busybody, but I'm concerned. I wanted to understand your feelings for Rafe because, to be honest, though he would likely deny it till he's blue in the face, I think he's starting to care for you. I want to see him happy again. Caleb and I both do. And I think you're just the woman to accomplish that."

Alison went stock-still. She gaped at Ivy. "Y–you're quite mistaken."

"No." She shook her head with a soft smile. "I see the signs."

"But we argue all the time."

"Yes," Ivy said pensively. "It stands to reason that in such a sticky situation such as you two have made for yourselves there would be strife. But, Alison, even the closest couples argue. Caleb and I bicker. It's the forgiveness that comes afterward that counts. Do your arguments last a long time?"

Alison listlessly shook her head. Often they were over as quickly as they began.

"I—I appreciate what you're saying, but I assure you nothing exists between us."

"If you say so." Ivy smiled as if she didn't believe her then began packing into the basket what little remained of the food.

Clarissa ran for the blanket as if she'd been wandering in a desert and not playing a game of horseshoes, sparing Alison from further awkward interrogations. The child collapsed onto the patchwork quilt, clutching her throat as if she might expire.

"Thirsty," she rasped.

Clarissa was no better an actress than Alison.

Ivy pulled a container and tin cup from the basket and poured apple cider into it. "Here, dear. I know how much you like it."

The child immediately sat up and reached for the cup Ivy handed her. "Thank you, Aunt Ivy!"

Clarissa skipped away, happily refreshed, and Ivy turned to Alison. "I hope I haven't destroyed any chance of us becoming friends. I tend to say what I think, and sometimes that can be unwise—especially for a preacher's wife!" She laughed with embarrassment.

Alison *had* felt cornered by Ivy's questions but could relate to speaking one's mind when one shouldn't speak at all. She'd had so few friends. Those who had shown interest soon learned of her heritage and more often than not, so did their mothers, who then forbade their daughters to associate with a nameless foundling. When she grew older, those same girls, who'd been bred into accepting their mother's opinionated ideals, ignored her or treated her with contempt. The idea of having a true friend who accepted her for her past and present, the good and the bad, made the recent drilling Ivy had given seem inconsequential.

Alison smiled. "I should love having you for a friend."

Ivy grabbed her hand and gave it a squeeze. "Good. It'll be nice having a woman to talk to. Someone close, I mean. Family."

To Alison's relief, Ivy didn't resume their earlier conversation. They talked of Rafe's children, Ivy's approaching motherhood, and the harvest celebration. Alison hadn't realized at the time that it would be so grand an event, with the entire town involved; she'd thought only the families of the schoolchildren would be present for Sam's speech.

Again that niggling concern ate away at her conscience that she'd pushed Sam too hard. But she comforted herself that it truly was in Sam's best interest not to hide her talent. Sam had been quiet all afternoon, but Alison felt relieved to see her playing with the other children.

Her gaze went to Rafe, who played just as hard, now throwing a ball with his sons. His exertions made his shirt stick damply to his skin, bringing into prominence the finely toned muscles of his lean frame....

She looked away, shocked by where her thoughts had taken her. Had she a fan, she would put it to good use.

"Aunt Alison! Aunt Ivy!" Tucker ran up to them, breathless. "You seen my pet snake?"

Ivy dropped the silver she'd gathered and Alison jumped, as if she could feel the reptile slithering beneath her skirts. Her action woke Baby Lynn, who squealed at the mention of the grass snake.

A hasty search turned up nothing, and with a dejected expression Tucker crawled into the buckboard once Rafe announced the time had come to go home.

Alison glanced at the girls, amused to note that she wasn't the only one smiling at the absence of Tucker's pet.

Chapter Eleven

....

Rafe brought the wagon to a stop in front of the cabin. Alison jumped down swiftly without waiting for him to give her a hand, as he'd done that morning at church. Although he'd done more than give her a hand—he'd grabbed her around the waist without thinking, only realizing what he'd done when that same shock of awareness shot through his body as it had when he'd taken hold of her hands and helped her up from the ground.

He frowned and jiggled the reins to get the horse moving to the barn. All the while he unharnessed the mare and put things away, he thought of what he wanted to say to her once he got the chance.

The chance came sooner than expected.

The children, tuckered out from their fun afternoon, retired to bed while the sun still hovered on the horizon. Even Andy said his good nights early and headed for the barn.

"We should talk," Rafe said to Alison as she extinguished the fire in the cookstove that she used earlier to brew coffee. She'd improved at both tasks. But he didn't know whether to feel relief that she wouldn't set fire to the kitchen like she almost did the first time she'd stoked the already-blazing wood and a stick fell out, or if he experienced alarm that a woman now managed things well in Amy's place. But then, he didn't know what to make of half the feelings he'd been having since Alison invaded his cabin two weeks ago.

Rafe went outside to wait. It wasn't long before he heard the creak of the door and her light step on the ground. She came into his line of vision, smoothing her skirts in a nervous manner. Before he could speak, she did.

"You're probably upset about today, but Lynn is only a baby, and right then she needed to be held. She's too young to understand if I'm distant or harsh, and I don't think she should be made to suffer. Do you?"

She looked at him then, her brown eyes wide and sincere. The sunset made her face glow rosier, bringing out the shine in her eyes. He'd never noticed how thick and curly her lashes really were.

He looked away, uneasy that he'd been staring. "No. Baby Lynn wouldn't understand, and she'd be hurt if you treated her badly. She didn't have anything to do with the children's scheme to get a ma. But that doesn't explain your time with Clarissa and Maggie. Playing that ring 'n' roses game...or whatever you called it."

"It was a game Amy and I played as children." The tone of her voice grew defensive, hurt, and angry, and he tensed, girding himself for another battle. "Even though she was older, she always found time to play with me, and I was paying that same respect to her children. Whether you like it or not, Mr. Munroe, I *am* their aunt. Yet just because I show my nieces and nephews consideration doesn't mean you've lost an ally for your plan."

The shine in her eyes grew brighter, and he realized with horror that she was close to tears. Before he could suggest they postpone their talk, not wanting her to cry, she continued.

"Have you ever considered that this plan could backfire on you? What if the slim possibility did occur that you fall in love again and wish to take a wife? What happens then, if your current plan succeeds and the children decide they don't need a mother? Wouldn't it be best to just talk to them, confront them with what you know, and explain your views?"

"They don't want to hear my views. They want to change them. And I don't plan on marrying again."

"But that's just it—we can plan many things in life. Plan to ride on a train. Plan to visit new frontiers. Plan the day-to-day chores and the picnics. But sometimes the heart doesn't recognize whatever 'plan' we make and doesn't care to know. Sometimes despite our best plans, we find ourselves in a situation we never expected. One that can wear on the heart, but despite rhyme or reason—there it is. Something we never planned and never wanted occurs!"

He stared at her, trying to follow her chaotic bends in the conversation. "Meaning?"

"Meaning," she stressed, almost angry, "that sometimes our plans all go to the river!"

"Go to the…"

At his slow, uncertain repetition of her words, she let out what came close to a growl.

"They count for nothing, Mr. Munroe! They get washed up and drown in a whirlpool of remorse and regret and—and…" She fumbled. "And foolish hopes." She gave a soft little laugh, as if making fun of herself. "Like your township. Hope. I thought it an odd name for such a rustic area, until I lived here these two weeks. Then I began to understand—about this land, about those dreams and why you never want to leave despite what trials the land can be. Despite the wind that blows and blows and never seems to stop. The sky is so blue and goes on forever, like hope. Hope can be like lifesaving water to one who thirsts.…"

He had never figured her for a poet. But now he began to understand something deeper with regard to what she didn't say. He tensed and took hold of her upper arms. She raised startled eyes to his serious ones. The expression in hers flickered soft then filled with uncertainty.

"I don't know half of what you're going on about with hope and skies and whirlpools...." He kept his tone low and grim. "But I want to make something abundantly clear. I'm *never* marrying again. Anyone. That includes you. So if you're getting any ideas of shirking this plan in the *hope* that I'll change my mind—"

She wrenched herself free of his hold. "Don't be absurd." High color stained her cheeks. "What makes you presume that I would marry a man with so many children? That I would wish to marry you for *any* reason at all?"

He'd seen the way she got along with his kids. It didn't take a highly educated man to notice her affection for them. Before he could contradict her, she spoke again.

"Believe me, Mr. Munroe, I may be nearing spinsterhood, but I'm not so desperate as to consider a future with a man who's made it clear that he wants nothing to do with me. It may surprise you to know that before coming to Kansas, I was betrothed."

"What happened?" Of all the questions he could ask and the replies he could give, why should he pick that one? The surprise mirrored in her eyes. Temporarily thrown off balance from her rant, she blinked, as if trying to get her mind focused again.

"What happened?" she repeated dumbly.

"To end things. I seriously doubt any man in his right mind would let you traipse off alone to the wilds of the Midwest to care for another man's family."

She blinked again, like a barn owl, as if trying to figure him out.

He felt the same way.

Why should he care if another man had made a claim on her

or not? Why did he ask such things that were none of his concern? Before he could retract his question, she spoke.

"His mother discovered I was a foundling from an orphan train with no true roots to call my own. Being from a distinctive family dating back to the founding fathers, she balked at her son marrying someone so common. He eventually agreed."

"You're not common by any stretch of the imagination. And her son is a dimwitted fool."

They both stared in dumb amazement after the words came spewing from his mouth like a leak on a roof that couldn't be stopped. Her mouth parted as if she might speak, but she only stared. A strange, electric warmth sizzled in the air between them. Rafe took a quick step back.

"We should discuss the plan another time, when we're both rested and thinking clearly." Clearly enough not to spout shocking declarations that would lead to great spans of awkwardness.

"Actually…" She cleared the huskiness from her throat. "On the ride home, I thought up a plan that won't cause me grief, because I won't have to engage in pretenses."

"Really?" Her words sparked his interest. "What?"

"No." She smiled, shaking her head. "You'll find out. Tomorrow."

His brow went up at her mysterious attitude. "Will I approve of this plan?"

She laughed. "As long as it does the trick, do you really care?"

"That depends"—suspicion laced his tone—"to what degree I'm involved."

"You'll know soon enough." She moved around him. "I should retire now, so I can get up in plenty of time to commence with *my* plan."

He faintly groaned, more in theatrics than in genuine dislike.

"This plan of yours doesn't involve flour and water and eggs, does it?"

"And whose idea was it to ruin that meal? But I'll have you know I've learned a good deal since that fiasco of a breakfast."

Rafe nodded his agreement.

"Can you give me any indication of what you're up to?"

Another smile. "Good night, Mr. Munroe."

He sighed. "Good night, Miss Stripling."

* * * * *

Alison frowned as she prepared for bed, her thoughts outside the cabin.

One minute they were arguing, though she'd done most of the talking and entirely too much of it. Then the strangest feeling had washed over her once he grabbed her arms—whenever he touched her at all, really. The moment passed after he so aptly discerned her thoughts, and in humiliation she retaliated with belittling words she immediately regretted. Then in a breath of time, their frustrations and anger with one another fled like shadows swept away by sunlight—in the moment he had made his startling remark in response to the reason for her broken engagement.

She didn't know what to make of their encounter, of him. He had sounded...angry? And had he actually paid her a *compliment*?

In all likelihood she made too much out of nothing. But why had such peculiar warmth rushed through her when they looked at one another, like the air tingled on her skin? She sensed he felt it too, by the manner in which he swiftly put distance between them, yet not so much that she couldn't still feel him though they hadn't touched....

Oh, bother the man! Even on the rare occasions he showed her kindness, he addled her feelings and thoughts and flustered her more than any man she'd known. She had hurried to bring back a measure of ease by airing the plan she'd devised, hoping to dispel the strange breathlessness that caused her to desire things she could never have. Things like his touch and his kiss...

Her eyes widened and she shot upward, sitting straight up in bed, then realized she'd forgotten to put out the lamp.

With her mind in a whirl and her heart leaden, she put her feet to the cold floor before reconsidering and kneeling beside her bed. Though she'd said her prayers to close the evening, she felt a desperate need to beseech God once more.

"Please, Lord," she whispered, "show me my true purpose for being here. If it's only to help Rafe in his plan, then please make my heart more tolerant to the idea. But if Your purpose is something far greater than what either of us thought..." She took a deep breath. "Well, then help us both accept whatever Your will is. I wish to be Your vessel, Lord. Blow the chaff of my ignorance away and refine me for your purpose. Amen." She began to rise then dropped to her knees again. "And please help me to curb my foolish tongue and temper so I don't ruin everything. Amen."

She extinguished the lamp and climbed into bed.

With the morning would come *her* plan. A faint smile tilted her lips at the thought.

She had no doubt the children would detest every bit of what was to come.

* * * * *

Before Rafe opened the door of the cabin, he heard Alison. She alternately hummed and sang little snippets of a song.

He stood still a moment, listening to her voice that had a quality all its own. Not angelic and crystalline like Amy's, but rich and deep and soft all the same. He hadn't heard music in the cabin for so long, it felt odd to hear a woman singing again. Not upsetting, just...strange. Whatever was going on, Alison sounded happy and confident, and he hoped it had to do with her anticipation of success for her plan.

The mouthwatering aroma of sausages, eggs, biscuits, and gravy reached him as he opened the door. He suspected that she'd had help, but Alison certainly had improved when it came to cooking. The scheme might have worked, had they continued with the first plan. Still, it was a relief to taste edible food once more. Again, he wondered what her plan would be.

He didn't have long to find out.

The boys lumbered past, making their usual dives for their places on the benches. Rafe took his seat at the head of the table.

"Mmm." Andy smiled. "I'm hungry."

"That smells plumb good, Aunt Alison."

"Just one minute." She whirled around from extracting biscuits from the oven with a dish towel. Her expression was stern. "Let me see those hands."

"Huh?" Tucker looked at his fingers curiously.

"Your hands. I want to see them."

Tucker obliged, clearly confused, holding up his palms for her survey. Andy did the same.

She took one glance and then planted her hands on her hips and shook her head. "Not only is there a goodly layer of dirt on them, but it's crusted beneath your fingernails, and your faces aren't much better. From now on, before you partake of any meal, you must scrub your hands and faces. When you return, I don't want to see a speck of dirt on them."

Tucker scowled. "We never had to before!"

"Well, that will change, starting today. You will learn to become dignified little gentlemen." She offered a warning glance to his girls, whose faces sparkled squeaky-clean. "And you will learn to be little ladies. Let me see your hands as well."

They glanced at one another before offering their hands for approval. Only Maggie she ordered to go with the boys to wash up.

"I don't see why we have to get dandified up just to eat breakfast," Tucker tried again. "'Specially since they're just gonna get dirty again. Besides, Pa don't have to!"

Rafe expected her to chide them that his business didn't concern her, or something similar. What he didn't expect was for her to turn his way, cross her arms over her chest, and lift her brows in silent command.

She had to be joking. Rafe opened his mouth to object then stopped short.

What was a few more minutes' delay and a little water if it would aid her plan, which appeared to be working. He smirked, stood, affected a slight bow from the waist toward Alison, and set his hat on his head. Clarissa clapped a hand over her mouth and giggled, Sam stared wide-eyed, and both boys gaped as if he were a three-legged horse. He'd been taught manners as a youth but hadn't practiced them in Kansas, except with Amy on occasion. Either his children didn't recall those days or they'd never seen him take on the role of a gentleman. Thinking of Amy, he realized how she would disapprove of her boys becoming anything less.

Alison smiled and inclined her head in acknowledgment of his gesture.

"Come, boys. We've got some washing up to do. Maggie." He looked her way and she sulked. Clarissa giggled again.

"Oh, hush up." Maggie bumped Clarissa's shoulder with her own before trudging outside.

Rafe barely paid attention to Andy and Tucker grumbling between themselves, his mind on his houseguest. Lately he'd been thinking about her a lot. Too much. With a stab of guilt, he realized he hadn't thought half as much about Amy, the occasions coming less frequently with each day that passed. Caleb would tell him that was a good thing; Rafe wasn't so sure. Whatever the case, he certainly shouldn't be filling in those gaps thinking about her sister!

The more Alison became part of his life, living in his cabin, sharing in their meals, taking part in his plan, the more difficult it became to ignore her. He *couldn't* ignore her, though God help him, he had tried. But she possessed a fire and spirit that refused to be ignored and always seemed to draw him out, whether in conflict or other ways.

As he washed up at the water barrel outside, his thoughts went to the previous evening.

Rafe frowned, remembering her jumbled words and how, for one insane moment he couldn't explain, he had wanted first to shake her, then pull her close and hold her. To assure her that she was every bit as good as those pedigreed Bostonians who'd snubbed her—better—and in that one fleeting moment the impulse shot through him to kiss her.

What had become of him, that such a faithless thought should tempt his besieged mind? Was he being disloyal to Amy's memory? Caleb would disagree, quoting Scripture of how it wasn't good for man to dwell alone, but this was Amy's *sister.*

…Whom she had loved and admired and respected and would approve of to teach her children….

Rafe groaned, putting his damp hands to his head. Good grief.

Now he was hearing his brother's voice in his head? Was there no end to the torment?

"You all right, Pa?" Andy's confusion broke through his thoughts.

"Couldn't be better, son." He smiled, though it felt forced. He just hoped Alison's plan worked, so she could leave soon and life could go back to normal.

Chapter Twelve

....

With a cunning smile, Alison surveyed the children's glum faces. It hadn't been an easy day for Rafe's "brood" so far.

It was about to get worse.

After breakfast, Rafe and his boys went to do their day's work, the boys eager to tend chores where they'd never been before. Alison watched them go with a sly smile. They may think they escaped the remainder of her plan, but she had the evening to engage part three.

But first, to initiate part two...

Once the dishes were washed, dried, and put away, she affected a severe countenance and studied each of the girls. "You may live on the plains, but there's certainly no call for you to run about like little heathens, with bare feet and a deplorable carriage, not to mention crude mannerisms. All too soon the day will arrive when each of you will step into womanhood. You must prepare in advance, so that when that day comes you will move into it with grace, becoming the little women God intended you to be."

The girls glanced at one another in doubt, clearly not eager to commence with the training.

"Our first lesson will be in carriage and good posture. Slouching is reprehensible and a sign of a poor constitution." As she talked, she walked in front of the girls and then behind Maggie, abruptly pulling her shoulders back and her chin up. Maggie's eyes widened, and she stood as still as a scarecrow. "Biting nails is also a deplorable habit." She plucked Sam's hand from where it hung by her side and studied the short, ragged fingernails. "Tsk, tsk."

Sam said nothing. She'd barely spoken to Alison since Sunday, and though Alison would remain firm with *this* plan, she resolved to help her niece however she could with her speech, also sharing with her from her experiences about how to surmount her fears.

"These," she said, lifting three books from the stack she'd unearthed from her trunk, "will help you to learn proper carriage—spine rigid, shoulders back, chin up"—Maggie jumped to attention like a little soldier—"and will be the first step to aid you in walking with poise, as a lady should."

The girls glanced at the thick leather volumes and then at each other, as if Alison had lost all reason. She gave each of them a book.

"You're to put the volume on top of your heads, like so." Alison took the fourth book and placed it atop her head. Their eyes bugged as she adjusted it until it balanced and then gracefully walked around the room, the book remaining as motionless as if it had been nailed there.

"Ooo!" Baby Lynn slid off the rocker, where she'd been sitting to watch. "I wanna play! Lemme!"

Alison regarded her small niece with gentle approval. She was much too young to learn such things, but Alison put the book in her outstretched little hands. "Watch me! Watch me!" She lifted it to her head and held it there, never letting go of the book, which shifted as Baby Lynn pranced across the floor.

Alison softly smiled, the warm maternal feeling she'd experienced at the picnic again threatening to spread throughout her body and choke her to tears. She cleared her throat before she could give in to the emotion and looked at her other three nieces with the smile dissolving from her face. "Shall we begin?"

Each of the girls took a turn, the books sliding off their heads as if their skulls were sloped. Each time, she made them start from their initial position, and they took no more than a few steps before the book slid and hit the planks with a *thud*. After a grueling half hour, with little progress and the admonition that they must work hard at the exercise each day, she silenced their moans and showed them how to sit in a chair properly. At Mrs. Perriwinkle's Ladies Academy, Alison had been taught not to let her shoulders touch the back of a chair, so the benches worked well for her purpose. She declared that they must hold their upright poses for ten minutes, as she'd been taught in her earliest lessons, and until they could do so they couldn't leave the bench.

And so, the lessons in deportment continued through the next hour, followed by lessons in penmanship. She had no degree in teaching but felt perfectly capable to instruct them on how to neatly form their letters. Sam's were the best of the three, and in glancing at her work, Alison recognized the familiar handwriting of the letter she received in Boston. She wondered how circumstances might have turned out had that letter been waylaid. But dwelling on what could never occur proved a colossal waste of time, and again she resolved to do her utmost to help her nieces and nephews while also aiding their impossible father in his plan.

After another hour, she instructed Sam to work on her speech, receiving a troubled look in return, but Sam obediently retrieved a clean sheet of paper. Baby Lynn soon grew bored with scribbling on her scrap of parcel paper and returned to the rocker to rock her dolly to sleep.

When it came time to prepare the evening meal, Alison called a stop to all lessons. The girls moved more stiffly than usual; even young bones couldn't withstand the rigors of learning deportment.

But they would recover quickly. The lessons not only helped in aiding "the plan" to rid her from Rafe's life but also were beneficial to the children, and she felt no qualms to proceed with diligence.

Rafe and the boys came inside near dinnertime. Again she demanded to see their hands. Again the boys grumbled as, with Rafe, they headed to the water barrel.

The family gathered around the table. Alison refrained from further criticisms so that the meal could be enjoyed. She set down the final dish, a bowl of corn pudding, pleased with the outcome of her endeavors. Only the loaf of bread had blackened on the bottom. Everything else had turned out well.

After dinner, Andy patted his stomach in appreciation, and Tucker smiled at Alison. "That was actually some good eating this time, Aunt Alison."

His remark earned him an elbow jab from Maggie.

"What? What'd I say?" he complained. "It was!"

"Ahem." Alison cleared her throat to gain everyone's attention. "Where I come from we often have music, which is considered a proper form of after-dinner entertainment."

The children got hopeful expressions on their faces with some darting uneasy glances at their father, whose features remained somber. Sam quickly looked at the pianoforte then away again.

Clearly Amy had kept up the old family tradition and they missed it.

"Pa don't play the violin no more," Clarissa announced sadly.

Alison glanced at him, astonished to learn he'd been providing music as well as Amy. His face remained a stone mask, giving nothing away. Whether he approved or didn't she had yet to find out.

She stood up. "Well, I assure you that from this point forward, while I'm a guest in your home, you shall have music every night."

"You play the pianoforte?" Maggie asked in surprise.

"No. Your mother tried to teach me, but I never excelled."

"The violin, then?" Andy also looked curious.

"No."

Clarissa cocked her head to the side. "What else is there?"

"Oh, there are many instruments that provide beautiful music. I'll show you. The dishes can wait." With a secret smile, she hurried to the bedroom and her trunk. She withdrew her thin black box, extracting her prized instrument from its bed of crushed velvet. "Forgive me for what I'm about to do," she said to the silver metal she caressed and, in spirit, to her absent teacher. "However, necessity is the mother of invention. And this is just one more necessity to ensure that the plan doesn't fail." The cheerless thought grieved her spirit, but she pasted on a smile and returned to the main room.

"What's that?" Clarissa looked at Alison's hand.

"A flute. Have you never seen one?"

The child shook her head.

"Well, then, you're in for a treat. Harps are usually associated with angels, but so are flutes. Allow me to demonstrate."

Putting the instrument to her mouth and fingering the proper holes, she began to blow. The most horrendous screeching filled the air. She tried not to laugh, to keep her lips correctly pursed at the mouthpiece as she continued her "song." Yet the expressions of pain and horror on the children's faces were almost too much to bear, and she found a need to close her eyes or double over from laughing.

Outside the cabin, Brutus began to howl. A peek out of her eye showed that Baby Lynn had clapped her hands over her ears and squeezed her eyes shut. Unable to prevent herself, Alison glanced at Rafe. He gaped at her, his look one of sheer, agonized disbelief.

Mission accomplished.

She deliberately had selected a long solo written for the flute. Once she lowered her instrument, she looked at them in wide-eyed innocence.

"That was from a concerto by Vivaldi. Would you like to hear another?"

"No! I mean, it's getting late and we've got those tools to mend tomorrow, don't we, Pa?" Andy asked almost desperately.

"And the dishes need to be washed," Sam added. "Tucker, go and get more water."

"Why do I always gotta fetch the water?"

"Stop complaining and get the water," Rafe instructed.

"I suppose you're right," Alison said mournfully, attempting not to chuckle. "Though I did enjoy picking up my flute again. I haven't played in ever so long." She hesitated, as if deliberating an idea. "I could play while you girls wash, to give you music to work by."

"It's gone patht dark. Time Baby Lynn wath in bed." Maggie grabbed the protesting tot's hand and moved with her to the stairwell.

Alison smiled. "Well, there's always tomorrow."

On her way to the bedroom to return her flute to her trunk, she chuckled to hear the children's frantic whispers and Andy's remark of it being the most awful sound ever made.

"I sure hope the angels in heaven don't play that bad," Clarissa woefully added.

"What are we gonna do if we have to listen to *that* every night?" Sam whispered back.

Day one of her plan a success, Alison tucked her poor, abused flute back into its case.

* * * * *

Five days into Alison's plan, Rafe noticed his brood beginning to crack. Along with the pressure of becoming little ladies and gentlemen, they suffered through the nightly torture of Alison's flute playing—hardly a lullaby and certainly not beneficial for good dreams. The keening high-pitched wails brought on thoughts of ghosts, not angels.

Upon spying the barn doors shut though it was nearing midday, Rafe drew near and then stopped when he heard noises within. This time his children made no effort to lower their voices.

"If I have to wash my face and hands one more time," Tucker complained, "it'll wear the skin clean off!"

"What are you bellyaching for?" Sam shot back. "At least you don't have to walk around the cabin all morning with a silly book on your head."

"She brought books?" Andy asked. "No wonder her dadburned trunk was so heavy."

"Learning to be a lady isn't so bad," Clarissa said so softly Rafe almost couldn't hear her.

"You're only thayin' that 'cause you can keep the book on your head," Maggie complained. "It's alwayth thinner than mine. Mine mutht hold every cotton-pickin' word in the English language!"

Rafe muffled a chuckle, bending his ear closer to the crack to hear.

"And that curt-thying is thtupid," Maggie continued. "Why should I want to curt-thy to thum dumb boy anyhow?"

"Next week she said she's going to teach us ballroom dancing," Sam said in horror. "And I'll bet she's going to play that awful flute when she does."

"Maybe we can sneak it out of her trunk and get Brutus to bury it," Tucker suggested.

"With the way our luck's been going, he'll just think we're playing fetch and bring it back—probably to her." Andy sounded sullen. "There's just too much gone wrong. Aunt Alison isn't ma material. All agreed?"

The immediate chorus of reluctant yesses should have given Rafe relief. Oddly, it did the opposite.

"But I don't want her to go back to Boston," Clarissa complained. "I love her."

"She doesn't have to go back, 'Rissa," Andy explained. "We *all* love her. She's our aunt, after all. She just isn't any good as a ma, and Pa's clearly not interested."

"She sings nice, and I like the way she smells," Clarissa insisted stubbornly.

"We need more 'n that in a ma!" Tucker protested.

"I don't know. Maybe we should give her more time." Sam sounded uncertain. "She *is* nice—when she's not giving those awful lessons."

"We've given her almost three weeks already," Tucker argued, "and things just keep getting worse."

"All right, then. Who do we pick next?"

"We've gone through every dad-blamed name on the list!"

"Watch your language, Andy," Sam protested.

"What about the new lady who came to town last week?"

"What new lady?"

"The seamstress," Clarissa answered Andy. "At least if we choose her she can make us pretty dresses."

"Who cares about purty dresses?" Tucker sounded aghast. "We should find someone who can *really* cook and not burn nothin' or make us eat our greens neither...."

While his children argued over new prospects, Rafe stared at the barn door in horror.

Of all the women in Hope, Alison was the most suitable for

the role. Truth to tell, if he were forced to marry, she wasn't a bad choice. She was a righteous, God-fearing woman and already family, so she cared about his children more than a stranger might. She did her utmost to give her best, even if that meant her worst. Anyone else would be sadly lacking in areas where Alison flourished and provide even more disastrous results. Couldn't his children see that?

Clearly not.

"When I was a child, I spake as a child, I understood as a child, I thought as a child: but when I became a man, I put away childish things."

The Scripture from 1 Corinthians rose to mind. His children were certainly being childish! But what else could he expect since they *were* children? Deep down, Rafe could understand their yearning to have a real ma look after them. Rafe was supposed to be an adult, their father, but in his desperation he had behaved just as badly and childishly as they had.

Their plan had been an unfortunate mistake, yes, but so had his. He could see that now.

He should march in there and tell them he knew of their scheme and announce that Alison was returning to Boston on the next train—and he would tolerate no more nonsense of plans hatched behind his back to find him a wife. He should...

His hand froze on the latch.

But he couldn't. He couldn't bring himself to follow through with putting an end to this farce and send Alison away. The reason for his reluctance, he refused to consider.

At the noontime meal, he didn't fail to notice his children's unease and Alison's frequent glances in his direction regarding his brooding silence. Afterward, Rafe left for the barn to make sure his tools were sharpened for the upcoming corn harvest; he was glad for the solitude so he could stew in his thoughts.

Later, the boys came into the barn to do their evening chores, and he looked up in surprise, figuring it must be nearing time for supper. He put away his tools and stepped outside, his attention immediately going to the darkening sky. His foul mood shifted to alarm.

"Andy—Tucker—come with me!"

The boys hurried to join him, and when they looked where he did, their faces went pale.

* * * * *

That evening, Alison went to her room. Rafe and the boys hadn't come in for supper, though Tucker had rushed inside nearly an hour ago demanding that Sam come right away, with no explanations to Alison. And so she sent the little ones to bed and decided to retire early.

In between every unkind remark she could utter beneath her breath about the insufferable boor in the barn, she ripped a pin from her hair and threw it into the little porcelain bowl she used to store them. She decided not to bother with plaiting her hair; she was so angry she might tear the strands from the roots!

She punched the pillow to get it just right, punched it again, then raised it high and flung it on the bed.

Was there no pleasing the man? She had *thought* he would be overjoyed that her plan was working and the children's desire to have her with them dampened more with each day. But he had behaved as surly as when she arrived, nearly one long, torturous month ago.

"He's a beast," she muttered, "an ill-mannered, rude, uncouth, vindictive beast!"

So it made absolutely no sense that tears should roll down her cheeks at the prospect of soon leaving his home.

Rain began to fall. Alison heard and felt the most horrific thunder shake the walls of the little cabin. A second bolt of lightning struck nearby.

She lifted her eyes to the beams in concern, wondering how sturdy Rafe's cabin really was and if the roof would suddenly come crashing down on her head. They had received rain before but never such a storm as the one that now raged outside.

The door to her room flew open, hitting the wall. Before she could do more than gasp or turn her head to see, she felt a small body hurtle against her.

"The rain is yelling!" Baby Lynn cried.

"Shh, it's all right."

"Why won't it stop? Is God angry?"

Alison had little experience with how to calm such a small child, but in giving comfort Alison grew calmer. She pulled back the blanket in invitation and the girl crawled in bed while Alison stretched out beside her. Baby Lynn clutched her around the middle fiercely, her little bare feet like icicles where they pressed against Alison's calves from where her skirts had ridden up.

"I'm scared." Baby Lynn sniffled.

Alison put her arms around the child. "Now then, there's nothing to be frightened of. They're merely having a concert in heaven." She soothed with words her nanny once told her. "The cymbals are the lightning, and the thunder is the drums. Those are loudest, so that's what we hear the most."

Baby Lynn sniffled. "What's the rain?"

"Hmm." Alison thought a moment. She'd never asked her nanny that question. "In Spain they have instruments called maracas.

I heard a Spanish musician play them once. He shook them in his hands. It sounded like pieces of shredded wheat tumbling inside hollow wood, with a whispering sound. So I think the rain must be maracas. And the wind, a stringed instrument—a cello, maybe? A cello is like a big fiddle, like a large version of what your father plays. And at times, when the wind grows high in pitch, it can also sound like a flute."

"But do the angels hafta play so loud?"

Alison chuckled. "Maybe it's the sound of victory. Victory is expressed loudly."

"I don' like victry. Victry is scary."

At that moment, Alison didn't like victory either. The victory of her plan.

Before she could follow that thought too closely, she heard the outside door blow open and the wind and rain increase in volume. Rising to close it, she began to move away. Baby Lynn clutched her hand, her eyes wide with fear.

"It's all right." Alison gave as reassuring a smile as she could muster. "You stay here, sweetie, safe in bed. I'll be back soon."

Once in the main room, she noticed Clarissa and Maggie in their nightgowns.

"What are you two doing down here?"

"Sam and Baby Lynn aren't in the loft," Maggie explained, worried. "I think Sam's still outside."

"Baby Lynn is in my bed. You two keep her company. I'll check on Sam."

At another burst of thunder, Clarissa ran past and dove under the covers.

Alison hurried to where the door had been thrown wide, the

wind pushing it to and fro. With the distant lightning as a backdrop, she made out the figures toiling in the field.

She blinked in shock then guessed the situation. Rafe depended on his crops to provide for his family. Clearly, he was trying to save what he could.

Alison hurried back to the bedroom, finding her long woolen shawl and wrapping it around her head. "You three stay here. I'll be back with Sam soon."

They nodded solemnly. Another wild burst of thunder made all three girls screech and huddle close. Alison breathed a prayer for protection for everyone involved and hurried into the storm.

Chapter Thirteen

....

The wind blew rain into Alison's eyes as she struggled toward the corn rows, the faint beam from Sam's covered lantern barely discernable. Rafe swung a scythe against the hardy stems like a wild man, his sons using smaller tools to slice ears of corn from them. She met Sam running toward the barn, her arms full of sheaves of corn. Alison grabbed her, bringing her face level with Sam's.

"Go to the house. I'll take over," she yelled above the storm, though she had no idea what to do.

Fear twisting her face, Sam nodded and ran for the barn. Alison picked up the curved tool the girl had left on the ground. She watched Andy, to see how he did it, then did the same, also running to the open barn doors and dumping what she'd cut in the middle of the floor where the children had thrown what they'd gathered. Her hands weren't yet toughened enough to withstand the sharp papery husks that sliced against her soft, wet skin as she worked to break the ears of corn free from the stalks Rafe had cut down. Sawing frantically, she used the curved knife while the rain battered against her back and the wind threatened to push her down.

She lagged where the others excelled but worked diligently. The storm grew wilder, a raging beast, and her desperation peaked. With her numb hands, she tugged and twisted and sawed and pulled the corn however she could to break it free.

Suddenly she felt a hand on her arm and looked up to see Tucker.

"Pa says go back!" he screamed above the wind.

Tucker ran for the cabin and Alison looked for his father. Rafe now ripped corn off the stalks, and Andy was running with the corn he'd gathered toward the barn.

Rafe hadn't quit, and Alison could save more too. She *had* to try. She had to... Just a few more...

The wind picked up speed, the rain stinging like needles. A hand on her arm startled her along with the knowledge that Rafe had come up beside her.

"It's hopeless!" he called above the wind.

She couldn't explain the urgency she felt to continue, as if she'd planted the seeds and nurtured this crop as her own. "Just this stalk..." She persisted with her task as though compelled.

He grabbed her arm, harder this time. "Stop! Now!"

She shook her head in refusal, unable to see him well, and might have tried to break away again when suddenly he pulled her up and close in a hard embrace, holding her tightly as if realizing she *couldn't* stop. The curved blade dropped from her cold, nerveless hand. It was then she knew the heat wetting her eyes were tears and not the rain.

The shock of his nearness didn't fully register as the wind died and the rain decreased, but the change felt more ominous than comforting. The skies had turned a strange dark-gray–green, and she realized something was amiss when his muscles tensed against her. She felt him turn then heard him silently curse beneath his breath.

"Run!" He released his hold, grabbed her shoulders, and shoved her toward the cabin.

Her skirts were plastered against her legs. Her limbs trembled

PAMELA GRIFFIN

so hard she could scarcely keep her hold on the corn. Rafe grabbed her arm again, trying to pull her along with him. She stumbled in an effort to keep up and dropped the corn. She tried to bend over to retrieve it, but his hand on her arm remained tight, forcing her to keep up with his swift pace.

"Forget the corn, woman—*run!*"

She felt a strange shift in the wind, the air around her going static. It grew louder, whistling eerily. Fear made her heart hammer against her chest, making it hard to breathe.

They barely made it to the edge of the corn row when suddenly Rafe wrenched her forward, throwing her down to the soaked earth. He fell hard on top of her, knocking the trapped breath from her lungs. With his entire body he covered her, his hands clutching hers, her cheek pressed into wet soil. She barely noticed the discomfort, as to her horror the strangest wail met her ears and the wind blew with tremendous force, whipping up the earth above their heads. She squeezed her eyes shut and prayed for it all to end.

The rain began to beat down again with force, harder this time. A piece of ice struck her hand; it had begun to hail.

"Run for the cabin," Rafe ordered in her ear, loudly enough for her to acknowledge with a bare nod.

He scrambled to his feet and grabbed her around the arm and waist, pulling her up to stand as she gripped his arm and shirt—anything her hand met to regain her balance. Keeping his hold on her strong, they stumbled and slid over treacherous ground to the cabin door that Andy held open for them.

Once they were inside, Andy shut the door with effort. Both he and Tucker lifted a beam into place to prevent the door from blowing in. Someone had done the same to the boards that covered the window.

"Did you see it, Pa?" Sam asked above the cacophony hitting the roof. "Was it a cyclone?"

"It sounded like it."

His low, rasping voice snapped Alison out of her shock. Her shivering suddenly came in earnest, and her body began to ache from Rafe's rough treatment—which had most assuredly saved her life. She knew she would have bruises come morning. She looked at him, where he'd taken a seat not far from where she huddled, and reached a hand toward his face without thought.

"You're bleeding."

He grabbed her wrist before she could make contact with his jaw, where little prickles of blood formed thin trails on his skin. His hold on her wasn't strong like before, but he didn't let go, instead lowering her hand to see it better. His brows drew together in a frown and she looked down. For the first time she noticed that her palm was red and swollen. Thin cuts ran along the inside. She wondered if the knife had slipped to make the ones that now seeped beads of blood mixed with water.

His troubled gaze lifted from her palm to her eyes. "Why didn't you stop when I told you to?"

"I couldn't. I just…couldn't…." She shook her head, unable to express her feelings when she barely understood them herself. Her explanation sounded foolish; certainly it made no sense, but he nodded as if he understood.

"Pa?"

The frightened query came from Alison's room where Baby Lynn suddenly appeared in the doorway. Spotting her father, the child ran and threw herself at him, winding her arms around his neck.

Rafe held her tightly, trying to offer what comfort he could, while the storm raged outside and the wind hammered against the small cabin, whistling oddly through the eaves. Still, Alison felt safer inside the log walls with the glow of the lantern now casting a calm pool of golden light nearby.

She wrapped a dish towel around her hand and looked at the children; worry was etched into each face.

"You think my kitty's okay?" Clarissa asked in a frightened whisper near the doorway.

"And Brutus?"

"Brutus is up in the loft," Maggie answered.

"I'm sure the cat is snug inside the barn, filling up on the mice there. Come." Alison motioned to Clarissa on her right and to Tucker on her left, noticing that his hands also looked raw. "Come closer."

From some inner well she drew up the strength needed to offer support to her nieces and nephews, sensing that Rafe had withdrawn to some dark place within himself. The strength he exerted when rescuing her seemed to have seeped from him. He remained silent, his stare unfocused as his gaze latched onto some faraway object in the room, and Alison realized she had become the one to guide them all. God help her. God help them.

She knew they must call on the One who ordered the weather and controlled the heavens while watching over all of them. The Lord had calmed a storm when his followers became panic-stricken. She would ask for the same.

She bowed her head and sensed the children do the same. "Almighty Father, we humbly commit our lives to You and beseech You for Your continued guidance and protection, for all those suffering from this storm. We ask that You stretch forth Your mighty hand to calm the skies and keep us safe beneath the shelter of Your wing." She recalled the verses of a psalm that Amy had once made into a sampler when she first learned needlepoint. Her Bible sat on the hearth, by the rocker, where she'd left it, and upon retrieving it, Alison opened to the Ninety-First Psalm.

"'He that dwelleth in the secret place of the most High shall abide under the shadow of the Almighty,'" she read, her voice growing stronger with conviction. "'I will say of the Lord, He is my refuge and my fortress: my God; in him will I trust....'"

She continued to read and the children quieted, as though grasping the comforting words. Clarissa still hovered near the doorway, looking extremely frightened, but moved closer to Alison as she read. Alison held out her arm in invitation. Clarissa darted to her, falling to her knees and nestling under Alison's arm. Alison held the girl close, gaining revelation of the verses she'd just shared: God wanted to gather His children against Himself, shielding them from dangers, and He asked that they trust in Him and stay close so that He could.

The knowledge brought solace. She began to hum then softly sing what verses she remembered of her mother's favorite hymn.

God moves in a mysterious way
His wonders to perform;
He plants His footsteps in the sea
And rides upon the storm.

Ye fearful saints, fresh courage take;
The clouds ye so much dread
Are big with mercy and shall break
In blessings on your head....

Clarissa's trembling diminished until she lay calm. Across the circle, Baby Lynn pulled her head away from her father's shoulder and looked at Alison with huge, watery eyes as Alison sang the last verse.

Blind unbelief is sure to err
And scan His work in vain;
God is His own interpreter,
And He will make it plain.

Suddenly Baby Lynn climbed down from Rafe's lap and walked to Alison, dropping down beside her. Alison, hoping Rafe wouldn't be upset over his daughter's actions, put her free arm around Baby Lynn's shoulders, drawing her close to her other side.

Embracing the two girls, Alison waited for a moment before she lifted her gaze to Rafe's, a bit apprehensive about what she would see in his expression.

His eyes didn't condemn or scold; neither did they approve. His expression appeared...lost, though Alison didn't feel he was thinking of the damage to his crops to bring such a strange look to his face, especially since he stared directly at her. She wished she could decipher his feelings, but he flicked his eyes downward and kept them focused on the floor.

The storm lessened in intensity. The rain still poured, but she doubted anyone would be able to sleep, and the boys certainly couldn't go back to the barn.

"You sing nice," Clarissa said. "Not high like Ma sang, but warm."

Alison smiled. "Warm" seemed like high praise at the moment.

The sting in her hands increased as the numbness disappeared, and she remembered the soothing oil. Memory of that night and the intent look that had been in Rafe's eyes when he saw her with her hair down made her face grow hot. It also reminded her of her current appearance and the wet woolen shawl she wore still knotted at her throat.

"Clarissa," she said near her ear, "please go retrieve the bottle of oil on my trunk."

"Andy, Tucker," she said more loudly, "please start a fire in the stove. Sam, Maggie, would you see about making coffee?"

She watched as the children set about their tasks, hoping it would help take their minds off the frightening situation. Pulling the knot beneath her chin loose, she let her wet shawl slide heavily to the floor. She lightly fingered her disheveled mass of hair, wishing now she'd had the foresight to plait it. Yet the sorry condition of her locks paled when compared to the Munroes' suffering. The crops she could do nothing about. Their bodies she could help, with what little she knew to do.

"Sam, Tucker, Andy, come here," she ordered softly once Clarissa returned with the bottle and handed it to her. Sam approached first.

"Hold out your hands," Alison instructed, noting the girl's hesitance. She assumed she feared the possible sting of the oil, which had no sting to it. "It's all right, honey. This won't hurt." She tipped the bottle to soak her fingertip then rubbed the tip over the slightly pink welts and light cuts the girl bore. She offered her a warm smile before looking at the boys. "Next?"

"That's Ma's hand oil, isn't it?" Sam whispered, gaining Rafe's sudden attention. He looked Alison's way.

"Yes, it is."

"Her perfumed *special* oil?" Sam continued nervously. "She never let us use it before."

Alison offered another reassuring smile. "Well, I would imagine that's because a need like this never arose before, did it?"

The girl shook her head.

"I'm sure that your mother would have done exactly as I'm doing now. My sister was generous with her belongings and put her loved ones' needs above any trifles she owned."

That seemed to mollify Sam, who smiled as if she'd set her mind at ease.

"Boys?" Alison looked at Tucker and Andy.

"Don't need no sissy lady-oil," Tucker replied, affronted.

"Well, if you would rather not… I don't know what this contains, but the oil is astounding. It helped my hands to heal after wash day." Alison winced at the memory of the chore she had yet to master and looked past the young boy. "Andy?"

"Sure, I'll take some."

Tucker looked at his older brother as if Andy had betrayed all of their gender. Alison tried not to laugh as she dabbed oil on the boy's large hands.

"Are you certain you won't change your mind, Tucker?"

He shook his head emphatically and scowled.

"What about Pa?" Maggie insisted. "Don't forget Pa! His hands need healing too."

His hands and so much more. Why the child's prod should send a strange tingling charge through Alison, she didn't know. "Mr. Munroe?" She worked to keep her tone natural, noticing also how his hair curled at the ends when damp.

"I wouldn't want to use up what you have," he said at last.

She blinked and realized she'd been staring. Had he forgotten that he gave her practically a full bottle? Or perhaps he used the excuse as a polite refusal. Alison nodded, preparing to close the bottle with the stopper. Her own hands were already oily from administering aid to the children.

"There's plenty, Pa," Maggie assured. "You should put some on too. Your hands don't look so good." She approached Alison. For a moment, Alison hoped she would ask for the bottle to doctor her pa's hands. "I'll take Baby Lynn to bed," the child offered instead.

"Don' wanna go to my bed," the tot whimpered sleepily against Alison. "Wanna go to Auntie Al–son's bed."

Alison glanced at Rafe. Nothing in his expression showed whether he approved or opposed the idea. She nodded to Maggie. "Put her in my bed."

"My dolly!" Baby Lynn cried. "Where's my baby dolly?"

"You probably left her upstairs," Sam soothed. "I'll get her."

Clarissa went with Maggie, both children helping the sleepy Baby Lynn to walk to Alison's room. Andy moved toward the stove and Tucker followed, harshly whispering to him beneath his breath—likely confronting him for breaking down and using the "sissy lady-oil."

The reminder made Alison hesitate. She studied Rafe, who sat hunched over with his elbows propped on his thighs, his hands hanging between them, his manner dismal.

She looked at the bottle in her hand.

Would he feel the same as Tucker and not wish to be bothered with using the remedial oil? Or would he behave like his eldest and be grateful for the opportunity?

This is ridiculous, she fumed to herself at the drama she was building. So much devastation had occurred, producing a need for them to come together, to help one another, and she shirked from treating his hands?

She stood up and approached him with purpose.

He looked up slowly when she stopped before him. The helpless expression in his eyes made her heart melt. Before she could consider her actions, she sank to her knees before him and gently took one of his large, limp hands in her small one.

The resulting warmth that shot through Alison also made her mouth go dry. She found she couldn't speak, recalling the reason for her earlier hesitation. That hesitation had a name. A name she felt loath to air, even silently in her mind. To wish for more than he would ever agree to give was folly and only caused the new, dull ache in her chest to throb more.

How could she be so insensitive? Rafe had lost so much…and she, selfish wretch that she was, pitied herself for the absence of his affection?

It had come upon her so suddenly, the shock, the awareness, the knowledge she'd fought for days. She wasn't sure when her feelings had begun to alter. But any fondness for this man should never have been allowed the chance to cultivate. Any change with regard to how she viewed their situation was solely her fault, and she must uproot all stubborn seedlings of hope that would ultimately lead to her humiliation and his discomfort. She *must*!

She focused on her task, applying oil to the angry welts on his palm and fingers with such featherlight strokes as to be almost nonexistent. But she felt the touches down to her soul. He had the hands of a farmer, hard and toughened by work and weather, but she knew his touch could be gentle too.…

"Your other hand, if you please." She snapped the words out, keeping her tone low, flustered by the direction his close proximity and her far-reaching thoughts were taking her.

He did as asked, still without a word, though she sensed that his eyes never left her face.

Alison didn't risk looking up. If she did, she feared she would be lost in those eyes, lost in this moment, and say something he wouldn't want to hear. Regardless of her nervousness to touch him, she strangely didn't wish to let go of his hand. She slowed her ministrations, allowing her fingertips to trail along his reddened skin, lingering only as long as she dared.

The silence grew oppressive. Her limbs felt leaden as she struggled to stand.

"I'll see about finding blankets for everyone." They still shivered in wet clothing, but she'd been too preoccupied with shock after escaping the deadly clutches of the storm to think clearly. She took a step, wincing at a sudden cramp in her thigh.

"Are you all right?" Rafe's voice came deep, gruff. "I didn't hurt you earlier, when I..."

Tackled me to the ground and shielded my body with yours? Silently she supplied the missing words to his question. "I think I'll survive our...fall. Had you not been there, I might not be here now." She grew bolder and lifted her gaze to his, noting the concern in his expression. "You most likely saved my life."

His eyes held hers a moment before flickering downward, his face again a mask.

"So don't you dare apologize," she warned, her tone going lighter in the hope of dispelling some of his misery. "Or I might misconstrue your meaning."

A slight answering grin tugged at the corners of his mouth, but he didn't let it grow, only giving a vague nod in return. After a moment, he looked up. "Thanks...for stepping up when I couldn't. For taking care of the children..."

Feeling the need to reply when his words trailed off, she kept her voice at a whisper so she wouldn't be overheard. "I'm sorry if my behavior tonight has hurt the plan."

He shook his head. "Forget the plan for now. The children need comfort tonight, not criticisms and complaints."

What about the comfort she could give him? Or could she? She could never be a substitute for Amy. Did she really *want* to be a substitute for anyone? She cleared her throat. "I know things look bad—"

He huffed in irony. "You have no idea."

"No, you're right about that. Even though I've been here for some weeks, I still know very little about crops except what you've told me. I'm sorry I couldn't have been more help in saving what you had. But at least you saved some." She smiled hopefully, though the pathetic amounts she'd seen in the barn likely wouldn't last this family several weeks and surely seemed nowhere near enough to sell. "God alone knows the end from the beginning. He's promised to be with us through every storm. Trust Him."

Rafe didn't respond, and Alison wondered if it had been a mistake to speak, what with his dour outlook on faith after losing Amy. But her parents had raised their girls to seek God's face at all times and especially in times of trouble. She could advise him no differently.

Clarissa padded out of her room, Maggie on her heels. "Auntie Alison?"

"Yes?" She turned sharply and stepped toward her nieces, aware of how close she'd been to Rafe and not wanting his children to get the wrong impression. She stoppered the bottle, amazed that with her awkward movements she didn't drop it from her oil-slicked hands.

"Baby Lynn wants you to sing to her."

"Of course." Maggie's request gave Alison the escape needed in what had become an embarrassing situation. "Girls, please find everyone dry blankets."

Without another look at Rafe, Alison entered the bedroom.

Chapter Fourteen
....

Rafe watched Alison go, curious about the woman who'd given her all in the fruitless effort to save his crop—to the point that her hands had swollen and bled. He felt bad enough that he wouldn't be sending her home in the shape she'd arrived, her hands now a far cry from the soft, pale ones she'd come with. But for her to apologize for something that wasn't her fault, especially after she'd done so much to help, well, it made him feel lower than a snake crawling on its belly.

It had been a mistake to try to save anything—a futility born of the need to provide for his family. After the poor crop he'd brought in last year, desperation had made him act without thinking, especially in ordering his children to help. Only one more week, surely, and the corn would have been ready for harvesting! When he noticed the storm gain in fury, he put a swift end to the mad scramble to save what they could, fearful for his children's lives. He'd been stunned at the similar wave of desperation and protectiveness that had rushed through him when Alison foolishly refused his order to go back inside.

Alison Stripling may have been bred in the city and enjoyed a pampered lifestyle, but she had the soul of a hard worker, due, no doubt, to her mission-minded parents. Yet she still wore the fancy dresses and fripperies of the wealthy, despite her change in status from Boston society to the Kansas wilds. Tonight, she'd gotten a taste of just how wild it could be.

His own hands had suffered worse on other occasions; it was part and parcel of farming the land. But when she had gently ministered to him, her faint touch both soothing and arousing to his senses, Rafe had been unable to refuse her.

For the moment he couldn't think of what the storm was doing to his crops, though that knowledge battered the back of his mind. If he focused on his hardship, he would sink into misery, and he couldn't do that again. His children needed him. He reminded himself of that every day, determined never again to become distant and lose awareness of the lives of his and Amy's offspring.

At times, his wife's sister reminded him of Amy; it wasn't difficult to see that they'd been raised in the same home. He could still envision Alison holding Baby Lynn at the picnic, the picture of motherly love, and again tonight, when his little girl had sought her out after hearing her sweet hymn. From the other room, he could hear strains of Alison's song now, her voice husky and warm, comforting. But on other occasions, Alison seemed nothing like his soft-spoken, gentle wife. At those times his houseguest bore a spirited fire equal to his that was both intriguing and exasperating. Lately, he'd come to realize he'd been thinking of her more often than he ought, more often than he thought of Amy, and he should feel ashamed for the slight to his wife's memory.

But the guilt no longer burned as fiercely as the first time he realized his oversight. Was he wrong not to feel blameworthy any longer?

Caleb would again say that the time had come to let go of the past. Yet Rafe still didn't know what that meant for his future.

Maggie came downstairs with blankets, followed by Sam

carrying Baby Lynn's doll. Sam disappeared into Rafe's bedroom, closing the door behind her.

"The roof ith leaking," Maggie announced. "It'th dripping on the bed."

Rafe sighed. "Did you put anything underneath to catch the water?"

"I came to get a bowl."

"Then hop to it."

Maggie grabbed the container and darted back upstairs.

She returned in time to join Sam, who went to the stove and poured two cups of coffee from the pot, which had begun to steam. She handed him one.

"Pa?"

He recognized her unspoken request, since she often asked the question. Amy had always insisted children shouldn't drink the strong brew, explaining how their fragile constitutions couldn't handle it. But on a night like this, when he felt it might have been better to build an ark than a cabin, he decided to bend the rules this once.

He nodded. "Go ahead. Pour some for everyone."

"Thanks, Pa!" She poured more into another cup then stilled, her mind clearly elsewhere, and set the pot down. "I saw it—the cyclone. It was so dark, but it looked like an angry black cloud spinning round and round. It was headed straight for you and Aunt Alison. I didn't know they came out at night too. I prayed, Pa. I prayed really hard, like Ma said we should when we need divine intervention. Do you think my prayers helped?"

Three thoughts rushed to him simultaneously. Amy's guidance still helped their eldest daughter…Alison had warned him that Tucker and Andy were falling away from the same faith that Amy instilled in them…and lastly, the memory came of Alison reading a psalm of protection from God's Holy Word.

"I've never seen a funnel up close," Sam said when he didn't answer. "I thought it was going to blow us all away."

"Well, it didn't." Wearily he tried to reassure her. "We're safe now."

"I wasn't skeered," Tucker announced.

"Sure you weren't," Sam scoffed. "I heard your teeth chattering!"

"You did not. Wind was too loud. Besides, they was chatterin' 'cause I was cold."

"Uh-huh."

At her skeptical response, Tucker scowled.

Rafe knew he should intervene before a quarrel began but felt too exhausted to deal with still more trouble. Thankfully, the children settled down.

"Pa?" Andy spoke. Rafe noticed his son help himself to the coffee that Sam had forgotten to pour for everyone else. "You think the crop is ruined?"

He didn't want to think about that probability. "Come dawn, we'll know more."

Andy nodded sullenly and took a long swallow of coffee. Being close to fifteen, he understood the ongoing consequences of such a dilemma, whereas the younger children could only see the moment in which they lived.

Rafe noticed Tucker wistfully eye the bottle of oil Alison had left on the table. He wondered if she'd done so purposely for his stubborn son.

He opened his mouth to instruct the boy to use some when the door to his bedroom opened and Alison appeared. Her features looked drawn, as weary as his, her eyes huge and girl-like in her pale face. Her hair, just beginning to dry, hung in tousled waves all around her.

"Is Baby Lynn asleep?" Sam asked.

"Yes." Alison's voice sounded hoarse.

"You don't have to tend to things here," Rafe assured her quietly. "Go on to bed with the girls. Since I don't see Clarissa, I'm assuming she decided to stay with you."

"Yes. They're both asleep. I smelled coffee and yearned for a cup. I don't think I'll be able to sleep, but I certainly can't sleep with my hair wet."

Her comment brought Rafe's attention back to the shiny tresses that fell in a dark waterfall all about her arms and back, much as it had on the night he'd brought her the oil. She moved to pour herself coffee, and he noticed that she'd changed from the ruined dress with its droopy bows into another dress—a simple, serviceable dark one, almost as dark as her hair. He looked away and toward the slow fire Andy was building.

"I can brush out your hair, if you want," Maggie offered shyly. "Bein' as how your hands have all that oil on 'em and mine don't."

Alison looked at her in surprise. Rafe recalled how Maggie liked to brush and plait her mother's hair. Alison's thick locks may not have been the same flaxen color, but they were glorious nonetheless.

"I'll be back with your brush." Maggie hurried to the bedroom.

Alison seemed nervous, as if she might reconsider, and Rafe wondered if his presence was the cause. He sure couldn't excuse himself to retreat outside. And he couldn't retire to his bedroom, because he felt awkward going in there while Alison lived beneath his roof. If he went up to the loft and heard the constant drips of rainwater coming from the ceiling and splattering into a pail, that might be what drove him over the edge of sanity.

With nowhere to go, he remained seated and watched Alison sink to the woven rug in front of the hearth. Brutus, who had appeared at some point, whined and thumped his tail, edging closer on his rump. Rafe held out his hand, and the mutt bounded forward to lick it. Absentmindedly he scratched the dog between the ears, his attention riveted to the quiet figure before the hearth.

Maggie returned with a silver-handled brush and sat down behind Alison, who stared into the struggling flames as Andy fed them more wood. A sudden blaze cast fiery light on her skin, bringing out a trace of the same shimmering color in the hank of hair Maggie held between her fingers. She meticulously brushed, starting with the ends and working her way upward.

Rafe watched in fascination as Maggie painstakingly brought the matted waves into a sleek shining cape, the ends touching the floor. Alison never looked away from the fire, only closed her eyes for brief periods.

In all likelihood she thought him rude, but he couldn't look away, however much he tried, though truthfully his attempts were pitiful at best. Watching Maggie brush out her aunt's hair with long fluid strokes soothed Rafe's own tattered nerves. It helped to focus on something other than the storm, which had lessened by degrees and now came as a gentle pattering against the roof.

Maggie sectioned Alison's hair into three thick ropes and plaited them. The fleeting thought crossed his mind that it seemed a shame how women bound up their hair to confine it, especially hair as lovely as Alison's.

He blinked, took another swig of coffee, and found it had gone cold.

"Thank you, Maggie. You have a tender touch." Alison spoke into the silence, her voice strained...the first time she'd said anything since Maggie began her task. Alison smiled at her and spoke again. "I think I'll lie down now. You need to get some rest too."

"Can't," Maggie explained. "It's raining where we thleep. Roof ith leaking."

"Oh?" She glanced at Rafe, then away again. "Stretch out in front of the fire, Maggie. I don't think there's room for one more soul on that bed."

"I don't mind thleepin' on the floor. I done tho before, and we got blankets."

"The fire will keep you warm." Alison hesitated as though she might say more and then slowly looked Rafe's way again. "If there's nothing else…"

"Go on to bed. We'll manage."

She gave a jerky nod, her smile hardly genuine, leaving Rafe to wonder what he'd said or done this time to cause her aggravation.

* * * * *

Once inside the bedroom, Alison shut the door and fell against it in relief. The entire time Maggie brushed out her hair and plaited it, she'd felt his eyes upon her. Several times she had closed her own, thinking that when she opened them he would have looked away.

But he never did.

Why?

Had he been comparing her to Amy?

Did he find her lacking?

Had he given her reason to believe he cared?

She groaned in disgust. It seemed absurd and shallow to concentrate on such inane questions, especially at a time like this. But her mind continued circling in an odd carousel, starting with the moment he saved her life, whirling to later when she doctored his hands, and still later, as he watched her in front of the fire. Over and over, around and around, she thought about those unsettling, breathless moments. She tended to constantly question what she didn't understand, and she certainly didn't understand the master of this household!

"Oh, Amy, what have I gotten myself into? Is it wrong to feel like this? Would you be angry if you knew?"

The patchwork quilt moved near Clarissa's leg, and Alison's attention abruptly shifted to the foot of the bed. She stared in confusion then gave a short laugh as a yellow-and-cream-colored furry head appeared.

"I see you managed to find refuge," Alison said to the tabby that Clarissa had named Peaches. Alison sank to the edge of the mattress. "This bed is getting more crowded every time I look. At least Clarissa's mind will be at ease, though I'm not certain her father would agree to this arrangement."

"Meow?" Peaches seemed to question and stretched his sleek body in lazy contentment as if he had every right to be there. Alison ruffled his fur. The cat lightly batted her wrist with his paw, showing his fangs slowly and pausing, as if wanting to play. Alison stroked his warm silky side, sensing that he tested her. A rumbling purr soon rewarded her theory as Peaches closed his eyes in bliss.

"Tell me," she mused, "are all the males of this household so difficult to figure out and so uncertain of what they want?"

She had no idea why she asked such a silly question—of a cat no less—but airing it helped to settle her nerves, and she finally felt she might be able to sleep.

She looked at the bed.

Somewhere...

She shed her dress and managed to slip onto a section of mattress that gave her as much space as elbow to hand. She only hoped she could manage to remain on the bed through the night.

Chapter Fifteen

....

Alison woke three times during the night. Once when Baby Lynn's knee lodged in the small of her back, almost knocking her off the bed. Once when Baby Lynn's arm flung across her throat. And the last time when Baby Lynn actually crawled on top of her in her sleep, as if she were a comfortable pillow.

She would have thought that after passing such a restless night she would be irritable, but she awoke feeling cozy and very wanted—by two warm little bodies sandwiched on either side of her and a cat that slumbered on her stomach. She squelched the urge to laugh, not wanting to startle the cat into unsheathing its claws into her belly or the girls into accidentally kicking or strangling her.

"Well," she whispered, "what to do now?"

A tap on the door gave her the opportunity needed. She doubted Rafe would knock and so quietly. He had steered clear of this room except to offer her the hand oil weeks before.

"Yes?" she asked, hopeful of a rescue by one of her nieces.

The door edged open and Sam appeared. At the sight of Alison and her companions, her eldest niece laughed outright. "I should have warned you about Baby Lynn. She tends to take over the whole bed."

"So I've noticed."

"You found the cat!"

"Hmm. Yes. Help me out of this predicament, please."

Sam removed the cat from Alison's belly. It let out an annoyed, sleepy growl, clearly not happy about being disturbed. Alison sat up and pushed errant tendrils of hair from her face that had escaped the braid. "What time is it?"

"Past dawn. Sun's been up for at least an hour."

"What?"

"Pa said to let you sleep."

"Oh my." Quickly, Alison moved all small limbs from her body so she could slide to the foot of the bed. She hurried to the trunk, where she'd tossed her discarded linen dress, slipped it over her head, and fastened it. She pondered the suitability of asking a twelve-year-old about her father's state of mind and reasoned that she would rather be prepared for what awaited her. She phrased the matter carefully. "Tell me, Sam, about the crop. Is there any hope?"

The girl's woebegone expression told her all she needed to know.

"Andy, Pa, and Tucker have been trying to clear what they could. The stream must've overflowed, 'cause there's water everywhere—almost ankle-deep!"

Alison's heart sank. She worked at pulling her hair free from the messy plait so she could brush it, roll it in a twist, and pin it up out of the way. Her hands still stung, but thankfully the damage was no worse than a few shallow cuts.

"I kept some cornmeal mush warm for you." Sam smiled proudly. "I didn't burn it this time."

"Thank you, Sam."

"I put on a fresh pot of coffee too. I thought it'd be wise to keep some available all day."

"That sounds like a good idea."

"You want me to wake them?"

Alison looked toward the bed, where Baby Lynn now curled up against Clarissa in their slumber. "Let them sleep a little longer. They had a difficult night, tossing and turning." And she had the sore muscles to prove it.

She followed Sam into the main room and took a seat at the table, feeling guilty about having the girl wait on her. Sam brought her a plate and pulled away the cloth covering it. The corn mush *did* look appealing. After a silent prayer of thanks, Alison poured honey over the crusty square and edged some off with her fork, taking a bite.

"It's delicious," she said in sincere appreciation.

"Oh!" Sam exclaimed softly. "I near forgot. The cyclone took away part of the barn. There's a great gaping hole in the west side, and the roof slopes funny. And the henhouse fell apart too."

"*What?*" Alison blinked at the news.

"The animals are okay, just shook up. The chickens were wandering around outside, but we gathered them. But the cow gave no milk, and the chickens were squawking up a storm—no eggs either."

Poor Rafe. Not only had he lost his crop, he'd lost use of his barn.

"What can I do to help?" Alison asked.

"I don't reckon there's much you can do. Clearing the land, that's men's work, and, well, today is wash day, but the ground's too wet to build a fire. I don't reckon we ought to wash indoors, like we do in winter. Not today, 'cause Pa has to fix the roof. The barn too, so they can sleep in it tonight. He and the boys took the wagon into town for supplies."

Sam sounded entirely too pleased, and Alison couldn't help but also feel relieved that wash day might slip by this week. But she wondered what that meant for the availability of clean linens and why Rafe's fixing a leaky roof in the loft would prevent her and the girls from taking on the despised chore in the main room.

"Any idea when they'll return?"

"Pa didn't say. Around noon, I reckon. I'm going upstairs for a while."

Alison nodded and finished her breakfast while contemplating some way to aid the Munroe family. The floor could certainly use a good scrub from the many muddy footprints of last night. When the rooms were neat and orderly, it always made her feel better; she hoped this one small act might brighten Rafe's outlook as well.

She located a broom and made thorough work of dispensing with the dirt. Opening the door, she prepared to sweep the mess outside. With a gray sky as a dome to shed light, she saw a wide path where the high grasses and land had been torn and tossed up. The neat little rows of the crop Rafe painstakingly raised now resembled the back side of a canvas tapestry, with the colored threads all gnarled and in knots with no idea of what belonged where. Near the barn, she spotted part of the destroyed wall, and as she looked over the land, she saw that rainwater lay at least an inch deep atop its surface.

"Oh my," she whispered, shocked by the tremendous devastation.

Her eyes grew moist but she straightened her spine. Crying over Rafe's predicament would benefit no one. There was work to be done. Her determination unquenched, she sloshed her way over to the barrel.

A glance inside the coverless container filled to the brim with rainwater told her that Tucker had forgotten to retrieve stream water again and—good heavens! Was that a snake she saw floating beneath the gritty depths? Had Tucker found his slimy friend? She decided she would rather not know and replaced the cover quickly.

Retrieving a pail, she felt thankful she'd worn her button-up shoes and not her slippers. She supposed she could skim water from the ground, as much of it that stood there, but likely she'd get a goodly amount of soil mixed in, which defeated the purpose of cleaning.

The trek to the back of the cabin and narrow ribbon of water in the distance took longer than she presumed. The marshy land sucked at the soles of her shoes as if to steal them. Debris of leaves and twigs lay everywhere from the cottonwoods, elms, and hackberries that grew along the creek.

Once she finally arrived at the bank, she took a few minutes to catch her breath before dipping the pail in the fast-moving, swollen stream. She felt relieved to see that the little springhouse Rafe had built to keep food cold stood intact.

The weight of the water ground the pail's handle into her still-tender flesh. Perhaps she would have been wise to wear her thickest gloves, even if the sight of her toiling in the white elbow-length coverings would have been rather preposterous...though no one but a stray chicken would have seen.

She gritted her teeth, determined not to be such a citified Easterner. For goodness' sake, she wasn't the only woman to suffer from chafed and cut hands! Amy had needed to endure much to become a farmer's wife. But with a man like Rafe to care for her, she could hardly be pitied....

"No," Alison announced to the dragonflies that flitted along the water's surface. "I will *not* travel that road of self-pity and regret again! You decided on the life of a spinster, Alison. Best to remember that. Remember what that faithless cur Stephen did to you. Remember also that the children's father can be a boor and wants nothing to do with you."

Alison briefly closed her eyes. She felt foolish for chiding herself aloud, thankful no one stood in the vicinity to hear, but if her short soliloquy ended such outrageous thoughts, the better for everyone involved. It *hurt* to acknowledge any burgeoning feelings of affection for the man when such feelings were not reciprocated and never would be.

The children… The children were all that mattered.

More slowly than before, she sloshed her way back to the cabin, attempting to keep the water inside the pail. At least the sun now peeked from beyond gray-tinged clouds to warm her. By the time she reached the cabin door, her hands stung dreadfully and a good third of the liquid had joined the water on the ground.

"It's enough," she said, resolute to make it so.

Gathering soap and a scrub brush, she winced, hissing through her teeth at the first contact of the harsh soap on her poor hands. A pity someone couldn't invent a soap that felt as good to the hands as the fragrant oil did—and one that smelled as nice!

She started scrubbing near the hearth. The light slaps of bare feet on the planks had her look over her shoulder and see Baby Lynn and Clarissa. Sam came downstairs from the loft, and Alison wondered if she'd heard her sisters.

"Please see to getting the girls something to eat while I finish this."

Sam looked at her a little strangely but set to work. The girls sat down at the table, waiting for their food. Perhaps she should have them dress first, instead of eating breakfast in their bed gowns, but she supposed *one* morning of slothfulness couldn't hurt. Then a thought occurred to her.

"Your bed linens, Sam. I assume they're very damp?"

"It rained on them before we got the pail to catch it."

"We should hang them to dry. Perhaps we could hang them outside?"

"When the ground's not muddy, we use the bushes by the stream sometimes. Or the branches of the trees."

Alison had no desire to attempt another messy trek to the stream. She could just imagine dropping the blankets on the sodden ground or having them trail behind her.

"Have you a ladder?"

"A ladder?" Sam looked confused. "In the barn, maybe."

"Why do you need a ladder, Auntie Alison?" Clarissa asked.

"The roof isn't so high it can't be reached nor the ground so low the bed linens would touch."

"You're going to hang the blankets from the roof?" Sam looked at her as if she'd been tippling the cooking sherry, if there were any cooking sherry to be tippled.

"We'll weigh them down with something heavy so they won't blow off. That way the sun will dry the linens in no time."

"Don' want corn mush," Baby Lynn announced as Sam set the plate before her.

"Just eat it like a good girl," Sam said patiently.

"Want cider, like Aunt Ivy has!"

"We don't have apples to make any."

Alison recalled the jug of cider she'd found the first day and wondered why she'd never thought of retrieving it before now. She remembered Clarissa's eagerness for the sweet drink Ivy brought to the picnic and hoped also to dispel Baby Lynn's grouchy mood.

"Actually, there's some cider behind the sack of flour," Alison told them.

"Oh. I'd forgotten about that." Sam foraged in the cupboard. "All right then, Baby Lynn, it looks as if you shall have apple cider with your corn mush."

The tot clapped in excitement. Alison smiled, relieved that problem was so easily resolved, and went back to her chore. She had developed a habit of alternately singing and humming while she worked, often without consciously taking note of it until later, and suddenly realized she had indulged again when the girls started humming off-key with her.

Clarissa frowned. "Cider's warm and tastes funny."

"You just ate honey with corn mush," Sam explained. "That's probably why it tastes strange."

"It's not like Aunt Ivy's." Baby Lynn wrinkled her nose.

"Just drink it and stop complaining," Sam told her.

Baby Lynn frowned and did as ordered, slowly at first, but then drank down what she'd been given. Clarissa did the same then asked for more.

"Don't drink it so fast, 'Rissa; you'll make yourself sick," Sam admonished. "I thought you didn't like it that well."

"Umm," Clarissa answered, putting the cup to her mouth, "not so much."

"After you girls finish breakfast, you need to get dressed," Alison instructed. "It wouldn't do for your pa to catch you in your nightgowns."

"Um-hmm."

Needing a rest from crawling on her hands and knees, Alison put aside her menial task for the moment. "Let's get those bed linens dried."

The roof sat fairly flat, and Sam was quite a climber even without the aid of a ladder. In no time the bedclothes draped from the roof, facing the sun that blazed from the sky. The wind wasn't blowing as strong as on some days, and with the heavy weight of some rocks found in a pile near the barn, Alison felt sure the blankets would stay put.

She instructed Sam to remove her muddy shoes at the threshold and did the same, setting both pairs just inside the door. Clarissa and Baby Lynn still sat at the table eating corn mush. Fits of sporadic giggles overtook them as they whispered to one another. Alison considered ordering them to stop talking and finish eating, but after the fright they'd suffered from the horrendous storm, a little merriment might be a good dose of medicine to help cure any lingering bad memories.

She lost track of time, involved in finishing her task. The unmistakable whicker of a horse brought her attention upward. She scurried to the door before the missing Munroes could enter the cabin in order to instruct them to take off their shoes first.

She had opened the door no more than a crack when a barking mound of fur shoved its way inside and knocked the door against her.

"Brutus—no!" she cried in dismay as muddy paw prints filled the floor, with the dog catching sight of something to make him run in a chaotic frenzy.

"Brutus is funny!" Clarissa laughed and jumped up from the bench, losing her balance when she stepped on the hem of her nightdress and fell to the floor. Baby Lynn, deciding she wanted in on the game, fell onto Clarissa's back. The two began rolling around the damp floor of muddy paw prints, laughing and tickling each other. Brutus lost interest in whatever had intrigued him and ran to the girls as he took turns yipping and lapping honey from their messy faces.

Alison hurried forward in an attempt to shoo the dog away from the children and get the girls off the floor. The cur jumped up on his hind legs, pouncing on her sore one, and she fell to her backside.

"Mind telling me why the bedding is hanging from the roof...?" Rafe's curious question preceded him as he stepped inside and then stopped, dead still. Alison looked up to see the master of the house gaping at her as if she'd gone mad.

She did feel a little insane and couldn't help the bubble of nervous, embarrassed laughter that escaped her throat.

* * * * *

Rafe took in the sight of Alison sitting on the floor, her feet bare, long bits of her hair falling from her upswept twist as she fought off the eager dog that licked at her face. His gaze swung to his two youngest rolling on the floor in their nightdresses, acting for all the world as if they were liquored up. An overturned pail of water and a scrub brush lay on the floor by the table, and an erratic path of muddy paw prints covered the entire area.

"Is there a problem?" Caleb came in behind Rafe, and he too stopped dead at the sight. "Oh my." Rafe heard the amusement in his brother's voice and saw Alison's eyes widen in horror at the realization that he'd brought company.

"I just have that one other basket, if you'd be so good, Caleb— oh, dear…" Ivy, with a basket of food hanging over her arm, came to a swift halt beside her husband.

All three looked at the scene as Alison futilely tried to sweep up the ends of her hair and secure it with her hair pins while fighting off the dog and standing to her feet. The girls continued to roll around and giggle, until Baby Lynn spotted him. "Pa!" She broke away from her sister and lurched to her feet, running to him and swaying as if dizzy.

He scooped her up and she threw her arms around his neck, kissing his cheek. He smelled the odor right away.

"Have these girls been drinking?" he asked in shock.

His question brought Alison out of her embarrassed stupor. "Of course not! How could you ask such a thing?"

Caleb leaned over and took a whiff of Baby Lynn's breath. "Hard cider, unless I miss my guess."

"How would you know?" Rafe asked.

"I wasn't always a preacher, little brother."

Alison paled, her defensive manner crumbling. "Oh—my—stars…" Her gaze went to the jug on the table. "I, um, think I know. I found some apple cider—"

"Cider?" Rafe then remembered the jug Amy prepared right before she'd taken ill and he'd shoved to the back of the cupboard, unable to part with it, unable to bear looking at it.

Suddenly a horrendous screech sounding as if it came from the very pit of Hades itself made them all jump in shock. The cat came out of nowhere and raced in a golden blur past their legs and out the door. Barking like a crazed dog, Brutus ran close behind. Ivy gripped Caleb's shoulder before she could be knocked over.

"Kitty!" Clarissa leaped up, grabbing the table as she lost her balance and lumbered to the door.

"No, you don't." Rafe easily caught her with his other arm. He noticed his eldest coming downstairs, her eyes wide as saucers. "Sam, help 'Rissa and Baby Lynn get dressed. Then we have to figure out what to do to get them…clearheaded."

"I'll go start the men on the wall," Caleb said, amusement bubbling in his voice.

"The *men*?" Alison squeaked.

"Friends who came to help Rafe get the barn wall up and the roof fixed before nightfall," Caleb explained.

"Oh." Her reply sounded like a lost little girl. She looked the part, with her damp skirts, hair in disarray, and her bare toes peeking from beneath the hem of her soiled skirt. Rafe blinked in disbelief. Had this woman really been raised in high-society Boston and dressed the part since arriving in Kansas?

And why in the world wasn't anyone wearing shoes?

The dog's sudden frantic barks, followed by his friends' loud laughter, took his attention outdoors. Rafe followed Caleb, who by this time also laughed outright. Rafe didn't know whether to groan or join in the hilarity.

In its escape the cat had managed to claw its way up a blanket draped over the roof. The mutt held one end of the blanket in its teeth, viciously wrestling with it, bringing part of it down to trail in the water.

"Well, one thing's for sure," Caleb managed to say through his laughter, "you can't say things are ever dull with Alison around."

His brother couldn't be more right about that.

Chapter Sixteen

....

"Oh," Alison bemoaned to Ivy as both women cleaned up the spilled water with dry towels, "what have I done? Not only did I make a catastrophe out of attempting to bring the cabin to order, I managed to get my small nieces inebriated through drinking old cider!"

Ivy tried to hide a smile but failed. "Don't go blaming yourself. It wasn't your fault. Rafe should have thrown that jug out long ago."

"And I manage to find what he'd hidden for at least two years and offer it to his little girls," Alison said miserably, wringing out the sodden dish towel into the pail. "Oh, Ivy, how could everything have gone so wrong?"

"It's just a little cider gone bad. They'll be themselves again in no time. Drinking milk will help. You go and pull yourself together, and I'll fetch them each a cup once they come back downstairs."

"The cow didn't give any milk this morning."

"Good thing I brought some, then. I wasn't sure what provisions you'd lost. I also brought some peach preserves."

"Thank you; you're a godsend."

Alison looked down at her bare toes, embarrassed to realize that Rafe, that his *company*, had seen her in such an outlandish condition. She considered her former acquaintances back East who hadn't hesitated to besmirch her name regarding much less than what her present appearance would surely kindle, and she thanked God for a true friend like Ivy.

If only she could stay in Kansas and get to know her better.

With a sigh, she ignored her muddy boots by the door and moved into the bedroom. It didn't take much time to change into a fresh dress, stockings, and slippers or to refashion her hair into an acceptable style to receive guests. It took far longer to work up the courage to return to the main room and face them.

What must all of Rafe's friends think of Amy's crazy sister? Well, she had faced a good deal of censure and disapproval in her short lifetime. What did one more day's worth matter?

She moved into the main room to find Ivy busy sorting through one of two baskets of food she had brought. With her back to the table, she didn't see a curious Tucker pick up the jug of cider.

"I'll take that." Alison swept over to the table and removed it from his hand.

He looked confused. "It's just apple cider."

"Yes, I know exactly what it is."

She stopped up the jug and took it to the bedroom, setting it behind her trunk. Once everyone left, she would dispose of it. She returned to the main room at the same time Clarissa and Baby Lynn trudged downstairs.

"I don't feel so good," Clarissa moaned.

"Me too," Baby Lynn added.

"Drink this." Ivy set two cups of milk on the table. "It'll help."

"Thank your aunt Ivy," Alison gently prompted.

The girls gave halfhearted thanks, scrunching up their noses but drinking the milk.

Ivy returned to making sandwiches. "When Rafe told us what

happened I was horrified." She kept her voice low so the girls wouldn't overhear. "I don't think anyone was hit as bad as you were."

"If not for Rafe, I'd be dead," Alison said distantly, her mind on the previous night.

At the shock in Ivy's eyes, Alison realized that Rafe hadn't told her.

"He saved my life."

"Really…?" Ivy seemed pensive and glanced at Clarissa and Baby Lynn. "Would you two be little dears now that you've finished your milk and tell the men I have food waiting for them?"

"My tummy still feels funny," Clarissa said.

"The fresh air will do you good. Go on."

The girls' movements were slow, but at least they no longer tee-tered when they walked. Once they disappeared outside, Ivy looked at Alison. "Tell me, what's changed?"

"Changed?"

"Since the picnic. When you tried to convince me there are no feelings between the two of you."

"There *are* none."

"You sure about that?"

"Of course. He couldn't very well let the children's aunt die, could he? Besides, he would have saved anyone who needed saving."

"Hmm." Ivy didn't sound convinced.

Alison shook her head in exasperation. "Even if there were feelings on my side, and I'm not saying there are, what difference would it make? Amy has been and always will be the one love of his life. He would never settle for a replacement, and I don't wish to be a substitute." She hated the jealous edge her tone carried, especially when she spoke of her sister. "The reason we initiated the plan," she emphasized, "is because *neither* of us wants that."

"I agree."

"You do?" Alison looked up, surprised to hear her say the opposite of what she'd implied.

"Of course. Despite the startling popularity of mail-order brides and other marriages of convenience, it's my personal opinion that no man and woman should be joined in holy wedlock unless it's for the right reasons. Rafe must come to regard and respect you for your own merit, not as a fill-in for Amy."

Heat swam up to Alison's face now that Ivy had made their conversation more personal by using his name and no longer speaking of him in pronouns. "The chance of either event happening is slim to none. He doesn't want a wife, as a substitute or otherwise. I don't want a husband. Besides, after today's fiasco, I've hardly proven to be a woman of true worth."

"Why? Because after all that Rafe is suffering due to last night's tragedy, you wanted to present him with a clean, orderly home to help him feel better? Or because you wanted to give the girls a treat for breakfast and opened an innocent-looking jug of cider? Or maybe it's because you have control over all the animals and ordered that cat and dog fight so they could add to the chaos?"

Alison laughed over the last absurd statement. "Just exactly what are you trying to say?"

"Only that we don't always have control over the fixes we find ourselves in or over how things happen or progress, but how we respond to those trials is how others perceive our character. That's what makes the lasting impressions, Alison. Not the quandaries we find ourselves plunked in the middle of."

Alison smiled. "You have a gift for making a person feel better."

"Oh, good. Hopefully that will make up for my intrusive prying?" Smiling, Ivy arched her brow, and Alison chuckled.

"We all have our troublesome little quirks, I suppose."

Ivy laughed outright. "A nice way to sugarcoat the truth. I'm a busybody." She shrugged. "But only because I care."

"I know." If not for Ivy's sincere concern, Alison might take offense by her embarrassing tenacity. But in the short time she'd known her, she'd grown somewhat accustomed to Rafe's sister-in-law and what to expect. To her surprise, discussing such matters with another woman who had more than a passing interest and understanding of the situation and had been friends with Amy helped Alison to better sort things out in her mind.

Further conversation died as the door opened and both girls walked in. Clarissa's look toward Alison seemed anxious. Rafe strode in behind them. The sight of the sopping wet blanket he carried made Alison close her eyes and groan. She didn't know whether to laugh or cry. She had begun to hope that this was all some bizarre nightmare from which she would awaken.

"I'm not even going to ask again what this was doing on the roof," he said, "but Brutus got hold of it, so it needs to go in with the wash. Which—I thought was today?"

He still looked baffled, as if uncertain whether he was in the right house or not.

"Sam said the ground was too wet to light a fire for the kettle."

"Ah." His puzzled expression didn't falter.

"I don't mind lending a hand," Ivy offered. "We'll wash indoors, after the men eat their lunches. It might get a tad stuffy, but we can leave the door and window open. It'll help."

Alison had hoped she could evade the laundry for another week or at least until the ground dried, then felt awful for the selfish thought. The family needed clean clothing, and at least she didn't have to undertake the dreaded chore alone. She had the girls to help and now Ivy.

"Let's do that," she agreed.

Sam's groan came clear from the opposite side of the room.

* * * * *

Rafe worked alongside the other men, grateful for such friends. Tomorrow he would lend a hand at Jedadiah Greer's home, to help patch up what damage the storm had wrought there. He and Jedadiah were the only farmers to get hit so badly. While Rafe felt thankful to hear that the damage wasn't widespread, he worried over his predicament.

He had enough to see them through winter, thanks to the wheat harvest, but what he had planned to save had been put toward supplies at Mr. Eisenhower's store for fixing the barn and roof. At least he hadn't needed to put the items on credit. He didn't like owing any man, but with no more money, he wouldn't be able to buy seed come spring. He should have grown more wheat than corn, especially after last year's hot-blowing simoon destroyed that crop. Some farmers had given up on growing corn altogether.

And always, the children kept growing, needing clothes and shoes. Along with food.

If he kept dwelling on his dilemma, he might lose all hope. That morning, after seeing the destroyed crop he'd long toiled over, Rafe had come close to weeping…something he hadn't done since Amy's death.

At times like this, he asked himself the question Alison had posed her first week there. Why persist on farming this land, which could be a cruel temptress at best, promising to meet his every expectation? When he turned his back, in foolish confidence, it robbed him blind.

The storm had come upon them unexpected, out of nowhere, like a thief. But something in his blood—determination? adventure? insanity?—wouldn't let him surrender. The natives who once lived in these parts said no man could own the land. Rafe at last understood. The land sought to own men, pushing new inhabitants to strive harder, often beyond their limits, to succeed and flourish when all seemed impossible. That's why Rafe never returned East as some settlers had done, settlers who succumbed to defeat, weary of fighting wildfires and cyclones and other disasters of nature.

Amy had been his encourager, keeping him strong. But Amy wasn't here any longer.

"God, what do I do?" he whispered, somewhat shocked at his whispered prayer, if he could call it that. He worked a short distance from the others and, with the ringing blow of his hammer, knew no one had heard him but still felt strangely exposed. He had returned to the habit of attending church meetings, chiefly for the children's sake, but had yet to breach the distance he'd placed between himself and God since Amy's death.

He didn't understand why she'd had to contract a fever in her eighth month. Maggie, Clarissa, and Tucker had also taken the fever, but through Ivy's care, they pulled through. Only Amy and their stillborn babe had perished. He couldn't understand how God could allow that to happen, could allow his children to suffer without their mother's love.

He slammed the hammer down on the nail with more force and hits than it required.

He had berated the heavens, wept for his lost love, and gone silent inside and out, closing the door on the comfort friends and family tried to offer. Through these last several months, he'd found a place past the pain and bitterness. An empty, hollow place, but one that allowed him to associate with people again.

Last night's losses brought back the anger.

He slammed the hammer home again.

"Rafe?"

Unaware that Caleb had come up behind him, he turned to look. The usual amusement didn't dance in his brother's eyes, which were filled with concern.

"The men are going home. They need to get back to their families."

Rafe nodded and prepared to go thank his three friends who'd given of their time and labor.

"You all right?" Caleb didn't move aside.

"What do you think?" Rafe shot back bitterly.

"I think you've been hitting that same nail for the past few minutes and maybe you should talk about what's bothering you."

"I need to go talk to the others."

Caleb nodded and let Rafe pass. He thanked the men and assured Jedadiah he would be at his farm after dawn to return the favor. Once they left, before Rafe could retreat indoors, Caleb grabbed his arm.

"Ready for that talk?"

"Have I got a choice?"

"We always have choices."

"In that case, I'll have to put this off to another time."

"Rafe—"

"I need time alone to think."

He moved away before Caleb could prevent him leaving a second time and felt surprised when his brother didn't follow. To be fair, Caleb usually gave Rafe the time needed to simmer down and never forced advice on him, waiting until he asked for it. Problem was, Rafe eventually asked, even when he knew he wouldn't like the answer. Rafe wasn't sure if doing so was a masochistic tendency to thrash his logic or the conviction of his spirit to hear what, deep down, he already acknowledged as truth.

He did need God again.

He couldn't run forever.

His children did need a ma.

But marriage was out of the question.

Stalking to the cabin, Rafe glimpsed clothes hanging from the lines they had rigged inside but didn't feel like facing the women either. He ended up leaning with his back and shoulders against the outside wall. Closing his eyes, he tried to collect his chaotic feelings into a manageable order.

"You sure hum and sing a lot, Auntie Alison." Clarissa's voice drifted to him from the open window.

"Was I humming again?" Alison laughed. "I often don't realize I'm doing it. While I waited to board the orphan train, before your mother's parents found me, they told me I was sitting on a crate with my legs swinging and humming a happy tune. I was very little, so I don't remember. But they said it's what drew them to me. Perhaps that's why I do it still—after having been so blessed to become a member of their family and singled out for that reason."

"Ma sang, but she didn't sing as often as you," Sam replied.

"Singing is something that's a part of me. It also helps to pass the drudgery of tasks I don't like. When I was little and had to study my lessons, I would often start humming. It exasperated my tutor, but I didn't do it to be unruly. I didn't even realize I was humming, until he would threaten to slap my palms with a willow switch if I didn't maintain silence."

"What's a tutor?"

"A private schoolmaster."

"Private?" Maggie asked.

"Amy and I didn't go to school with other children. Our father employed professionals to come to our home and teach us the rudiments of learning. We also had a music teacher."

"Oh."

The sounds of scrubbing continued.

"Ma said her parents were wealthy," Sam said after a moment, "but she never talked about her childhood, except about you. I wonder why?"

"Perhaps because your mother was very happy to be here with you and didn't feel the need to dwell on days gone by."

"Are you happy to be here with us, Auntie Alison?"

The scrubbing stopped. "I'm happy to have finally met my nieces and nephews and to have gotten this chance to know you, Clarissa. I suppose you might say these have been some of the happiest months of my life, and I'll treasure them."

"You won't be staying?" Clarissa sounded worried.

"One day soon I must return to Boston. It's my home."

"It was Ma's home too, but she thtayed."

"That's true, Maggie. But ours is an entirely different situation."

"You mean 'cause of Pa," Sam said matter-of-factly.

"Because of your father?" Alison repeated, her tone coming a pitch higher, as if nervous.

"'Cause you're not married to each other by now."

Rafe heard Ivy's unmistakable laugh. She immediately stifled the sound.

"If Pa marries you, will you stay?" Clarissa practically begged.

Whatever Alison must have been holding splashed into the tub of water.

"Girls, you shouldn't set your hopes on such a far-fetched idea—on your pa ever marrying again. It isn't suitable to push someone into doing something they would rather not do, especially if it concerns your pa. And Sam, I owe you an apology, because I did exactly that to you, by telling your teacher you would give that speech for the harvest celebration. At the time, my reasons weren't completely selfless, I'm ashamed to admit. Though a great part of why I volunteered your participation is because I do want the best for you."

Rafe noticed how she managed to evade the awkward topic of marriage, apologize to Sam for her interference, and, in doing so, punch holes in the plan all at the same time. For some reason it didn't infuriate him, as it would have weeks ago. Strangely, he didn't feel anything at the knowledge that she'd done something else to win his children's admiration. Not annoyance, not relief... nothing.

"I just don't know what I have to say that anyone would care to hear," Sam admitted. "The idea of speaking in front of so many people makes my flesh crawl."

"Since my meddling got you in this dilemma, I'll help and advise you however I can."

"Thank you, Aunt Alison."

"Oh, I wish we didn't have to have a blasted wash day!" Maggie's irritation rang through in her voice. "It's tho darn hot in here! If only there was a breeze."

"Little ladies shouldn't use such inappropriate words," Alison gently scolded. "Next week we should be able to resume with wash day outdoors."

"Won't matter much," Maggie complained. "I'll thill hate it."

"Then what do you say to making the chore more pleasant?" Alison suggested.

"How could something so awful as washday be pleasant?" Sam agreed with Maggie.

"Remember what I just told you—how singing helps to dull the drudgery of a despised task?"

"There was a song Ma used to sing," Sam suggested, her voice a bit brighter. "Can't recall the words to all the verses, but it was somethin' about Polly Wolly doodling all day."

Alison laughed in delight. "I remember that one! For the life of me, I can't remember where I first heard it, but it was such fun to sing." And with those words, she began to hum a few lines of the melody and went into the first verse.

"Sing it with me if you know it," she encouraged after a few lines, and Sam and Maggie joined in, at first quietly hesitant, then boisterously with glee.

The glum atmosphere inside the cabin underwent a dramatic change as Alison went through the verses while they continued their chore, his girls' voices stumbling then drifting away when the lyrics became unfamiliar. The only accompaniment to Alison's warm, husky voice was the sound of her keeping time to the beat with her scrubbing on the washboard.

> *...Ohhh, aaaaaa—grasshopper sittin' on a railroad track*
> *Sing Polly wolly doodle all the day,*
> *A pickin' his teeth with a carpet tack*
> *Sing Polly wolly doodle all the day.*

The girls laughed in delight at the nonsensical words Alison made even sillier by the exaggerated way she drew out the syllables. Hearing her now, Rafe found it hard to believe she came from a refined home. He heard Baby Lynn, fully recovered from the cider experience, giggle and clap her hands in appreciation.

"More, Auntie Al–son, more!"

Fare thee well, fare thee well,
Fare thee well my fairy Fay,
I'm going to Lou'siana for to see my Susyanna
Sing Polly wolly doodle all the day.

Be-eee-hind the barn, down on my knees
Sing Polly wolly doodle all the day,
I thought I heard a chicken sneeze
Sing Polly wolly doodle all the day.

Clarissa laughed loudly. "A chicken sneeze!"

Oh, he sneezed so hard with the whooping cough
Sing Polly wolly doodle all the day,
He sneezed his head and his tail right off
Sing Polly wolly doodle all the day....

All of his girls, by this time, were laughing as their merriment increased and their loathing of the dreaded chore dwindled. Rafe realized he was smiling and straightened from the wall a mite disoriented. His earlier bitterness had, at some point, washed away as if it never happened.

What had not been apparent for weeks became astonishingly clear. Alison most assuredly was a godsend to his children, and he would be a terrible father to send their aunt away, to deprive them of a relation who cared about their welfare and loved them dearly... enough to work so hard at making their workday pleasant. If he must marry again to give his kids a ma, Alison would be the best prospect.

He frowned. No matter, he could not, *would not* be forced into the position of marrying anyone.

In aggravation, he stalked away from the cabin as Alison and the girls went into another light ditty, this time of Polly putting the kettle on to have some tea. Their bright voices followed him then faded away the farther he walked from the cabin.

If only all of his problems could disappear so easily.

Chapter Seventeen
....

"Teach us another song, Auntie Alison!"

"Later. You must study your lessons, and we still have to practice your etiquette."

Maggie groaned. "Do we hafta?"

Though Rafe had advised Alison to dispense with the plan for the present, she felt that every young girl benefited from learning proper behavior. Moreover, she knew Amy would approve of her persistence. Regardless of the fact that her sister had become a hardworking farmer's wife, from this family's memories of Amy she had never ceased to be a lady.

"Now then, no more grumbling," Alison chided. "Studies first, etiquette later." She set slates and chalk in front of Maggie and Clarissa. To Tucker she gave a McGuffey Reader she'd found while cleaning.

Alison moved behind Sam, noticing how she scowled at the paper that held her speech. With her other hand cupping her forehead, she clutched strands of hair in frustration. Alison took a seat next to her.

"What seems to be the problem?"

"Miss Proctor says I should speak about thankfulness and hope, since that's the town's motto—but I can't think of anything to be thankful for, not since we lost so much." She turned her head to look at Alison. "How come God wants to punish us all the time?"

Alison's heart ached for the child. "I don't think He wants to do that."

"Seems that way. Besides Jedadiah's farm—and he's a drunkard —ours was the only place hit so bad."

Although Alison had smelled the whiskey on the man when she'd briefly met him and Sam could be stating the truth, she felt she ought not let the incident go unchallenged. "You shouldn't speak of your elders with disrespect, Sam."

The girl shrugged. "Makes sense, though, that God would punish *him*, since he gets all liquored up and that's one of the seven deadly sins."

"Be that as it may, it's not our place to judge or gossip. I was raised to believe that God is almighty, but He's not just watching and waiting for us to go astray so as to bring down a gavel on our heads like a stern arbitrator."

Clarissa looked up. "What's an arbitrayer?"

Alison smiled. "An arbitrator is a judge—like your great uncle. He gave me that illustration when I was young and questioning the troubles of life, just as you're doing now."

"What troubles did you have, Aunt Alison? I thought our grandparents were wealthy."

"They were, Sam, but money can cause more problems than it solves. It isn't the answer to all of life's woes." At their confused expressions, she went on to explain. "The mother who gave birth to me and the father who sired me—I never knew them. I was found in a basket on the doorstep of an orphanage. My sister, whom I loved, moved on to live another life here with you, but it was difficult for me because she had become the center of my world. Then our parents died five years later in a horrible accident."

"Our grandparents," Clarissa added solemnly.

"Yes."

"And you went to live with our grandmother's sister?"

"Yes." She should put an end to the discussion and encourage them to continue their studies, but some opportunities in life allowed for more important lessons than reading, writing, and arithmetic could give—lessons to nurture their faith. "You may not believe this, but my childhood growing up in Boston was difficult. Many of the people my family associates with judge others for appearances alone. Since I was an orphan, my acquaintances and their parents treated me as inferior. At first I was angry and bitter, but my parents, and later my aunt and uncle, helped me. They were strong Christians and raised me to believe as they did. I learned to grow from hardships. Instead of laying the blame at others' doorsteps, I learned to accept their ignorance and made my own peace. Those trials I suffered helped to shape and build my character, making me stronger. And they can do the same for each of you, if you'll let them."

She had their attention now, as each child looked her way with mixed expressions of somber reflection and hopeful anticipation.

"Sometimes God allows troubles to help us grow and not be so feeble in our faith. I'm convinced that the outcome of this hardship will result as a step toward all you children becoming the fine, honorable men and women that God intended, and you'll be stronger for it. You're a family. You'll always have each other. You love and support one another, and that carries with it its own bond of strength. You children will never be alone."

They glanced at each other, a few faintly smiling.

"But, Aunt Alison," Sam said, "if things were so bad in Boston, why do you want to go back?"

"Yeah," Maggie agreed. "Them people were dumb to call you names."

"We love you," Clarissa added. "You're family too!"

"So why don't you want to stay?" Sam regarded her with confusion.

Their avowal of love made her heart melt, while their questions raised her anxiety.

"It's best. It's the life I know." She stood up from the bench and turned toward the stove, smoothing her skirts. She decided to put on some coffee to give her hands something to do. Rafe and Andy would be home from helping Jedadiah soon. "With all your father has gone through this summer, he certainly doesn't need another mouth to feed this winter."

"You don't eat much," Maggie argued. "You hardly eat at all."

"Well, in any case, I'm certain the boys don't want to spend their lives sleeping in the barn."

"Yeah," Tucker agreed.

"So can't they move back to their side of the loft?" Sam asked. "I don't see why they had to move out anyway."

"Don't forget about your father," Alison reminded, hoping that would end further arguments. "He wouldn't want to sleep in the barn forever. Especially with the cold weather approaching."

"He can move back too," Maggie insisted. "You two can get hitched and share his bed."

As hot as her face flamed at the innocent remark, Alison felt relieved that her back was to the table. Her skin must be the color of persimmons by now. She scooped coffee beans into the grinder. "I've told you not to interfere in your father's affairs; it isn't suitable."

Maggie sighed. "Yes, ma'am."

"So," Clarissa took up where Maggie left off, "why can't Auntie Alison sleep with us in the loft?"

"Aw, there's barely enough room for us, 'Rissa."

"Well, I don't care. I still think if we put our heads together we could figure out a way so she can stay," Maggie insisted. "Maybe Pa could build another room?"

"I doubt it," Tucker put in.

"I just remembered," Sam said. "Could we make a special dinner tomorrow?"

Curious, Alison looked at Sam. "Special how?"

"It'll be Pa's birthday, and I was hoping we could bake him a cake, like Ma used to. She wrote down everything, so we have a recipe."

"She wrote it down?"

"In her journal."

Alison's breath lodged in her throat. "Your mother kept a journal?" She'd never seen one, though she'd never gone through Rafe's trunk or armoire in the hope of spotting her sister's things. She felt peculiar enough occupying his bed while he slept in the barn.

Sam nodded. "I'll get it."

Before Alison could stop her, Sam ran into the bedroom. A long creak followed from what Alison assumed was the clothes cupboard. In less than a minute, Sam returned with a slim leather-bound book. She opened the flap and pulled out a piece of folded paper.

"Here it is."

Alison looked from Sam's helpful smile to the book.

"Would you mind?" She hesitated, realizing it wasn't Sam's place to give permission, but couldn't resist and held out her hand. "I would like to see the journal."

Sam handed it over without a word.

Alison stared at the small book then clutched it to her heart.

"So can we make a cake?"

"I think that would be splendid." Alison's voice came barely above a whisper.

"Can I draw Pa a picture?" Clarissa asked.

"I'm sure he would be pleased. I'll get a sheet of paper." A small pile sat up on the highest cupboard shelf, parcel paper that had been neatly straightened and stacked.

"And I can darn his spare set of socks," Sam exclaimed. "I'd best get started now, if I want to finish in time!" Evading her speech once again, she hurried back into the bedroom.

"Should I give him the scarf I'm making him for Christmas?" Maggie wanted to know. "It's not done yet."

"Christmas isn't far away," Tucker pointed out. "Wait and give it to him finished. What's the good of having a half-knitted scarf?"

"But what can I give him now?"

"He likes them berries by the stream," Tucker pointed out. "I could pick some and you put them in a pie."

"Think the storm might've damaged them too?" Maggie asked.

"Won't hurt to look. I'll probably be sent to go get more water soon anyhow…."

Alison could see that further studies would be difficult if not impossible. Perhaps this once she should relent and allow them the joy of planning their little surprises to please their father. She only hoped that their hopeful endeavors had the desired effect. Rafe had been so sullen of late, with good reason.

"Very well." Alison retrieved a piece of parcel paper from the shelf and laid it in front of Clarissa, also giving her Sam's abandoned pencil. "There isn't much time before your father returns. Tucker, you may go to the stream and hunt for salvageable berries. Take the extra bucket, and do remember to fill the water barrel. Be sure and get that snake out too."

"There's a snake?" Tucker's eyes grew round with hope.

"No, it was just a twig," Clarissa said. "I saw it too."

"Aw, too bad." Tucker shoved his hands into his pockets, and Alison wondered what else he might be hiding in them. To her immense relief, his missing pet had never been replaced with another of a similar species.

"What about me?" Maggie asked.

With such short notice of tomorrow's celebration and likely just a few hours until Rafe's return, Alison didn't have much time to think up ideas.

"How are you at stitching? Such as a letter on cloth?"

"A letter?" Maggie's brows drew together in confusion. "I can knit. Aunt Ivy taught me."

"Have you ever done embroidery?"

"Not sure what that is."

"Well, there's no time like the present to learn. I'll be back shortly. Don't go anywhere."

Taking the treasured journal with her into the bedroom, she pondered her idea for Maggie, hoping there would be enough time to accomplish the task. Gently she laid her sister's journal on the foot of the bed, giving it one longing look before riffling through her trunk. She found the desired items and returned to the main room, setting cloth, thread, and needle down in front of Maggie.

"This was my uncle's handkerchief. He gave it to me at the train depot when I couldn't locate mine. You could stitch your father's initials on that corner, there." She pointed to the bottom. "Many of the dignified gentlemen of Boston personalize their belongings."

Maggie fingered the handkerchief. "It's so soft and shiny. As pretty as one of your dresses."

"It's made of silk, some of the finest. It would make a lovely gift for your father."

"Won't your uncle mind?"

"No," Alison assured her with a smile. "He has plenty. I'm sure he would be delighted to know that his handkerchief went to such a worthy cause as your father's birthday."

"But—won't it be more from you than me?" Maggie looked troubled.

"If you embroider the first letters of his full name on that corner, it will make the gift personal and from you."

Maggie beamed, the space between her two front teeth now filled with the beginnings of new ones. "All right, if you're sure it'll be from me."

"It will."

"Will you show me how?"

"Of course." Alison studied the cloth, her practice at making hats an aid to her. "First we'll trace the letters on the cloth, to use as a guide. Clarissa, may I?" The child handed her the pencil and also watched as Alison lightly formed Rafe's initials. "Like so." She held up the cloth for Maggie's approval. The girl nodded, smiling. "Next, we thread the needle…." After three tries she met with success. "We'll start at the end of the letter, making tiny stitches, like this. I'll do the first ones to show you; then you may continue."

Maggie scrutinized Alison's every move, and when Alison handed her the cloth and needle, Maggie took over with confidence.

With the children busy at their tasks, she should start dinner. However, the knowledge that Amy's journal lay in the next room provided too great a temptation, and Alison drifted into the bedroom. After looking at the book for endless moments, she picked it up and opened to the first page.

The recipe fluttered away, to the floor, revealing the date of the first entry. Her heart gave a jolt at the familiar handwriting and the manner in which Amy always ended her words with curlicues. The date coincided with the time Amy and Rafe traveled to Kansas.

Should she be reading the heart's treasures of her deceased sister? Was it wrong?

Certainly, without Rafe's permission, it must be wrong since the pages likely contained personal moments he might not appreciate sharing. Yet to have found this unexpected connection to her dear sister after so long wishing for something like this proved too great a lure, and she read the first page. It contained details of their journey to "this blustery land of endless sky and towering grass" and Amy's first impressions of the land—similar to Alison's thoughts upon seeing it from the train window.

"Aunt Alithun?" Maggie called from the other room.

Alison snapped the book shut. "Yes?" Guilt for giving in to her desire put a high pitch to her voice.

"I need help."

Alison quickly snatched up the recipe and set down the journal. She resolved not to go near the book again until she'd had a chance to speak with Rafe...whenever that might be. They hadn't spoken alone since the night of the storm.

Tonight would change that.

* * * * *

The moment Rafe stepped through the door with Andy he sensed something afoot.

The girls ceased whispering to one another. Maggie hurriedly hid something in her lap, and Clarissa slapped her arms over the paper she'd been writing on. Alison blushed deep red—and he didn't think the heat from the stove caused the effect. Even Tucker seemed unnaturally jittery.

"Hi, Pa," he boomed in a voice louder than usual. "Did you get things fixed at Mr. Greer's?"

That Alison seemed a part of the new mystery set Rafe's mind at ease that his children weren't courting more trouble. No doubt his family's sudden fidgets and nervousness to see him had to do with something they'd planned for tomorrow.

Rafe took a seat on the bench next to Clarissa, ignoring her squeal as she grabbed up whatever she'd been working on and scurried upstairs.

All eyes watched her departure. Rafe looked over at Alison.

"Anything happen here while I was gone?" he asked innocently.

"What would make you ask that, Pa?" Tucker sounded anxious.

"Excuthe me, please." Maggie clutched something in her skirts as she awkwardly moved off the bench. She raced upstairs after her sister.

"Oh, I don't know, son," he drawled. "Just a hunch."

Alison must have caught on that he'd figured out the reason for their secrecy. The uncertainty left her eyes and she regarded him with gentle warning. "Be nice," she mouthed.

He swiped at his jaw, feeling a smile begin. "I should go take care of some things in the barn while there's still daylight. I want to take another look at that wall. I felt quite a draft last night, so caulking up any cracks should be the next order of business. Andy, Tucker, I need you to give me a hand. We'll need plenty of water to make a good mud paste, so fill both pails."

Tucker looked at Alison in alarm.

"You and Andy go on ahead, Mr. Munroe. I'll send Tucker for the water. He'll join you soon."

"All right." At her calm attitude of command, he felt more curious than upset. He looked back and forth among his brood and Alison, deciding by the cautionary look in her eyes it would be wise not
to question.

He really didn't want to ruin any of their surprises.

The rest of the evening, until dinnertime, he spent in the barn.
With the boys' help, he patched all the walls. Once he returned to
the cabin, he noticed a change had come over his daughters. They
seemed more at ease, apparently finished with whatever they'd been
hiding. Alison, however, was distant, as if her mind were in the next
county. Three times he had to repeat her name and gain her attention for a question asked. He wondered what would cause her to
become so absentminded that she toyed with her food, tonight's fare
meeting all standards for good eating. Nothing burned on the bottom, nothing hard or crusty. But for all the enthusiasm she gave her
meal, it might as well have been a mud pie.

After dinner, Rafe retreated outside, as was his habit, though
he didn't look toward where his crop once stood, as he used to. He
didn't need the image of the battered cornstalks to put him back in
a foul temper.

The door opened and Alison appeared.

"I hope you don't mind company?" She hesitated. "I have something I need to discuss with you."

He nodded. With the sun just beginning to set and the sky melting
into vibrant reds and violets, it brought out a blaze of color in her hair
and a rosy glow to her face. In the last light of day, she seemed uneasy.

"I just learned of this." She took the few steps separating them,
her arm outstretched, a book in her hand. "I thought you should
know. Also, I wanted to seek your permission, to see if there was any
chance..." She took a deep breath. "I'd like to read it if I may."

He recognized Amy's journal as he took it from Alison.

"It didn't feel proper to do so without first securing your permission," she explained when he remained silent. "Did you know of this?" she asked more softly.

"I knew she kept one." His answer came quietly. On a few occasions he had tried to read it, but the pain had been too fresh and he'd put it back in the cupboard. "I don't know what's inside it."

"I thought that might be the case. Which is why I thought you should have it, to do what you feel is best. Sam knows about it. She brought it to me. I wasn't sure if you wanted the girls looking through their mother's journal. I don't know if Sam's read it; she didn't say. But apparently that's where Amy kept a recipe Sam wanted me to have."

Rafe nodded. "Is there anything else?"

He saw the disappointment settle in her eyes. But he couldn't let her read Amy's journal, not when he didn't know what it contained.

"I've done my best to tutor the children, but I have no teaching license and can only instruct them based on how I remember being taught. While I'm visiting, I think it would be beneficial for *all* of the children to attend school."

He considered her suggestion. "You would be all right here by yourself every day, with Baby Lynn and Clarissa underfoot?"

"It's only for several hours, and yes, I think I can handle the situation with the little ones." Her face darkened a shade. "I dispensed with the remainder of the cider and washed out the jug last night, so we won't have that problem again. I can't tell you how horribly ashamed and terribly sorry I am for what occurred—"

He lifted a hand to stop her apology. "If anyone was to blame, it's me. I should have gotten rid of it long ago." He shook his head, letting out a tired sigh. "None of it was your fault."

She gave a faint nod, the barest amount of relief filling her eyes. Still, she seemed upset.

"Is there something else?"

"It's just that—it's rather silly of me to feel this way, I suppose, since the idea all along has been for me to make errors to ensure your plan is a success. Yet it's unsettling to me when I make mistakes without trying."

"You're learning a new way of life in complete opposition to how you've been raised. It's understandable. When Amy first tried her hand at pioneering, she made mistakes too." He chuckled at a memory. "Once, shortly after we settled here, she put almost as much yeast in the bread as she did flour. She didn't know it only took a pinch. The dough was bursting out of the pan and liked to have taken over the table, maybe the entire cabin—it was a sight!"

Alison laughed, her eyes sparkling in relief. "Really?"

He nodded. "Another time, she mistook the salt for the sugar—not sure how, since they come in different-sized canvas—or maybe she wasn't paying attention. She never did say, and she tended to do a bit of daydreaming, you might remember. I expect that's where Sam gets it."

Alison grinned. "Do tell?"

"Well, let's just say the persimmon pie was awfully bitter that night."

Again Alison laughed in delight. "Thank you for telling me about Amy's little mishaps. It helps to know that my perfect sister also had to learn by trial and error. I don't feel like such a dunce."

He looked at her strangely. "Everyone who comes to the Midwest has to learn. I did. Amy did. Even if someone has experience, it's a whole new set of rules. It takes time to catch on, but you're doing all right."

She beamed at his praise. He didn't know why he added the last—it came out before he thought—but she deserved to know. He'd seen how hard she'd been trying, even when she didn't try, thanks to the plan.

"I'm pleased you think so. Well…" She turned to go. "I should help Sam with the dishes. Oh! Before I forget, there is one last matter. You know that I worked in a millinery shop before coming to Kansas?"

"Amy might have mentioned that you liked to make hats."

"Yes, I do. And I've noticed the girls' bonnets are in a deplorable state. They should have something to cover their ears, once the cold weather sets in especially. I'm not suggesting you buy the material," she hurried to say, as if afraid he might refuse. "Actually, I have a dress made of material that would suit well for bonnets."

He stared at her in astonishment that she would suggest the idea. "You want to cut up one of your fancy gowns to make hats for my girls?" He shook his head, flustered. "I can't let you do that. It wouldn't be right." He hesitated then made a swift decision. "Take one of Amy's."

"Of course I could, but I truly don't mind using my own. I rarely wear the dress I have in mind. But since you did offer one of Amy's dresses, there is another matter…."

He raised his brows when she didn't continue. "What?"

"I thought perhaps I might take one up to fit Sam? For her oral presentation. I think it would help lift her spirits if she had a new dress when she gave her speech for the harvest celebration—a dress of her mother's. Since I did volunteer her for this project, I would like to make the day as easy for her as possible."

"I still don't like the idea of you cutting up one of your dresses."

"Please, it's no problem. I have so many, and it would be my gift to the girls. Something they can remember their aunt by, once I've returned to Boston."

"When you put it like that, I can hardly refuse."

She smiled. "And with regard to the matter of a dress for Sam?"

"You're welcome to look through the clothes cupboard and find whatever you need." The idea of anyone touching Amy's belongings didn't fester as it once had.

"Thank you, Mr. Munroe. I'm sure Sam will be pleased. I would ask for one more favor: please don't tell the girls. I wish this to be a surprise."

In that regard, Alison and Amy were alike.

"I won't say a word."

She nodded her thanks and went back indoors, leaving Rafe to his thoughts and the sounds of the approaching night. Strange how he'd never noticed before, but the keening of the wind seemed almost lonely.

Chapter Eighteen

Alison spread her green brocade over the table. The skirts were so full they hung over both sides and would yield plenty of material for four bonnets. With the colored stick of wax she'd brought with her from her millinery days, she marked the inside of the dress, using a worn bonnet as a guide. With the celebration four weeks into the future, she should have enough time to devote a few hours to her sewing each night.

It both amused and encouraged her to learn of Amy's little disasters, and she'd been pleasantly surprised Rafe shared such moments. Since her arrival, he'd never brought up Amy to speak of her in any great depth. Tonight had been his first time to do so and without the somber expression the mention of her name usually produced.

She hoped his heart was at last healing; she prayed for his welfare and the children's each night. If she could make a difference in their lives in her time remaining here, then her journey to Kansas would have been worth any sacrifice. Though in all honesty, she couldn't figure out where she stood with Rafe Munroe.

At times he could be a congenial host, amusing, entertaining, and she could understand what Amy had seen in the man to surrender all she knew to travel to the prairie wilds with him. At other times, Alison seriously considered trying to saddle a horse herself and ride into town to find passage on the next train heading east.

Yet for all her determination to leave on those occasions, her heart betrayed her, and she knew she would never go as long as he needed her, in whatever capacity. She felt guilty to have feelings for Amy's husband; she could no longer deny that truth. Those silent words she could never utter, had dreaded even to consider, now taunted her every day, and she worried what Amy would think if she knew that Alison had fallen in love with Rafe.

Would she be troubled? Angry? Resigned?

Love…it seemed inconceivable, but of all the men, east or west, it had to be Rafe who captured her heart. She had never felt this way about anyone. Even if Amy could somehow know what occurred in the lives of the loved ones she'd left behind, it failed to matter. Rafe wanted nothing to do with Alison.

She certainly did have a propensity for choosing unwisely when it came to men! First Stephen, who rejected her because of her lineage; now Rafe, who refused her because he still loved her dead sister.

Could life possibly become more complicated?

She stewed on her dilemma as she cut the last piece of cloth.

Perhaps in Boston she could find something useful to keep her hands occupied and her heart fulfilled. Yet how could she return to her previous lifestyle? She felt forever changed, her hands the physical proof of labors learned. Despite the toll it had cost her, the price was trivial when compared to the joy of having her life and work truly matter.

Her mother had told her that when God closed a door on what could hurt His children, He opened a window to let in something much better than ever could be expected. Surely, though, it hadn't been God who closed the door on Alison's desire to remain in Kansas? And what if He had? She didn't want any other windows opened. Her present location suited her just fine!

Foolish thoughts—all of them. It didn't seem to matter what she wanted. Not to Rafe, in any case. Though she continued to nurture a flicker of hope.

She resided in a town called Hope, for mercy's sake. Ivy had told her, after discussing the loss of Rafe's crop, "There'll always be hope in Kansas." But did any hope really exist for Rafe to open his eyes and see what was right under his nose?

Once she put away her things she decided to sort through Amy's dresses. The armoire appeared to be well made, and she wondered if she witnessed the result of Rafe's handiwork.

Amy had a goodly amount of dresses but less than she owned in Boston. Alison carefully scrutinized their condition. A gray woolen frock seemed good for nothing more than rags, the moths having feasted on it. The stitching had loosened on a blue cotton, also minus a button at the cuff and collar. Pushing aside the forgotten dress, she saw a pretty green frock sprigged with white flowers, which would suit Sam's red hair and ever-changing eyes well. Her niece had the most remarkable eyes, which turned from blue to green depending on her surroundings. The dress was in good condition; a simple tie at the back would help fit it to Sam's girlish form.

Decision made, she closed the cupboard, remembering it had held Amy's journal. She couldn't help but be disappointed that Rafe hadn't given her permission to access the connection that would make her feel close to her sister again, but she understood his reluctance.

As she readied for bed, she noticed a guest curled up at the foot of the mattress.

She brushed out her hair. "Don't think this is to become a regular routine." She gave a stern look in the cat's direction and raised her eyebrow. "Tonight, however, I'll allow it."

The mouser gave a huge yawn, as if her opinion bored him.

With the course her thoughts had taken and the desire not to visit there again, even the companionship of a lazy-lidded ball of fur was preferable to being alone.

* * * * *

Rafe woke from a fitful sleep, his mood grim. Dreams of Alison and Amy had tormented him all night. In his sleep, he'd seen his wife in the distance, standing with her back to him. Shocked, he would run up to her, only to turn her around and come face-to-face with Alison.

He picked up the journal he'd stashed in the hay near his temporary bed. He'd actually been able to read the first several pages, farther than he'd ever gotten, the experience not as painful but bittersweet regardless. He assumed Amy's book brought on the strange dreams he didn't want to experience again. Although, now that he'd made that difficult first step, he planned to read more.

Alone in the barn, he tended to his morning grooming and headed for the cabin.

Inside, Clarissa gave a surprised little squeal and hid something. Baby Lynn beamed from her place at the table. "Mornin', Pa!" she cried. "It's a special day!"

"Shh," Maggie warned.

"Special?" Rafe asked in mock ignorance, determined to push aside his despair so the children wouldn't see. He had actually forgotten what day it was until Baby Lynn mentioned it.

"Don't ask so many questions, Pa," Clarissa instructed with a giggle.

"You're not back-talking me, are you?" he teased with a growl. He tousled her hair and she giggled again. "Something sure smells good."

"Auntie Al–son is making scrammled eggs," Baby Lynn explained.

"Oh?"

Alison laughed. "Don't look so worried. I've been practicing."

"Really?"

"Yes, the girls and I held a little tea party."

"A tea party?" He sank to the bench, his back to the table. "Well, that's news to me."

"I've been giving the children lessons in etiquette. That was part of a lesson."

"At least I didn't have to take part," Tucker said in relief from where he sat across from Andy and filled his mouth with bread and peach preserves. "Tea parties are for girls."

Sam slapped his hand. "Wait till we all start eating," she admonished her brother.

"You used eggs for your tea party?" The thought made Rafe grin when he recalled what Amy had said about her childhood tea parties and the crumpets and pastries their cook made.

"Yes, among other things. I needed to teach them the proper way to handle a fork."

"And the tea?" He knew they had none left.

"Coffee served its purpose as a substitute."

He opened his eyes wider. "You gave the children coffee?"

She laughed. "No. My mother had strong opinions on the subject. I used it to fill the cups so they could learn to pour and not spill. They didn't drink any." She hesitated. "Well, maybe a sip, but no more."

Rafe didn't bother to ask what use his girls would have for learning about fancy tea parties in the wilds of Kansas. He figured it must be part of Alison's plan and knew Amy would approve of their daughters learning anything that would help them to behave like little ladies. They'd been running around like hoydens far too long.

At the thought, he looked at the two girls nearest him. "Where are your shoes?"

"Shoes?" They repeated the word as if it were unfamiliar to them.

"Yes, shoes." He nodded at their bare feet.

Clarissa and Maggie exchanged glances.

"Mine has a hole at the bottom that's too big to stuff with a rag. It flaps like this." Maggie put her palms together and flapped her fingers, clapping them together.

"Mine hurt my feet," Clarissa complained. "My toes get all scrunched up like this." She put her hand to her feet and scrunched her toes together. "It's hard to dance in them."

Rafe winced at the news. "Sam, what about you?"

"I don't like to wear shoes."

"You'll be thankful for them come winter."

"Well..."—she seemed reluctant to say the rest—"they feel funny on my feet too."

He sighed. "Will they fit Maggie?"

"Maybe. But there's something sharp inside, like a thorn."

He made a swift decision. "Miss Stripling can check the clothes cupboard after breakfast. Your ma had some new shoes that might fit one of you."

All of his children stopped what they were doing and stared.

"Did I say something peculiar?"

Wide-eyed, Maggie shook her head. "Really, Pa?" Sam asked.

"I said it, didn't I?" Feeling uneasy with the manner in which they were treating his suggestion, he shifted around to face the table. "Will breakfast be ready soon? I'm starved."

Alison used a dish towel to grab the handle of the pan. "It's ready right now."

"What are you doing today, Pa?" Sam wanted to know.

"Not much. Thought I'd just relax around the cabin for a change. How's the roof working out? I noticed we got a light rainfall last night. That repair holding up?"

"We stayed dry." Maggie looked at Sam then back at him. "Maybe as you don't got nothing to do you should go visit Uncle Caleb till dinnertime."

"Dinnertime?" He lifted his brows in surprise. "I imagine he's getting his sermon ready."

"Oh, I'm sure he'll want to see you," Sam hurried to say. "He asked you to come by when he was here last, remember?"

"I think someone in this cabin has awfully big ears," he drawled. "Sharp as a wolf's. I sincerely doubt that your uncle Caleb..." He caught Alison's rapid-fire glance and brisk shake of her head, as if in warning. "...Will remember he said that." He finished the sentence with something other than he had planned to say. "Maybe I'll go into town anyhow and drop by the postal office to see if anything's there."

"You expectin' a letter, Pa?" Andy asked.

"No, but Miss Stripling might have gotten a post from Boston. I also need to check up on the news in town and see what's going on."

"Think they might have canceled the harvest celebration?"

At the hopefulness in his daughter's voice, Rafe shook his head. "'Fraid not, Sam. This town knows how to rally, and not everyone was struck as hard as we were."

"How come you call Aunt Alison 'Miss Stripling' all the time?" Clarissa asked suddenly. "And she calls you 'Mr. Munroe'?"

The unexpected question staggered Rafe. Alison also looked

confused as she finished setting food on the table. She glanced at him.

"It's a sign of respect," Rafe explained.

"You don't call Aunt Ivy 'Mrs. Munroe.'"

"That's different."

"I don't see how. She's our aunt, just as much as Aunt Alison."

"It's a formality," Alison attempted when Rafe couldn't think of how to answer. "Polite society requires gentlemen and ladies to address one another by titles."

Clarissa thought on that as long as it took for Rafe to take a sip of coffee to fortify himself. "So don't you respect Aunt Ivy, Pa?"

"'Course I do!" Rafe set down his cup with more force than necessary.

"She's a lady."

"She's also my brother's wife."

"Aunt Alison is Ma's sister. So it seems there'd be no need for those kind of formalities." Sam flushed red when Rafe swung his attention her way. "Just saying…"

Rafe crossed his forearms, settling them on the table, and eyed his brood. "What brought this on?"

"It's just…" Maggie looked to Sam for help, and he wondered if this was a new plan they'd concocted. Had they changed their minds again about wanting Alison for a mother?

"It sounds funny hearing you call her 'Miss Stripling' all the time," Sam took up where Maggie left off. "And Aunt Alison always calling you 'Mr. Munroe.'"

"'Cause Aunt Alison is your family too, right, Pa?" Maggie added.

He knew once his girls got bees in their bonnets, as Amy used to say, they would never surrender their cause.

"Yes, I suppose you're right about that. She is family." His low admission brought Alison's surprised gaze swinging to his steady one. "And I suppose, if your aunt has no objection, we can drop the formalities, since this isn't a Boston parlor."

As one, his children turned to look at Alison. Her skin went a shade rosier.

"I have no objection," she all but whispered, taking a seat and dropping her attention to her plate.

"Good. That's settled, then." Rafe clapped his palms to the table, leaning forward. "*Now* can we eat? I'm starved."

His enthusiasm brought the desired response as the children laughed and reached for the platters.

"Ah-ah-ah," Alison quietly reprimanded. "First we offer thanks to God for His bounty. Mr. Mun—" At Sam's slight cough in reminder, Alison tried again. "Er, that is, um…Rafe, would you do the honor?"

His name on her tongue came out a bit raspy, but he decided he liked the casual use better than the proper title. Surprised she should ask him to say grace, he nodded and gave thanks. It had been a long time since he'd said the blessing, not since before Amy died. But he found he didn't mind, even if all the words about "bounty" and "mercy" didn't quite ring true in his heart.

* * * * *

After breakfast, Rafe rose from the table and placed his hat on his head. "I'll be heading to town now."

"Bye, Pa!" Baby Lynn hopped off the bench and gave him a hug.

He put his hand to the back of her curls. "I'll return before evening. G'bye, children." He hesitated then glanced at Alison, nodding once in acknowledgment. "Alison."

She felt a rush of warmth flood her face at his casual mention of her name, her first time to hear him say it, but managed a faint nod in return.

Once he left, Clarissa looked at her. "You have such a peculiar look on your face, Auntie Alison."

She smiled to cover her embarrassment. "I'm thinking of all we need to accomplish before your father's return. But first come lessons."

The children's groans of disappointment were her response.

"Now then, none of that. Only an hour's worth today," she relented. "Then we'll bake the cake and you can finish working on your presents."

"You think Pa will be surprised?" Clarissa's excitement shone in her eyes.

"Ma used to do special things for him too," Maggie added.

"I think he'll be quite pleased. Our parents always made a celebration out of Amy's birthday and mine. When we were little, they took us for a ride around the park in the carriage. Later, they gave us parties with ices and cake, and when we grew older, they held tea parties for us. Sometimes we would attend the opera."

Clarissa looked at her curiously. "What's a park?"

Alison regarded her with surprise, realizing that Amy's children only knew this plot of land on which they'd been raised. She wondered why Amy never spoke of her childhood home but realized she might have shared something of her past without the younger girls remembering. The thought saddened her, and she resolved to tell them all they wanted to know of their mother's childhood and the memories she had with her sister.

As they washed and dried dishes and the boys tended to their outside chores, she told the girls about the park she and Amy had frequented and the thick trees that reached to the very heavens, as well as the evergreens that never lost their leaves but remained green all winter long. Their eyes grew round at the idea that such a tree existed, and she wondered if they'd never seen a Christmas tree.

"I remember Ma once talking about Christmas in Boston," Sam answered. "She said the tree had prickly fronds and you decorated them with candles and strings of red berries and fancy glass balls."

"Yes, they were prickly but the branches were so lush, they looked something like feathers. Your mother and I used to string berries and Father would loop them around the tree." Alison smiled in fond remembrance of happier times.

"Will you be here for Chrith-mas?" Maggie asked suddenly in worry.

"Oh, you must stay for Christmas!" Clarissa pleaded.

"Why, I…" Alison tried to frame a response, taken aback by the question. "I don't rightly know. I should return to Boston before the snows start."

"Please stay!" Baby Lynn grabbed her around her skirts. "Don't leave us."

Alison's heart felt close to brimming over with love for the children. Surely, before winter set in, Rafe would want her gone. At the woebegone faces and cheerless eyes that regarded her, Alison forced a smile.

"We needn't think of such things now. We have a special day to prepare for."

The gentle reminder prodded the girls in continuing with their lessons. The boys soon returned and took their places at the table amid the usual grumbling, which Alison responded to with quiet chastisements about not complaining because it wouldn't change what needed to be done.

Silently she urged herself to do likewise and not show resistance or distress at the idea of leaving Kansas. If she attempted to display optimism she didn't feel about returning to Boston and promised to write often, it might not be so hard on her nieces and nephews once she left.

She wondered how she would ever be able to say good-bye.

With the children now silent, Alison planned the special meal with Rafe's favorites—deciding with Sam's help to try to roast a leg of pork. She cut carrots, turnips, and wild onions, thankful for Ivy who'd brought them.

Once Sam collected the meat from the larder and Alison popped it and the vegetables in the oven, she told the children they could cease with their schooling and resume the preparation of their gifts. Books enthusiastically closed while slates were pushed aside in relief.

She gathered the latter, glancing over them to assess any progress, though she felt sadly lacking as their teacher. If only Rafe would relent and allow the older children to attend school.

Tonight, she resolved to discuss the matter one last time.

For the present, she had a cake to prepare.

Chapter Nineteen

....

Rafe rode home under a cloud of dejection. He had looked for work, but no openings were available, unless he wanted to travel with a group of men to work the mines in another town. He'd left his children once through his neglect, after Amy's death, no better than orphans for all the attention he paid them. He wouldn't do that to them again. There had to be other means of securing work.

But today, especially, he wouldn't dampen the merry spirit of his household with the problems he faced. He forced a smile as he opened the door to the cabin.

Pleasant aromas of baking filled his senses. Alison sat by the hearth. His children were scattered throughout the room.

"Pa's home!" Baby Lynn squealed and ran to him.

He scooped her up in a bear hug, her eagerness to see him always lifting his spirits, even if it didn't last.

"Happy birthday!" Clarissa exclaimed with a wide smile. The sentiment was echoed by all his children.

"Come see what I made you!" Maggie grabbed his hand, pulling him toward the table.

"Give your father a chance to catch his breath! He's barely stepped through the door!" Alison laughed from where she sat in the rocker with the cat purring in her lap. Rafe lifted his eyebrows at sight of the sleek animal, wondering when the barn cat had taken run of the house. On second thought, with the chickens in a temporary wire coop until he could build another wooden one, he supposed it was a good idea.

He took a seat on one of the benches. Clarissa approached.

"Have you caught it yet, Pa?"

"Caught what?"

"Your breath?"

He chuckled at her enthusiasm and drew her close. She half stood, half sat in his lap, too excited to be still.

"Give your father time to relax," Alison gently chided a second time. "How did things go today?" she asked him. "Are Ivy and your brother well?"

"I didn't see Caleb. He was out visiting one of his flock, but Ivy is well. She sends her love."

Maggie cocked her head in curiosity. "What did you do today, Pa, if you didn't go fishing with Uncle Caleb?"

"Were you gonna go fishing without taking me?" Tucker asked sullenly. "You said I could go next time."

"Did I say anything about fishing?" Rafe asked in confusion. "If there's any fishing going on around here, it's from you children." He tweaked a strand of Clarissa's hair and she giggled. "As a matter of fact, I was looking for work." He directed the last part of his answer to Alison.

"How did that go?"

"It didn't."

Clarissa shifted to look him full in the face. "Why not just stay home with us till it's time to put seeds in the ground again?"

"You're sure full of questions today." He arched his brow in mock disapproval, earning him another giggle. "To get those seeds takes money. Money I need to earn." He again directed his attention to Alison. "The prospects weren't promising. No one needed an extra hand."

"Something will come up, I'm sure of it. God never leaves His children forsaken when they call out to Him for help. He'll show you what direction to take."

Her stalwart faith, much like Amy's, encouraged him. Both women held strongly to their parents' ideals. He'd never had a mother to teach him such matters, and his father had been too busy at his trade to try. It had been something of a miracle for his brother not only to seek the faith but also become a preacher of it. Through Caleb and Amy both, he had found God. Through Amy's death, he had lost Him.

"Now, Aunt Alithun?" Maggie begged, breaking his morose train of thought.

She grinned. "Your father looks as if he can breathe again. Now," she agreed.

Amid a flurry of squeals from the girls, Clarissa jumped off his lap and ran upstairs, he presumed in order to retrieve something, while the rest of his children eagerly flocked around him.

Alison laughed. "Don't suffocate your father before he gets a chance to see!" She rose from the rocker and moved toward the high shelf mounted near the stove, pulling the stack of plates from above. He heard the clatter of each dish as she set them at their places on the table.

"Look at mine first," Maggie begged, shoving a wrapped parcel into his hands.

"All righty, then." Rafe untied the string.

In her excitement, Maggie hopped from one foot to the other. Once Rafe had the wrapper halfway open, as if his daughter couldn't stand the suspense any longer, she blurted, "See the corner? Look at the corner. I wanted to do both letters, but there wasn't time and I just did one."

With no idea what she chattered about, he unfolded a white cloth. The material appeared to be of the finest silk, like Amy used to own when he courted her in Boston. At the sight of a man's handkerchief, he blinked in confusion. No way could his little girl afford to buy something of this price. He doubted any general store in town even owned such material.

In the corner, carefully stitched in black thread, he noticed the letter "R" and traced with lead, angled beneath it, a faint "M."

A sliver of worry pricked at Rafe when he remembered all the trouble his children had found themselves in before Alison's arrival. He hoped his little girl hadn't resorted to thievery.

"Don't you like it, Pa?" Her tone came anxious when he only stared at the cloth, his brows gathered in a frown. "I know I didn't get it finished on time, but I can do the other letter this week."

He sighed and looked at her. "It's a handsome present, Maggie, but where did you get something so fine?"

His quiet words brought a relieved smile to her face. "Aunt Alithun gave it to me. She helped me learn to stitch the letter, too. She said all the fine gentlemen of Bothton have these, and you're just as fine, Pa."

Relief, curiosity, and a strange irritation worked through Rafe as he pulled Maggie to him with one arm and gave her a squeeze. Alison had a man's handkerchief? Why? Did she have a beau waiting for her in Boston? Had he been the one to give it to her? Rafe recalled her recounting of the situation with her ex-fiancé, but that didn't mean another man might not have approached her with interest. She was a lovely woman with many fine qualities.

The idea that she might have an admirer never occurred to him, and he didn't wish to speculate why the thought didn't please.

Clarissa walked toward him, a piece of paper in her hand. "I drew this for you." She offered it to him with a shy, hopeful smile.

The sketch of a large family in front of a cabin, the picture shaded in areas to appear more real, looked as if it belonged to someone older. He felt constantly amazed by his little girl's talent, which seemed extraordinary for one her age, and if he had the money, he would buy her art and music lessons like Amy had taken in Boston. He studied the tall man with the hat and suspenders surrounded by six children. A woman stood in the background. "Is that your mother?" he asked, a catch in his throat.

"No, Ma's in the sun shining down—see? I made her face there." In the corner of the paper, she'd sketched a sun with the faint lines of a woman's face. "That's Auntie Alison standing with us. She belongs here too—don't you think, Pa? Since she's family."

Her words held a hopeful note. He heard the sudden clatter of a dish, as if Alison had set it down too rapidly, and he glanced her way.

"Dinner's ready." Her announcement came hoarse.

"It's a very nice picture, 'Rissa." He kissed the top of her head. "You draw well."

"You certainly do," Alison added, her voice a little more natural. "You have your grandmother's talent. My mother—your mother's mother—enjoyed sitting in her garden in the springtime and painting the landscape. In winter, she would sit inside, by the picture window, and paint the nearby wood covered in snow. I see her talent passed down to you."

Clarissa beamed at the praise.

"I darned your spare socks, Pa." Sam held them out. "I wanted to write you a poem, but I've had to spend so much time on that dumb speech." She wrinkled her nose, and Rafe struggled not to laugh. Sam loved everything literary, and Rafe was sure one day she would succeed in her latest aspiration of becoming a writer. But even reaching that goal took money. He wished he had a fortune, so he could dole out to his children everything their hearts desired.

"Thank you, Sam. These will definitely come in handy. Now, let's eat. I'm starved."

His brood eagerly flocked to their usual places around the table, and he shared in their enthusiasm. No underlying burnt odor lingered in the air, the aroma of roast pork and baked vegetables most satisfying. Once he spoke the blessing, he discovered the taste was even better. Alison had improved significantly since her first attempt, and he told her so.

She blushed. "I had help. With dessert as well."

"Sounds good. I can't wait." Rafe rubbed his hands together in anticipation, having smelled the sweet scent too.

She cleared the dishes away and brought out a cake sitting pretty in the middle of a plate. The sight brought a slight pang to his heart. The last time he'd been presented with such a cake, Amy had baked it for his birthday. Two years ago.

"I hope you like it," Alison said shyly.

"It's good," he approved after the first bite. Soon all that remained were crumbs.

"We have a pie, too, if you'd like a piece."

"A pie as well?" Rafe blinked. "Did Christmas come early this year?"

"No, Pa," Baby Lynn exclaimed as if he should know the difference. "It's your birfday cebel-ration!"

Everyone laughed and Andy swung his baby sister high from the ground in a whirl. She gave an excited squeal.

"Andy—careful!" Alison instructed. "She's just eaten."

With their bellies content, Rafe decided to save the pie until later. Alison and the girls washed dishes while Rafe and the boys set a fire in the hearth, to help offset the evening chill. With all quiet again, Rafe stared into the steady flames and pondered his dilemma.

"I was thinking," Alison said as she moved toward him, wiping her damp hands on a dish towel. "The clothes armoire in your bedroom—did you make that?"

He nodded.

"The craftsmanship is superb. Amy once mentioned that you were your father's assistant at his carpentry shop." At his second nod, she continued, "Maybe you can find work from someone who needs a carpenter."

"I tried. No one in town does."

"Did you talk to Miss Proctor, Pa?" Sam finished wiping off the table.

"Now, why should I do that? Are you in trouble at school?"

"Of course not." Sam responded as if the idea were absurd. "I heard her say something about how the schoolhouse could use more desks, and that's the truth of it, Pa! Some of us have to sit three to a desk. She put me next to Matthis Daugherty—he must take up half the bench, though both me and Lucy Travis sit there too—and he belches an awful lot."

Rafe managed to contain a laugh. "Well, now, if Maggie, Tucker, and Andy are soon to be joining you at the schoolhouse, that might be a worthy endeavor to look into."

Maggie's eyes grew huge. "Honest, Pa? You're gonna let us go to school with Sam?"

"I don' wanna go to no schoolhouse," Tucker complained. "Can't we just stay here and do our book-learning?"

"I agree with Tucker," Andy seconded. "I don't need no fancy learning at any school."

"If your ma were here, she'd disagree." Rafe gravely eyed his eldest son. "Every day your grammar gets worse."

"A farmer don' need to know 'rithmetic and writin' to plow fields and raise crops."

"Is that so?" Rafe settled his back against the pianoforte. "Well, I learned both. Not only does it help to understand how to add and subtract numbers when figuring accounts, but knowing how to read and write well can make a marked difference in your future, son."

"Aw, horsefeathers."

"Andy, none of that." Rafe grew stern. "You'll go to school and you'll like it, and that's the end of the matter."

"Aww…" Andy's grumble came more subdued this time.

"I'll talk it over with Miss Proctor tomorrow. Come to think of it, I could visit some of the widows and spinsters who don't have a man about and see if any are willing to take me on for hire."

"I think we could use some music," Alison announced suddenly. Did he imagine it, or did her tone have a bitter edge? "I'll get my flute."

Rafe thought fast, scarcely able to believe what he was about to do. "No need for that, not tonight. Sam, would you bring me my case? It's at the back of the clothes cupboard."

The children all stopped what they were doing and gaped at him. He recalled another occasion in the not-so-distant past when they'd reacted the same. But he figured the time had come to make an attempt at restoring another part of his life, and right now he didn't think he could stand another night of Alison's sour notes on that silver pipe of hers.

Chapter Twenty

....

Alison noticed the children's shock and wondered to what "case" Rafe referred. Sam hurried to his bedroom and soon returned with an instrument case. She handed it to her pa as if it were the crown jewels of London. He opened the worn leather and pulled out a violin. Alison stared with eyes just as wide.

"The one thing I brought with me from my days of living in Boston," he explained. The instrument looked well-made, of great expense, the mahogany glowing in the lamplight. "It's how I met Amy; did she tell you?"

Alison shook her head in wonder.

"I was visiting a friend, playing a song in the servants' area of the house where he worked. Amy was in the main house, visiting her friend. They heard me and came into the kitchen to listen. We were a strange mix that day—the upper crust of Boston and the lower crumbs of society." He chuckled. "But neither Amy nor her classmate cared for rules that prohibited who they could associate with, and the four of us formed a connection some disapproved of or found hard to believe." He grew silent, and Alison dwelled on his words in fascination, amazed to hear this story for the first time.

"When I could spare time from my father's cabinetmaking shop, I would meet up with them. I was his apprentice until he died. Debtors came out of the woodwork, and I lost the shop—all my father had left me. This"—he held up his violin—"was my grand-father's, when he lived in the old country. Before that, it belonged to his father, and before that his father—passed down in our family. I hid it so no one would take it away. I'd heard about the great adventures west, about wide-open spaces and free land to those who claimed it, and decided it was better than the polluted streets of the city. I asked Amy to come with me. We made it as far as Kansas, deciding to settle here."

Alison listened in bewildered amazement. He spoke so freely of the past, when he'd never been forthcoming with it before. The unexpected glimpse into his history fascinated her. Amy had never told her how she and Rafe met or that they'd first been good friends, and Alison wondered why, since they shared many secrets. Of course, it had taken awhile for Alison's bitterness toward Rafe to ebb. By that time, other events occurred about which Amy wrote, such as the birth of their first child, Andy, several months after arriving in Kansas and the reason Rafe decided to put their roots down in Hope. He hadn't wanted Amy to endure the long trek farther west, anxious for his fragile wife. When Alison learned of his decision, her heart at last began to soften toward the man, though it would be a long time until she experienced total forgiveness.

Further thought scattered as he tuned his instrument. She watched him pluck the strings and tune the keys. How had she never noticed what long, slim fingers he had? A musician's graceful fingers; a farmer's roughened hands. Rafe was an intriguing mix of gentleness and ruggedness, and she pondered all he'd told them.

Once more her mind's wandering drew to a swift close when the most expressive, haunting music issued from the instrument as he drew the bow across it. She blinked in awe, having expected a rousing tune and not a piece from a violin concerto by Mozart.

Unable to pull her attention away, she watched his fluid movements, his telling facial expressions as he closed his eyes and appeared to become one with the music.

After a few stanzas he stopped. "I'm afraid I'm out of practice."

Alison shook her head in astonishment that he would think such a thing. "You play as if you've been part of an orchestra your entire life."

He chuckled. "Not that good, surely, but thanks."

"No, don't laugh. I'm serious. Who taught you to play like that?" She voiced the question that had been whirling in her head since he first began.

"My grandfather. He was a music teacher in the old country, poor in material wealth but rich in his knowledge of music. He gave me lessons for as long as I can remember, and when he died, he bequeathed this to me. It's the one material good of any worth I've ever owned."

"It's a beautiful instrument."

"A Stradivarius. Now I'll show you how it can play."

He moved into a fluid piece, the notes rich and lingering like the breath of a keening wind. Clarissa began to dance, floating like a cloud on her bare feet. Recognizing a waltz, Alison decided to take the opportunity to combine pleasure with education.

She approached Clarissa, whose steps slowed as she looked at Alison in curiosity. Holding out her hands for the child's, she nodded in encouragement. Clarissa smiled and laid her hands in Alison's.

"Follow what I do and I'll show you how dancing is done in the ballrooms of Boston."

The child's face glowed with excitement, and she nodded eagerly.

Alison sensed the eyes of everyone in the room on them as she patiently took her niece through a simple waltz. Clarissa proved to be a fast learner, and Alison nodded in approval then looked at the boys.

"Next?"

"Do we hafta?" Tucker complained.

"Proper gentlemen and ladies know the etiquette of the dance."

"Pa don't."

"Who says I don't?" Rafe stopped playing

"I ain't never seen you dance before."

"Just because you haven't seen something doesn't mean it didn't happen, Tucker."

The boy grumbled, and Andy stepped forward.

"I'll try."

"Aw, you're just wantin' to learn so you can impress Abigail Greer."

"Hush up," Andy growled beneath his breath, his face flushing red in embarrassment.

"Now, I'll have none of that," their father warned. And once again, he began to play—another waltz.

Alison took turns showing each child the proper steps. Andy did well and possessed Amy's grace. Tucker dragged his feet, his hand clamping around hers until she thought the blood might have stopped flowing. She did the same with the girls, taking the part of the male lead and showing them how to follow—especially Maggie, who forcefully danced her around the room.

"You boys dance with your sisters. When you approach a lady, you bow like I taught you and say, 'May I have the pleasure of this dance, Miss Munroe,' for example. You always give the lady the benefit of the decision. Never force her will."

The entire time, she felt Rafe's eyes on her and wondered what he thought of her impromptu lessons. Andy danced with Clarissa, the two of them almost floating. Tucker clomped around the floor with Maggie.

"Ow!" he cried. "You stepped on my foot."

"Maybe if you'd go faster I wouldn't have to."

Sam took Baby Lynn's hands, twirling her around and earning happy squeals from the youngest Munroe. Rafe's bow stilled on the strings as he brought the music to a close.

"What about you, Pa?" Tucker wanted to know. "You gonna dance too?"

"I can't very well dance and play at the same time."

"Sam can play!" Clarissa suggested.

"I can't play the violin."

"Not the violin, silly—the pianoforte!"

Sam looked at her then at her father, as if nervous. "I can't play."

"But I've seen you," Clarissa insisted. "Before Aunt Alison came—"

"I. Can't. Play." She enunciated each word between her teeth with a sharp look at her sister.

Clarissa's mouth drooped into a resigned frown.

Rafe said nothing, acting as if he didn't hear the conversation.

"Well, I can!"

"You play the pianoforte, Andy?" Alison asked in surprise.

"Nope—this!" From his pocket he pulled out a harmonica, astonishing Alison once again. In the month she'd lived in their home, she hadn't once seen him play and wondered why he would keep it hidden.

"Please, Pa!" Clarissa enthused, as eager as Tucker at the prospect of seeing Rafe take a turn. "It's your birthday. You should get to dance too!"

As much as Andy's revelation surprised her, it was nothing compared to the shock Alison received when Rafe rose from the bench and moved across the room to where she stood, instead of approaching Clarissa as Alison had expected.

His storm-colored eyes were intent as they met hers, affecting her ability to draw breath. He bowed slightly from the waist as perfectly as if he were in a Bostonian drawing room.

"Miss Stripling, may I have this next dance?"

The power of speech failed her. She brought her hand to just below her throat, hoping the action might somehow slow her rapidly beating pulse. Feeling the children gawk and expectedly await her reply, she nodded.

"I would be honored, Mr. Munroe."

"I'll be dogged!" Tucker exclaimed. Andy blew a few notes on his instrument while a few of the girls gasped in relief as if they'd been holding their breath.

Rafe held out his hand and she set her small one in his large palm, feeling the tingle that nipped under her skin. She wondered if he felt it too. Never breaking eye contact, he moved his other hand to press lightly against her waist. Her heart beat hard and fast, as if they'd danced the entire night, though they had yet to move to Andy's lyrical tune that resembled Rafe's earlier music. Alison preferred Rafe's violin, but somehow, it ceased to matter. The moment he began to move with her, she forgot all else.

Keeping time to his steps required no conscious effort, and Alison soon realized it must be a combination of both their parents' lithe grace that Clarissa and Andy had inherited. The children took places on the benches, making as much room as possible while Rafe twirled her around and around. Never mind that the whistling tune hardly resembled a waltz and at times faltered, Alison felt mesmerized and knew a dance had never affected her more...so enjoyable, and at the same time, disconcerting.

Andy brought the song to a close and Rafe spun her in another dizzying whirl. Whether by accident or on purpose, he brought her close on the last step, so that her skirts whisked around his legs. Alison inhaled a startled breath, but he didn't let her go. He seemed to have forgotten their rapt audience.

"Were you wantin' to dance another, Pa?" Andy's innocent words acted like a cold dousing of water on Rafe. He released her so suddenly that if her head weren't already spinning, it might have been jarred from his abrupt movement. Thankfully, she didn't fall.

To cover the awkward moment, Alison looked at the children. Sam's and Maggie's eyes were shining, while the others looked curious. "And that's how it's done where I come from. But enough merriment for one night. Time for bed."

The children groaned. Rafe held up his hand to stop their complaints before they could start. He still hadn't glanced in Alison's direction since they parted, though during the dance he'd never once looked away from her eyes.

"Mind your aunt. No more complaining." His voice came gruff.

A chorus of "Yes, Pa" filled the cabin and the six each went their own way to prepare for bed, leaving Rafe and Alison alone. She braced herself for a confrontation, his sullen silence the precursor to such a grim probability. But he merely inclined his head, still without looking at her, and mumbled good night.

She watched in disbelief as he left the cabin. For a long time she stared at the block of wood, comparing the door to the thickness of a certain man's head.

"Well, what did you expect?" she muttered to herself. "An explanation of his actions? A proclamation of his feelings? You'd sooner get the dog to speak and recite poetry."

Thinking of Brutus, she recalled the juicy roast bone, all that remained of their meal, and decided to give the mutt a treat. She collected it and swung open the door. Her eyes not yet adjusted to the darkness, she looked to the left, where the dog usually came running from, and not ahead, closing the door at the same time. She bumped into something solid—realizing instantly that Rafe stood there.

He swung around, further upsetting her equilibrium. She dropped the bone, and he grabbed hold of her upper arms so she wouldn't fall.

"I'm so sorry!" she blurted in shocked embarrassment, but he didn't release her. "I thought you'd gone to the barn." Recalling his odd behavior earlier, she warily eyed what she could make of his face. His eyes were half in shadow, and it unnerved her that she couldn't read their expression. "I–I'll leave you alone to your thoughts. I didn't mean to intrude."

He didn't reassure her, as he'd done in the past. Nor did he offer rebuke, further unsettling her mind. Instead, he remained disturbingly silent, though she felt the tenseness of his body, hard and taut like a whip.

"S–sorry."

Alison took a little sideways step, hoping to break free of his hold. The sole of her soft slipper made contact with the greasy bone. Letting out a shocked gasp, she felt her ankle turn and staggered, bringing a minor stab of pain. She would have dropped to the ground if not for his grip on her arms. In saving her from a second fall, he pulled her closer…and held her tight against him.

She blinked as one of his large hands moved to her lower back, spreading across it. Her heart beat like a trapped, wild thing inside her breast. Her breaths seemed to take a life of their own since she could do little to control them. She looked up in question, finally able to see, and noted his stormy dark eyes fixed on hers.

"Rafe…?"

"You all right?" His voice came huskier than normal, making her strangely shiver though she felt so very warm.

"I…"

When she didn't continue, his intent gaze dropped to her mouth.

"…honestly don't know," she finished in a whisper, answering him from her heart, her reply stemming from much more than her near tumble.

A breath of time elapsed, the span of several erratic heartbeats, and then suddenly his mouth covered hers. She gasped at the sweet invasion, her startled response allowing him deeper access. His hand clutched the back of her head, and she felt she might melt.

Her senses swam with the maelstrom of feeling he evoked, her knees going weak, and she clung to his shoulders in order to remain standing. His kisses came as no gentle brush of the lips, no tentative instigation, but a hungry, masterful assault that triggered her every nerve ending and some she didn't know she possessed.

Trembling, she kissed him back, moving her hands from his shoulders to wrap her arms around his neck, to press closer, never wanting this astonishing moment to end, never wanting him to let go—

When suddenly he broke all contact.

Their breathing ragged and heavy, they stared at one another. Shock and confusion clouded his eyes. He took a step backward, almost defensive.

"I *can't* marry you." He sounded miserable, uncertain, looking like a troubled little boy who'd just learned his beloved pet had run away—looking as if he, too, might bolt and run.

"I never asked you to." She breathed the reply, scarcely aware of what she said, while pressing her palm to the door behind, her weakened limbs barely able to offer support.

He gave a curt nod and then shook his head, as if fighting off a voice inside it. Without another word he turned and retreated to the barn, his stride long and quick, almost a run

That was it? No apology, no explanation—nothing? Yet if he had remained and attempted either, she didn't feel she could have borne what he had to say.

Slowly, her legs feeling as if they weren't part of her, Alison retreated indoors.

While readying for bed, she moved sluggishly, as if in a dream. She brushed out her hair in gradual strokes, forgetting to count to one hundred, her mind still absorbed in his earth-shattering, whirlwind kiss. Like a cyclone that came out of nowhere and struck, whipping her feelings into a blind tumult, rendering her without breath or thought or speech.

She had been kissed before, during her engagement, but platonically. Never so possessively or passionately!

Alison grabbed the edge of the bedpost as she relived the startling moment. Her lips still tingled, and she pressed her fingertips to them.

Oh, what did it all mean! How could he kiss her like that when he had no intention of marrying her, when he'd made clear his disinterest in the idea—his disinterest in *her*. But his actions screamed the opposite, confusing her all the more. Had the spontaneous gaiety of the evening made him act out of character?

For Alison, his kisses made her feel more than she would ever admit, and she flushed with embarrassing warmth when she remembered how freely she had returned each one. She had certainly behaved out of character as well, and like no proper Bostonian lady!

Much later, unable to sleep, she lay in his bed and stared at the dark ceiling. Once the shock ebbed by slow degrees, she didn't know whether to be angry with Rafe, hopeful...

Or both.

* * * * *

Rafe didn't go directly into the barn, sure his sons would see his agitation if they were still awake. He stood silent just outside it and stared up at the globe of the harvest moon. Almost full, it hung large and orange in the sky.

He didn't want to dwell on the last few minutes but couldn't prevent his mind from whirling in that direction.

What on God's green earth had compelled him to kiss her like that? To kiss her at all?

The mistake had been in asking her to dance; that had been the start of it. To feel the touch of her soft hand, her body warm and pliant, her doe-brown eyes huge and shining with delighted confusion—all of that had scrambled his senses. At the close of the dance he had given in to the insane urge to draw her closer, to breach the gap that society's dictates demanded of the proper dance. Proper? Ha! "Proper" had been the last thing going through his mind, the need to excuse himself immediate.

He had remained outside, needing time alone to collect his chaotic emotions. It had been almost two years since he had touched a woman in so personal a manner. And his body, traitorous fiend that it was, wanted more. He recalled past sermons his brother preached about wickedness of the flesh and the need to keep it under control.

He had tried, he honestly had. Maybe if he'd had more time to gather his wits he wouldn't have behaved like a selfish rogue. She had appeared so unexpectedly at the door, stammering in her flustered state, almost falling into his arms not once but twice, and the temptation to hold her, to taste of her lips, had at last been too great to resist.

He sternly told himself the kisses meant nothing lasting—only a need to fulfill a temporary desire—nothing more. But one relentless fact drummed through his mind: he hadn't wanted to kiss just any woman to satisfy that longing. He'd had the opportunity countless times in the past year for female companionship and chose to pass up each one. He had only wanted to kiss Alison. Amy's sister. Not by blood, but nevertheless—her *sister*.

Was that wrong...?

Of course it was wrong!

He had treated Amy's beloved sibling with dishonor, without the respect due her, acting like a wild animal in need of having its yearnings fulfilled. Such an intimate, heated kiss might have been acceptable if they'd made plans to marry, might have been...or not. And he hadn't imagined it when she melted against him and kissed him back just as feverishly. That sort of kiss led to one thing. Experience told him that, even if it seemed like a lifetime ago.

But he had no desire to marry again. Ever.

As often as Rafe told himself those words in the past few months especially, this time they didn't come across quite so forceful.

Chapter Twenty-One

....

After a restless night, tossing and turning with little sleep, Alison rose from bed out of sorts. She took her time dressing and putting up her hair, delaying the inevitable meeting. Her heart raced as the time came and passed to make her presence known.

Would he be remorseful? Certainly he wouldn't mention what had happened in front of the children! Would he watch her closely, as he had while she had danced with her nieces and nephews and later with him? Or would he ignore her, as he had after their dance, before he'd departed for the barn...or so she'd thought?

She closed her eyes, collecting her breath and her thoughts, resolving not to relive their kisses yet again. If only she knew what to expect...

Smoothing the back of her hair with nervous pats, she opened the door.

All six children were in the main room, the girls making break-fast and the boys lighting the fire in the hearth, since the mornings had grown chillier. Rafe was nowhere to be seen.

"Good morning." She worked to make her voice sound natural. "Is your father still in the barn?"

"He took off early," Andy answered. "Said he needed to talk to Uncle Caleb."

"Before breakfast?"

"Said he wasn't hungry and could eat something there if and when he was."

Mingled emotions of relief and disappointment filtered through her heart. Apparently Rafe had as much difficulty facing her as she did him.

"Well, then." She moved forward with purpose and forced a smile she didn't feel. "Let's finish with this meal so we may begin the day's lessons."

A chorus of the usual groans met her announcement.

"No use complaining, it must be done. And starting next week, you older children will be attending school with Sam." She paused in reflection. "We should also take today to ensure that you have everything you need for your first day there."

"I don' have a thlate," Maggie said. "So guess I can't go."

Alison hid a grin at the hopeful note in the girl's voice. "How much does a slate cost?"

"I don' know. A nickel, I reckon."

"Two cents," Sam said smoothly, earning her a baleful stare from Maggie.

"Only two cents?" Alison looked at her younger niece. "Since it's for a worthy cause, I'll give you what you need."

Maggie quirked her mouth in a resigned manner, clearly not happy with the outcome.

"After breakfast, I want to get a good look at all of your clothes."

"Huh?" Tucker scratched his head. "What you want to do that for, Aunt Alison?"

"Well, you can't attend school with the other children if there are holes in your trousers, can you?"

"Don't see why not," Maggie said. "Who cares about clothes anyhow?"

"I'll bet Andy does," Tucker teased in a singsong way, "since *Abigail'll* be there. He'll want to be all purty-fied for her."

Andy flushed beet red. "Shut up, if you don't want a hole in your *lip*."

"Andy," Alison admonished as she spooned batter into the hot frying pan, "that's no way to talk. Apologize to your brother."

"Sorry," he muttered.

"And you," she said, glancing toward Tucker. "Stop teasing Andy. There's nothing wrong with wanting to present a good impression. You want to start your first day there with your best foot forward."

Maggie wrinkled her brow and looked down at her bare feet, lifting one. "Which one's my betht foot?"

Alison laughed. "That's just an expression my uncle used. It means to give your very best right from the start. And you children want to give your best, don't you?"

They glanced at one another then looked to her and nodded.

"Excellent. After breakfast, we'll take inventory of your clothes. I'll do any mending needed while you study your lessons."

Maggie smiled, at last won over. "I'm glad you came to Hope, Aunt Alithun. I don't know what we woulda done if you'd never come. It's almost as good as having Ma back with us."

A chorus of agreement met her ears, and Alison felt her eyes tear up. "I have so enjoyed being with you children as well." But deep in her heart, she sensed her time with them would soon come to an end.

* * * * *

"You look like someone just shot your best horse," Caleb greeted Rafe in clear concern mixed with mild amusement after he opened the door to him. "The children, the crops, or the houseguest?"

"Where's Ivy?" Rafe darted a glance around Caleb's parlor.

"She's visiting a congregation member. We're alone. So what's wrong?"

"I kissed her."

Caleb lifted his brows in surprise. "That is serious. I hope you mean Alison."

"Of course I mean Alison!" Rafe snapped. "And it gets worse. She kissed me back."

His brother's eyebrows rose higher. "I see. So tell me how that's a problem?"

"Come on, Caleb!" Rafe snatched off his hat and slapped it against his leg. "How can it not be? You know how I feel about marrying a second time."

Caleb spread his hands wide. "Feelings change—"

"Stop right there. I don't want to rehash this again."

"All right, then. What do you plan to do about it?"

"That's what I came here for. I need advice."

"Why? I've given you bushels of it, and you never want to hear anything I have to say."

Rafe blew out a frustrated breath. "It's obvious she can't stay at the cabin anymore. I took advantage of her—"

"You *what*?"

"Nothing more than those kisses. I'm not a lecher."

"Glad to hear it. You know, there's more than one reason the Good Book says it's not good for a man to be alone. And to take a wife."

Rafe shook his head in exasperation, deciding to ignore Caleb since he wouldn't quit.

"Okay." Caleb held his hands up in surrender. "You want my advice? If you don't think you can inhabit the same space, do you think you should send her back to Boston? With six kids as constant chaperones and you sleeping out in the barn, the situation seemed proper, though a few of the older matrons might have disagreed. I should tell you, there's been some talk."

"Talk?" Rafe grew alert, his eyes narrowing. "What kind of *talk*?"

"From a few of the older woman, poor misguided souls who don't seem to understand the Bible's proclamation to not gossip. They've been casting aspersions of doubt on Alison's reputation. That she traveled without a chaperone to Kansas made matters worse."

"Alison is one of the most righteous women I've met!" Rafe exploded. "It's due to her that I found my way back inside a church again and grew closer to my children."

"Really?" Caleb remained calm in the swift blast of Rafe's anger. "Doesn't surprise me. She's good for those kids."

Rafe took a deep breath, attempting to calm down. "That's why I'm in such a quandary. After all they've lost, how can I take their aunt away from them too?"

"What about the infamous plan of yours?"

Rafe snorted. "That seemed doomed to fail since day one. I was wrong to start it."

Caleb took a seat at the table. "Sit." He motioned to the chair opposite. "Sounds like you've given this a good deal of thought. Does that mean you're giving up with trying to convince the children they don't need a mother?"

Rafe winced at his choice of wording. "I'm going to sit them down and talk to them like I should have done from the start."

"Sounds like a wise decision. I support it wholeheartedly."

"But it doesn't solve the problem of what to do about Alison."

"You might consider finding her temporary board as a companion for one of the elderly widows, until arrangements can be made?"

"You mean one of those women who criticize her behind her

back?" he scoffed. "Maybe I could set her up somewhere in town. Once I find work, that is."

"If you set her up in a hotel, in a room you pay for, that won't stop the gossipmongers from talking. It might make matters worse. Not to mention, the expense isn't something you need right now. Your children come first."

"Don't you think I know that?" Rafe slammed his palm on the table in frustration. "It's for *their* welfare that I'm trying to find a way to keep Alison in Hope!"

"So you're going to boot her out of your home?"

"Of course not. I would never hurt her like that. But it's clear she can't stay." Rafe's shoulders drooped, the fire leaving him as suddenly as it blazed. With cold weather coming, he had to come up with some solution fast.

"Are you afraid your feelings for Alison—whatever they are— are more than you can handle?" Caleb asked frankly, no amusement in his eyes this time. "Are you afraid you might kiss her again, might not be able to stop at that?"

Upon hearing his fears so bluntly put into words, Rafe slapped his hands on the table, using it to push himself up to stand. "I can't take that risk. Don't you see?" The thought drummed in the back of his mind—for Alison to have kissed him back could only mean that her feelings had changed. He had to be fair to her and squelch such feelings before they could develop. "I need to go look for work."

"No matter what you decide, I'm here for you. I'll talk it over with Ivy. Maybe Alison could stay here."

Rafe knew his brother and their wife could ill afford another mouth to feed, and they had a baby on the way. They relied on offerings from their congregation, which sadly weren't always forthcoming, but their generosity abounded with what little they had.

He clapped his brother on the shoulder. "Thanks for the offer just the same. You have your own family to consider. I'll think of something." He turned to go and then remembered why else he'd come. "Later, can you come by the cabin? And bring your wagon?"

"I could manage that." Caleb regarded him with curiosity. "May I ask the reason?"

Rafe sadly smiled. "A little matter of letting go of the past."

* * * * *

After finding several places to patch and rips needing to be sewn, Alison ordered the three children to shed their clothes and cover up with blankets. Huddled at the table, the chosen three studied their books while Alison threaded her needle.

Clarissa looked up from her drawing. "How come you know how to sew clothes but didn't know how to wash them, Auntie Alison?"

At the frank question, Alison let out a short laugh and lowered her needle. "Ladies from affluent homes aren't always only ornamental. We're taught ladylike accomplishments, to sew pretty things, like the doilies your mother made. But our mother was unique. Teaching us to make decorative mementos to embellish the home became the first step to greater endeavors with far worthier results. Our parents took part in charitable institutions. Often my mother and sister and I made blankets and clothing for the poor."

With her elbow planted on the table, Clarissa leaned her cheek against her palm and smiled. "I like when you talk about when you and Ma lived in Boston."

"There are many stories I could tell."

"Oh, yes, please!" Clarissa sat forward eagerly and the other girls chimed in agreement. Even Tucker and Andy had quit reading and looked interested.

"After lessons." Alison remained firm.

Tucker scowled and went back to reading his book.

"Are all well-bred ladies taught music?" Sam inquired. "Is that why both you and Ma had lessons from an instructor?"

"It is a great advantage for a lady of society to have musical skills as well as others, yes."

"Like walking with a book on her head?" Maggie asked.

Alison chuckled. "I use that method to help teach you good posture."

"So in Boston you really don't walk around with books on your heads?"

"No." Alison smiled at the image in her mind that created.

"Do only ladies have music lessons?"

"I had no brothers, but I would think some of the boys took lessons as well."

"Pa learned," Tucker announced. "And he lived in Boston."

"Well, that's true," she began carefully, "but his family didn't come from high society. His grandfather taught him, as he mentioned last night." Not comfortable discussing Rafe's past where she had no right, she smiled at Andy. "That was some lovely music you created with your harmonica. I had no idea you could play."

Andy shrugged, looking uneasy.

She persisted. "Why the big secret? I'm certain you would have preferred to play your harmonica rather than listen to my flute every night."

Her teasing earned her a reluctant smile. "I quit playing after Ma died, well, leastways I didn't play around Pa. He didn't want music in the house. He'd get mad when he'd hear it and yell for us to stop. Told us that all music died with our ma."

The news troubled Alison, and she looked at Sam. "Is that why you told him you don't play the pianoforte?"

Sam looked trapped, her eyes darting around the room to the others, before she nodded.

"That was awhile back, though," Andy hurried to say. "When he was really angry all the time, right after Ma died."

"Did he…" Alison struggled to say the words she couldn't believe. "He didn't harm you children?"

"'Course not! Pa would never harm us," Sam said. "But he stayed away a lot and was quiet all the time. He never smiled and sometimes, well, sometimes it was as if he wasn't with us even when he was in the room."

At the pain in Sam's voice, Alison ended the discussion. "Well, he's better now, and thank the Lord for that, because the man you described doesn't sound at all like your father."

A hopeful light glimmered in Sam's eyes. "It was good to hear him play the violin again."

Alison smiled, remembering. "He does play well. Now…" She cleared her throat at her wistful words and affected a stern countenance. "Back to lessons. Sam, finish your speech. The harvest celebration is fast approaching."

Sam groaned but dutifully picked up her pencil.

Time passed, the children's scribbles and page-turning all that disrupted the silence. Every now and then Alison fondly glanced at each small head bowed over studies, thankful for her nieces and nephews and this opportunity she'd been given to share in their lives. No one could take moments like these away. She would always have the wealth of these memories to cherish for what promised to be a lonely future.

With her mind absorbed in such thoughts, she didn't realize Rafe had come home until she heard Baby Lynn squeal and run for the door. Only then did she hear the rattling of a wagon outside. Her heart gave a harsh thump, seeming to rise and lodge in her throat. "You may close your books for the day. I'll finish the mending later. All of you get dressed."

Books slammed shut and papers and slate were pushed aside as the children eagerly hopped up from their benches. The three snatched up their clothes and headed off to different areas to dress. The door to the cabin opened just as Alison finished clearing the table. She turned and smoothed her skirts, surprised when Caleb walked in behind Rafe.

"Hello," she greeted, pleased to see Rafe's brother, who always seemed to be in good spirits. "Is Ivy with you?"

"No, but she sends her love. And this…" He set down a cloth-wrapped parcel. Alison detected the sweet scent of bread. "She's been in a flurry of cleaning and baking."

"I have something for her as well. Excuse me." She hurried to her trunk and retrieved the little booties she'd knitted with blue yarn that Amy must have put aside for her own child. She'd accomplished these while the children studied. Knitting never her strong suit, she'd been pleased not to drop any stitches.

"That was kind of you," Caleb said when she handed him her gift. He tucked the booties in his pocket. "It seems that today the Lord is blessing us with quite a bounty."

"Oh?" She raised her brows.

"I'm donating the pianoforte to Caleb's church," Rafe explained, his eyes somber. He moved toward the instrument, Caleb going to the other side. With Rafe's back to her, he didn't notice Sam's stricken expression, but Caleb did, since he stared her way.

"Sam, is everything all right?" he asked.

Rafe looked over his shoulder at her. With tears welling in her eyes, Sam bolted from the cabin, leaving the door wide. "Sam?" he called in worry. "I didn't think she'd take it so hard." His words came low and confused. Alison wondered if she should betray Sam's secret, when Caleb spoke.

"Let me talk to her. Maybe I can smooth things over."

Rafe gave a distant nod.

Alison noticed the children nearby, quiet and watchful. "Girls, please get the meal started. Boys, I'm sure you have afternoon chores that need tending?" The children looked curious but went to their assigned tasks, and Alison addressed Rafe. "May I speak with you?"

He gave another slight nod, not making eye contact. He had barely looked at her since he entered the cabin.

"Outside?"

He narrowed his eyes in a guarded manner but motioned for her to precede him. Once they stood outside, he spoke.

"I didn't think she'd get upset." He stared out over the land. There was no sign of Sam or Caleb. "I figured it was the right thing to do."

"It wasn't your fault—"

"Of course it's my fault!" He clenched and unclenched his hands as if he'd like to slam one of them into the wall. "If I knew my children better, I could have foreseen this. But I spent too much time away from them, lost in my own misery."

"You can't blame yourself for that."

He swung his attention her way. "Can't I? I wasn't there for them. They lost their mother, and I *wasn't there*. I *couldn't* be there, couldn't even cope with my own pain, much less handle theirs."

"And they understand that and forgive you and love you regardless."

He shook his head as if he couldn't believe it.

She desperately ached to reach out to him, to touch his shoulder in comfort, but memory of their unspoken kiss made things awkward, and she kept her hand clenched in her skirts at her side.

"It's true," she insisted softly. "They admire you a great deal—"

"What's to admire?" His chuckle came self-derisively. "I haven't been a good example these past two years. You showed me that. "

She winced that she'd caused him more grief and couldn't bear for him to berate himself for past faults any longer. "There's something you should know. About Sam. I don't think she was upset about you giving away the pianoforte because it belonged to Amy."

"No?" He chuckled without humor. "Then why'd she go tearing out of here with tears in her eyes?"

Alison hoped Sam would forgive her. "I think she might have been upset because she was hoping to learn to play it."

"What makes you think that?" His confusion was apparent. "Did she tell you?"

"Not in those exact words, but she made her interest clear."

"She never said anything to me."

"It is my understanding that up until the night of your birthday celebration, you preferred no music in the house," Alison began carefully, hoping not to make him feel worse but feeling he needed to know. "Sam was trying to respect your feelings."

His eyes closed in remorse. "Dear God, what have I done? It wasn't enough that my children lost their mother. I had to go and make things worse by killing their spirit and trust to confide in me. By stealing what happiness they had left. And now...this..."

Alison didn't know what he spoke of but sensed more importance lay buried beneath his words than a misunderstanding about a pianoforte. No longer quelling the desire to reach out to him, no longer able to, she laid her hand on his shoulder. His muscles tensed beneath her fingers, but he didn't pull away.

"Rafe, you need to stop this. Your motives were admirable. You wished to donate an instrument to your brother's church, where it can be of great benefit. Sam will come to understand and respect your decision. She's an intelligent girl."

"It's not just about Sam." His eyes again grew sad, breaking her heart. "Every day I see more proof of how I've estranged my children. And at a time when they needed me most. When it all boils down to it…" He shook his head in defeat. "I can't really blame them for searching for a ma and sending that letter to you. I intend to sit them down and tell them that I know—tonight. But I'm no longer angry. How can I be? When I was guilty of a far greater sin in neglecting my own flesh and blood?"

She inhaled a quick breath, lowering her hand to her side. "The plan is over?"

"Yes. From now on, nothing will be spoken in my house but the pure, undiluted truth."

She tried to gather her scrambling thoughts. "So where does this leave us—me? Are you sending me back to Boston?"

An intent look she couldn't define entered his eyes. "Is that what you want? To go back home?"

Home. Of course. She didn't belong here. She never had.

"Perhaps it would be best," she answered softly, lowering her gaze to his shirtfront.

"But not for the children."

"What?" Her gaze snapped up to his again.

"They've grown to love you, and you love them. It's clear to see. In town today, the schoolmarm was happy to receive my offer to build more desks. But I ran into someone else who came to visit just as I was leaving. A widow who owns a reputable boardinghouse. She needs a handyman to take care of things. I asked, and she said she'd soon have a room available."

Alison struggled to speak over the lump that thickened in her throat.

"You're throwing me out?"

"Don't think of it like that. I want you around for the children. They need you; I realize that now. But with winter coming, the boys and I can't stay in the barn...and I don't want your reputation compromised. People talk, even when there's no fire. We can't live under the same roof."

"Of course not." Warmth flushed her face at his blunt words. The memory of their kiss, which had felt very much like the start of such a fire, rushed to the forefront of her mind. "You're absolutely right. I can't stay here."

"But you can stay in Hope. You could find honest work, with your experience in making hats. And you can come visit the children whenever you like."

But not you.

She shook her head to dispel the thought. "I'll need to think about it." She told herself she was silly to feel rejected. He had never promised her anything other than that her stay at his cabin wouldn't be permanent.

She walked a short distance away, her gaze going to the field. Caleb and Sam walked together toward the cabin. Sam appeared calm, smiling up at her uncle as they talked. Alison was grateful to see her happy again but wished she could experience the same ease.

"So," she said as if it didn't matter, "if I agree, when is this new plan to commence?"

"After the harvest celebration."

She spread her hands helplessly and turned to look at him. "I still don't see how it would work. I don't have any way to pay for a room yet."

"I don't expect you to. I made a trade with her. I'll be going into town five times a week to make repairs there, in return for your room and board."

She frowned. "I can't let you do that."

"It'll only be until you find work. As talented as you are with cloth and a needle, that shouldn't take long."

She blinked. "You think I'm talented?" she asked softly.

"Yes, very much so."

The first true compliment about her skill she had received from someone other than her immediate family, and it came as a bitter-sweet balm to ease his words of ultimate rejection.

Alison gave a stiff nod. "I'll consider it."

"Fair enough."

But it isn't *fair,* she wanted to cry out.

It never could be considered fair that she'd fallen hopelessly in love with Rafe, when it appeared he would never get over her deceased sister.

Hope, for her, felt as if it would never belong to Alison again.

Chapter Twenty-Two

....

After the evening meal, Rafe instructed his children to sit around the hearth, and he took a seat, facing them. The empty space beneath the window looked odd, but he felt he'd done the right thing by giving the pianoforte to Caleb's church. He'd been relieved when Sam returned with his brother, excited that he told her she could come play the instrument any time, adding that Ivy had lessons as a child and could teach Sam. At the hope reborn in her eyes, Rafe gave her permission to visit Ivy after school. And so, one minor catastrophe had been swiftly handled, thanks to his brother. And Alison.

He looked at her, where she stood by the wall, her arms folded across her middle. She gave an encouraging dip of her head, and he nodded in reply before turning back to his children.

"It's high time we talked," he began, "starting with the letter you sent your aunt Alison this summer. The letter asking her to come to Kansas and be your ma."

Sam went as white as chalk. Andy didn't look so good either. Clarissa appeared as if she might cry. Tucker's gaze landed on his crossed legs, and Maggie bit her thumbnail, her eyes wide in apprehension.

"What you did was wrong, but I don't need to tell you that. If you thought what you were doing was right, you wouldn't have kept it quiet, now would you?"

Andy and Sam exchanged worried glances. "We were only trying to help, Pa," Sam explained quietly.

"I know that. And I know that in the past two years I haven't been the father you children needed. There's a lot that's gone wrong. But you can't go interfering in people's lives just because you want something. No matter how badly you want it or how much you think you need it. You did your aunt a grave injustice by sending for her when you knew I'd never approve of your plan...."

He watched as shame filled their eyes. Clarissa and Sam looked down at their laps.

"But I made a mistake too."

At his low admission, the girls' heads jerked upward, their mouths gaping in surprise.

"I took part in this by letting you think I didn't know what you'd done." Their eyes widened even more and he nodded. "Yes, I've known since the day your aunt arrived. I tried to fix your mistake and get you to see reason in a way I shouldn't have, instead of just sitting you down like this and talking to you from the start." His posture grew stern. "Before I say more, you owe your aunt an apology for using deceit to get her here."

With guilt-ridden glances, Sam and Maggie quietly told her they were sorry. Andy nodded in agreement and Tucker went red in the face, staring at his lap.

"But you're happy you came, aren't you, Auntie Alison?" Clarissa asked hopefully. "Even if we were being bad to ask you. You like it here with us, don't you?"

"Yes," Alison assured softly. "I'm happy to have come and gotten to know all of you."

"So you'll stay?" Maggie pleaded.

Rafe sensed her unease, realizing she'd not yet made a decision. "We're not through talking about your behavior."

"Will we have to pay hell?" Clarissa whispered in fear. Tears glistened in her eyes and rolled down her cheeks.

"What?" Rafe blinked in shock to hear such words come out of his little girl's mouth.

"Andy said that there'd be hell to pay if you found out what we'd done."

"Oh, he did, did he?" Rafe turned his disapproving gaze on his son, whose face, neck, and ears turned red. "We'll discuss your language and part in this later," he promised Andy. "For now, we need to talk about this."

He went on to expound on their reckless actions and the repercussions until he felt they understood their mistakes. Deciding they'd learned their lesson and feeling just as guilty for resorting to the same trickery with his own plan, he chose not to dole out punishment and quietly ordered them to bed. Once they walked off with subdued good nights, he gave a parting nod to Alison and left the cabin.

He felt no surprise when, moments later, the door opened and she joined him. The silence stretched between them as they stared out over the land. The moon shone behind clouds like the soft glow of a lantern in the sky.

"You handled that well," she said at last. "If it's possible that Amy is looking down from above, I know she would be pleased."

He quirked his mouth in a sad half smile and continued staring at the dimly lit sky. "I wish I could remember her, but it's getting harder.... Her face. The smell of her hair. Her laugh. The sound of her voice. Each month that passes steals a little more of her away from me." The worst of it was that the pain he felt about losing such important details had also begun to dull with time.

"But you do see her. Every day."

At Alison's astonishing words, he looked at her.

"In the children you created together," she explained gently. "I see Amy in all of them. Her love of music in Clarissa and Andy and Sam, her curly hair and blue eyes in Baby Lynn, her smile with its one dimple in Tucker, her skill with a needle in Maggie. And in all of the children, I see her devotion and loyalty to loved ones, her tenacity and strength of mind."

Her husky words calmed his heart, though he wondered why he confided in her. Oddly, doing so didn't feel as awkward or distressing as he might have thought. But he should address another matter before too much time passed and he lost courage.

"I owe you an apology," he began, "about what happened last night—"

"Please." Lifting her hand, she turned fully to face him. "I would prefer not to discuss it. You don't owe me an explanation."

He thought that odd, since clearly he did, but he felt more than willing to let the matter drop and pretend that reckless moment of intimacy never happened between them if she was just as eager to dismiss it.

"I should go inside and finish working on the bonnets."

He nodded in acknowledgment. Without another word, she turned and left.

As had happened before, a peculiar loneliness came over him. He had no cause to feel lonely, being the father of six, and should feel grateful for the quiet when it came. Usually he did. But this disturbing void had occurred, twice now, only when Alison left his company. Likely he'd grown accustomed to conversing frequently with another adult and that's why he felt the way he did.

Shaking his head, he went into the barn. He pulled off his hat and boots, slipping his suspenders off his shoulders. The boys were already bedded down in the hay, wrapped like cocooned moths in their blankets, but Rafe felt too alert to sleep.

His restless gaze fell on Amy's journal.

He reached for it and brought the lantern closer. Maybe if he continued to read what was inside those pages, he might gain a little of his wife back and begin to feel whole again, not so hollow and lonely.

The next entries expressed Amy's delight in reaching their new home and her distress over being unable to function in it well. She hadn't yet mastered the fundamentals of keeping house, and the following twenty or so pages were filled with her disasters, sometimes making him chuckle and other times making his eyes tear up in bittersweet pain. She expressed excitement over learning she carried his child and his eager reception of the news. The words of his dear wife that once brought terrible heartache now strangely brought comfort.

Unable to put the book down, he read long into the night, the details of their life together, the knowledge of each child conceived, the love she had for him. At times he couldn't help the tears that ran down his cheeks or the smile that lifted his mouth. The entries came fewer and farther between as the children kept coming, and she lamented how she rarely had time to sit down with her journal, though she wouldn't trade her life for anyone else's.

She'd often told him that, when he sometimes worried aloud that she might one day regret leaving a household of servants to take on a life of servitude. But by what she'd spoken and written, she didn't consider the care she gave her family menial labor. It was an act of selfless love. He read of their joys and sorrows, their triumphs and failures, experiencing their years as though Amy were beside him, speaking to him in reminiscence.

His heart grew heavy as he came to the last pages of the journal. The beginning of the end.

I haven't told Rafe my fears. They are likely nonsensi-cal and groundless, and I don't wish to worry him with my foolish qualms. Regardless, I cannot help but notice that with this new child I carry, I am wearier than before and my ankles have swollen to twice their normal size, although I'm barely halfway into my term. The midwife gave me a plant root she'd crushed for the swelling, but still I wonder and I worry.

Stunned to read what Amy never told him, he quickly contin-ued to the next entry, dated a month and a half later.

I've been remiss in writing but have been fearful to pen my thoughts. They trouble me. Yet perhaps in writing, I may at last vanquish them or at least come to terms with what might happen. I feel as if I might not survive this childbirth. I've not confided to Rafe my fears, but my heart palpitates strangely when I engage in too much activity, much like it does when he holds me in his arms. However, this peculiar beating brings with it not a feeling of pleasure but of pain. He has enough to manage, what with the upcoming harvest. I don't wish to burden him further, though I believe he senses something amiss. He continually asks if I'm well, and with a smile, I always offer the rejoinder that how can I be other-wise, with him for my husband. If these premonitions of my demise are inaccurate, then I will have accomplished nothing except to grieve him with worry, and if they are genuine, then

and only then will he be subjected to the pain of my passing.
I will not speak of this and elongate the process.

Terrible sorrow wrenched through his gut along with a smattering of anger to realize that Amy had known all along she was ill. How could she not have told him? He would have moved heaven and earth to help her, borrowed whatever money he had to in order to take her to the best doctor Kansas offered. How could she have kept her feelings secret?

He wanted to slam the book shut but found his hand turning the page. Only three entries remained. In one, she dismissed her earlier fears; in the next, she confirmed them. The final entry, the longest of all, made his mouth drop open in shock and his hands tremble.

I know now, deep within my heart, I will not survive this winter. At first I suffered such anger and self-pity. Besides my strange ailments, the midwife has needed to turn the baby once, and I fear it may be a breech birth. I've made my peace with God, but I have one final prayer: that Rafe again finds love and his heart is open to accept it. My death, should it come, will be very difficult for him and the children to bear. Samantha is strong-minded and has learned a great deal. I am confident she will take over in running the household when I'm gone, but at this moment my heart is heavily burdened that I shall soon leave my dear ones, and I feel as if I may weep with this secret I've kept. I allow myself the weakness of tears when I'm alone and tenaciously remind myself of Scripture—and how God will wipe away every tear with no place for sorrow in heaven. With that knowledge, I know I will experience joy after my death.

I told Rafe today that I want him always to be happy, that he must promise me he will never surrender to defeat. He smiled and held me close, kissed my nose, and assured me I had nothing to worry about. I fear, for him, it will be the worst year of his life. For I don't believe I shall be here much longer, and I know he will strongly grieve my passing. The love we share shines with a gentle brightness, like the moon in the darkest heavens, beautiful yet intense, and it is my utmost wish that Rafe will again find a woman with whom to share such love—a woman deserving of my husband and one I can trust to care for my children, someone like my sister, Alison....

Rafe almost dropped the book but kept reading, unable to stop.

I've been blessed a thousand times over. My life may be brief, but some who have lived twice as long have never found true happiness, such as I have known with Rafe.

I wish also for Alison to find such love. The man she writes of—this Stephen Sumpter—sounds as if he isn't worthy of my beloved sister. I hope she doesn't give him opportunity to harm her. She's endured so much sorrow and pain. If only Rafe could meet Alison and they could find a life together, this would be my ultimate wish. Yet with her in Boston and Rafe in Kansas, I fear such a hope is unattainable. Alison wrote to me that she no longer bears ill feelings toward Rafe, who she once said "stole me away." Yet I went readily, my heart a willing captive in Rafe's possession. One day, I pray my sweet sister may experience the intensity of a love so deep and passionate, which was all that could enable me to leave

*my family home and anticipate a future in a land unknown
to me.*

*It has been a good life. If I could live it over, I wouldn't
trade these past fifteen years with Rafe for a life of old age
without my dear husband. If my fears are groundless, then
I will write again, and if not, then let this be my last entry.
My final prayer would be that all those I love may seek happiness and find peace without me, knowing that I am truly
well and wait for the day when I will be reunited with them
in heaven.*

Rafe closed the book, his heart and mind too full of what he'd
just learned to try to sort it out. Tears ran unchecked down his
cheeks. Not wanting to wake the boys, he left the barn and stood
outside, turning his somber gaze toward the pale globe of the moon
that his wife had compared their love to.

"Oh, Amy, why?" he whispered into the wind. "Why...?"

There were no answers. And the saddest irony of all: there never
would be.

* * * * *

The days passed into a week. With each one, Rafe grew more distant.

It made no sense to Alison. On their last private encounter he
had confided in her. He had even almost apologized for kissing her,
something she had stopped because it would have hurt too much.
She didn't want him to feel remorse for showing interest in her, and
remorse seemed all he was capable of feeling.

With her morning chores done and both Clarissa and Baby
Lynn napping in the big bed, Alison withdrew a piece of stationery

from the small amount she'd brought with her. She had been remiss in corresponding with her aunt but hadn't known what to write.

To stay in Hope was tempting. If she thought any chance existed that Rafe might let go of the past and change his mind about her, she would gladly remain and wait for that elusive day. But sure of the impossibility, she faced only disappointment. Though Alison had adored her sister, she found herself fighting off moments of envy that Amy still possessed all of Rafe, which then made her feel ashamed for being so insensitive. Theirs had been a love Alison both admired and resented, because it had been so strong Rafe still couldn't let go.

So why did she stay?

The children, of course. Yet was it really in their best interest for her to remain in Kansas, giving them false hope that their dream of her becoming their mother could come true?

And yet…

She looked up from the blank page toward the missing space where the pianoforte once stood and the window open above. A ray of sunlight washed the floorboards in a pool of gold. She stared at the area for some time.

There were occasions when she discerned a look in his eyes, a fleeting sense that he also desired a relationship. His kisses had seemed more than a momentary lapse in judgment….

She blew out a disgruntled breath. This did her no good whatsoever.

With firm resolution she dipped her pen into her bottle of ink and put pen to paper.

My Dear Aunt Eliza,
 Forgive my delay in writing. There has been so much to

learn in living as a pioneer; I confess the execution of such tasks has taken up the greater portion of my time.

Amy's children are everything she told us and more. To meet and know them has been a true blessing and a period in my life I will never forget.

She felt it wise not to mention Rafe's plan, certain her aunt wouldn't understand and would instead be horrified to learn that Alison's appearance in Kansas had been a cleverly orchestrated scheme.

With regard to the future, I'm not certain what course to take. I have an opportunity to remain in Hope, and for the children's sake I've considered the prospect. I have come to love them, and they show great affection for me.

My other choice, of course, would be to return to Boston and pick up the pieces of my life there. I know I'll always have a place in your home and am grateful to you and Uncle Bernard for everything. If not for your generosity, I would not consider my return an option. I must make a decision soon and will inform you by telegraph once I have.

At the sound of a wagon, she looked up from her letter in surprise.

Chapter Twenty-Three

....

Sam entered the door first.

"Sam? I thought you were going to stay after school and take lessons with Ivy."

"Aunt Ivy wasn't feeling well."

Rafe suddenly came in behind her, further confusing Alison, since he didn't usually come home until late afternoon.

"Rafe?" Alarmed, she noted the grim worry in his eyes. "What is it? What's happened?"

"It's Ivy. Her time has come. I came to let you know. My brother's beside himself. I need to go back and be with him."

"Of course."

The other children moved through the door. Maggie hurried to Alison's side, putting her arms around her waist in fear.

"Don't wait supper on me," Rafe instructed. "I have no idea when I'll be back."

Alison held Maggie close. "Please tell Caleb that my prayers are with him and Ivy."

"I will." Rafe nodded in farewell and left.

"Will Aunt Ivy die?" Maggie asked, her voice wavering.

Alison glanced at the girl then at the other children. The same terror clouded their eyes, and she realized they must be remembering how their mother died.

"Of course not, sweetie." Alison forced a smile. "Your aunt Ivy will be just fine."

"Pa looked scairt," Tucker put in.

Alison recalled the fear burning in Rafe's eyes. "And you are too," she said rather than asked. The boy nodded, for once unashamed to admit weakness.

"Whenever I become frightened I take the matter to my Father."

Clarissa cocked her head. "I thought your parents are in heaven."

"I was referring to the Almighty Father. I pray and ask Him to intercede." She held out her hands to them. "Would you like to join me?"

A few of the children nodded. All of them drew close. Gathering in a circle and clasping hands, they bowed their heads while Alison uttered a heartfelt prayer pleading for Ivy and the babe's good health and protection.

Afterward, she instructed them to do their chores, wishing to keep the day as normal as possible. The boys left the cabin without grumbling and the girls were quiet during the meal preparation. After a meal where they barely touched their food, Alison realized any attempt at normalcy was impractical. The children needed a diversion to help take their minds off what occurred on the other side of town. Once the dishes were cleaned and put away, she retrieved the handiwork she'd stowed inside her trunk and brought it with her to the main room.

"I have something for you girls." She handed each the bonnet she'd made for them.

Her nieces stared at the dark-green material. Onto it she'd sewn simple but appealing details to make the bonnets different. Sam fingered the velvet-black cording that rimmed hers, and Clarissa smiled at her lacy frill. Even Maggie seemed happy with her plain one, and Alison felt relieved that she'd guessed correctly in keeping her bonnet simple.

"I got one too!" Baby Lynn squealed in glee. She turned to Clarissa, holding hers out in demand. "Put it on for me."

Clarissa knelt on the floor and tugged the bonnet over Baby Lynn's curls, tying the shiny yellow ribbons in a bow beneath her chin. "This looks like one of your dresses."

"It is." Alison smiled. "I thought the design was perfect for a bonnet."

"I love mine!" Clarissa put on her bonnet and held each end of the matching green ribbons, crossing them under her chin as if in a hug.

"You cut up your dress to make these for us?" Sam stared at her bonnet in confusion. "Why?"

"I love you girls. I wanted to give you something special."

"Because you're leaving?" Maggie asked sadly.

Their excited smiles to receive the bonnets melted away.

"Because I want to make you happy."

"Then you're not leaving?"

"I haven't decided," Alison began carefully. "But if that day does come, distance won't matter. We'll always be close. Here." She pressed her hand first over her bosom then Maggie's. "In our hearts. And we can always correspond with one another through letters."

The girls exchanged woeful glances.

"It won't be the same," Maggie insisted.

"Will it be like it was with you and our ma?" Sam asked.

"Yes, exactly."

Alison felt a hand tug her skirt and looked down into Baby Lynn's sad eyes. "Please don't go," she whispered.

Emotion clutched her throat like a hand gripped it, and Alison worked to curb her own tears. She bent to hug the child close and forced a laugh. "We don't need to be anxious about what might never occur." She looked up at all of them. "It's enough to live each moment as it arrives."

Alison turned to Andy. "Would you play your harmonica? Or, if you would rather, I could play my flute—"

Andy jumped up and retrieved the instrument from his pocket. "Sure thing, Aunt Alison."

"Can we dance?" Clarissa begged.

"Yes, please teach us more," Sam agreed.

Relieved to have diverted their attention from worrying over Ivy or fretting about her departure from Hope, Alison agreed.

She allowed the fun and frolicking to continue until they were exhausted and would sleep well. Baby Lynn had already fallen asleep, curled up as content as a kitten in the rocker, and Alison instructed Andy to carry her to bed. Once the rest of the children retired for the night, she put on a pot of coffee, intending to wait up for Rafe. Sitting in the rocker, she opened one of her books, to pass the hours in a classic her uncle had given her.

Two chapters into Dickens's strange but lovely tale of a young, selfless woman named Little Dorrit, she suddenly jerked awake when the book hit the floor.

Sighing, she picked up the novel, smoothing the creased pages. The aroma of strong coffee made her rise to pour a cup. The sudden pounding of horse's hooves nearly had her drop it.

A short time later, the door swung open and Rafe appeared.

Her heart gave a sudden jolt at the sight of him, and she clutched the back of the rocker. He looked tired, his eyes not as vibrant, his hair wildly mussed from his ride. She gripped the rocker more tightly at the fervent urge to go to him and smooth it from his brow.

"Ivy…," she whispered.

He gave a short nod. "Ivy's well. The baby too—a boy."

Alison's relief escaped in a sigh. "Thank you for coming inside to tell me."

"I was surprised to see a light in the window."

"I couldn't sleep."

"I doubt I'll be able to after tonight." He hesitated at the door he had yet to close. "Mind if I come in and get warm?"

"No, of course not." This was his home, after all. Thinking of the cup she'd just poured herself, she offered it to him once he closed the door and took a seat near the rocker. "You look as if you could use this."

He nodded his thanks and took the saucer, carefully taking the fragile teacup into his large hand and sipping the dark brew.

She watched how the firelight played over his features, picking golden highlights out of his hair. Even utter exhaustion didn't detract from his appearance. She wanted to reach out and touch him, hold him, had wanted to do so from the moment he entered the cabin.

Embarrassed, she averted her gaze to the low flames sputtering as they ate through wood. For long moments silence dominated the cabin.

"Everything went well? There were no problems?"

He looked at her strangely. "Why should you ask?" His voice came tight with emotion. "Did Ivy say something to you?"

"What do you mean?"

"I thought…" He expelled a weary breath. "I thought she might have confided in you."

She tried to follow where he led. "Well, yes, she did. Nothing with regard to any problems, though."

"There were problems, but she's all right now." He took another sip of coffee. "Did Amy confide in you?"

His question took her aback. His words came so low, at first she didn't think he'd spoken them, until he lifted his eyes to hers, awaiting her answer.

"She—she wrote of her fondness for the baby." Alison folded her hands in her lap, uncertain of how to answer.

"Did she tell you she was ill?"

She stared in shock. "What are you talking about?"

"While she carried the child. Did she mention…" He struggled with the words. "Did she mention that she thought she—might not make it through the ordeal?"

"No," Alison breathed.

"I didn't know about any of it either till I read her journal." He bowed his head, placing his forearms on his thighs, and wrung his hands together. "I had no idea she was sick. I knew she'd contracted the fever, of course, but before that, I didn't know. I should have known. I was her husband." He shook his head, closing his eyes. "Tonight brought it all back. And I've since wondered, if maybe I'd been less attentive to my crops and more attentive to my wife—"

Alison couldn't stand to see his misery and acted before she thought. Leaning forward she cupped her hands around his clasped ones, a little tremor going through her at the contact. He jumped a bit in surprise, lifting his eyes to hers in question.

"You're *not* to blame, Rafe. Knowing Amy, she kept the truth from you to spare your feelings."

"Spare them!" He raised his voice, anguish tormenting his eyes. "How could she have thought that *losing my wife* would spare my feelings? Had I known, maybe I could have done something to save her."

She shook her head in helplessness. "I can't speak for Amy, but

I know she never wanted to cause anyone a moment's distress. The day before she left Boston, she did her utmost to make me feel loved and happy. It was Amy's way."

He was silent a moment. "Do you ever still resent me for taking Amy away?" he asked quietly. "If not for that, she might still be alive."

Alison drew her brows together in concern, carefully framing her answer. "Perhaps so, but would she have been happy and lived a life fulfilled with anyone else? I think you were the only man who could do that for my sister." She shrugged self-consciously. "I was young and foolish when you left Boston. I thought as a child, with no knowledge of how the heart could lead. I may never have admitted it before coming here, but I think it was the hand of God that brought you two together."

At that moment she realized she was stroking his hand with her thumb. She ceased at once, though he made no remark about it, didn't flicker an eyelash. Slowly she removed her hands from his.

"You have a way about you, Alison, something that makes a person feel better about themselves."

At his quiet compliment, similar to what she'd told Ivy, she nervously smiled, the husky sound of her name on his lips bringing with it a shiver of warmth.

"I came home tonight grieving the past and what couldn't be changed, and you showed me that to change any of it might have made things worse. For both Amy and myself. Thank you for that."

"It's my pleasure to help however I can." Her gaze dropped to her lap.

"Have you made a decision? About staying in Hope?"

"I haven't given the matter a great deal of consideration," she hedged.

"The children would like it if you stayed."

A burst of courage pushed her to ask, "And what about you, Rafe?" Her voice came soft as she searched his eyes. "Would *you* like it if I stayed?"

He flinched. "For the children's sake it would be a good thing."

Of course. Always for the children. Never for himself. Yet what else did she expect? He had never led her to believe otherwise.

She rose quickly, surprising him, by the manner in which he raised his brows. But she couldn't endure a moment longer in his presence without feeling as if she might say something they would both regret. "I should retire."

"Have I offended you?"

"What could you have possibly said to cause offense?"

His expression was troubled. "I can see you're upset."

"I—I suppose it's because of all you told me. I don't blame you. Please believe that. I meant every word I said, but it's a lot to take in. And I have a decision to make. Go home to Boston or stay in Hope and find a way to secure a living."

"You could always make hats."

She huffed a laugh, a sound that came out as half a sob. "Oh, yes. My millinery work, I could do that. I'm certain there's no shortage of women in town in need of a fancy hat."

"Alison," he said in concern, reaching out to touch her arm before she could turn to go—but his fingers only brushed her sleeve as she jerked away from him.

"Forgive me, I'm not—feeling quite myself tonight. I'm exhausted and no longer aware of what I'm saying." Not daring to look at him should he discern the truth of her feelings, she struggled to speak. "The hour is late. My nerves are frayed. A night of sleep should improve my disposition considerably."

"I apologize if I hurt you." His voice came deep and resigned.

She managed a smile his way, her heart breaking. "It's not your fault. I went into this knowing the outcome and don't expect anything else." Her eyes widened when she realized her slip and hastily added, "Good night, Mr. Munroe. There's coffee on the stove if you want more." She purposely used formality to create distance between them, which she so desperately needed in order to pull herself together.

In the bedroom, she closed the door behind her and pressed her back against it, the tears she could no longer stanch quietly streaming down her face.

* * * * *

Rafe stared into the fire in sad reflection. He hadn't meant to hurt her and wished somehow to smooth over the awkwardness.

But what she wanted to hear, he couldn't say.

The flames shot up in a shower of sparks as the fire ate through some very dry wood.

The fire reminded him of her. At times mellow, calm, warming to the soul. In the next instant, spirited and wild, with a mind all its own and unwilling to back down when it encountered a rough patch....

He had no idea what to do. Her return to formality hadn't escaped his notice, nor had her slip of the tongue that she had begun to hope for more between them.

He'd grown accustomed to their talks and took pleasure in their budding friendship. But instead of acting selfishly and seeking only what he wanted, as he was prone to do, he must consider her feelings. If she needed him to keep his distance, he would at least grant her that. She'd been to his children, to *him*, more of a godsend than ever expected.

His harsh feelings toward his Creator had slowly diminished, in no little part thanks to Alison. He had come to accept, if not understand, Amy's death. And he took some comfort in the knowledge that his sweet, erstwhile wife no longer felt pain. He still couldn't understand why she hadn't told him of her fears, but it did little good to dwell on such questions.

A movement of white on the stairs captured his attention. He watched his youngest tiptoe down them, using the wall for balance and clutching her doll against her nightdress. She wore a pretty bonnet on her head, the ribbons dangling untied. With only the low fire lighting the room, she didn't see him as she reached the landing and hurried to Alison's door.

"Lynn," he said softly, startling his child, who swung around to look. "Best not disturb your aunt right now. Is anything the matter?"

"I had a bad dream," she whimpered.

He held out his arms and she ran into them. Holding her close, he lifted his little girl to sit on his lap. "Tell Pa all about it." He brushed the damp curls from her face and kissed her temple.

"I dreamed that Auntie Al–son went away and I neveh saw her again." She threw her arms around his neck. "Oh, Pa, don't make her go. Please!"

"I won't make her do anything. But, honey, if she wants to go, it would be wrong to try to stop her."

"Why would she want to go?" She lifted her face from his shoulder to look at him. Another tear dropped from her lashes and made a slow roll down her cheek.

"She had a life in Boston. We took her from that life." The words felt as empty as they sounded. From what Alison told him, she had been dissatisfied with privileged society. But she'd also told him she would never marry a man with so many children. He blinked.

Where had that thought come from? He didn't want to marry Alison.

"She has a life *here*," his daughter stubbornly insisted.

"Still, we can't make that choice for her. What your brothers and sisters did in bringing her to stay with us by lying to her was wrong. If your aunt is happier going home to her aunt and uncle, you'd want that for her, wouldn't you?"

"No!" Lynn's denial came sharp and on the verge of more tears. She pushed away from him. "She can't go—she can't! *This* is her home! With *us*!"

Before she could break entirely free, he tightened his hold and brought her close to his heart. She cried against his shirt for long minutes while he smoothed her back. Once she at last calmed, he kissed her forehead.

"Back to bed with you, Sweet Pea, but first put your pretty new bonnet away so it looks nice for Sunday. You don't want to sleep in it and get it more rumpled." By its present condition, she'd done exactly that.

She perked up a little. "Auntie Al–son made it for me. And it wasn't even my birfday!"

"I know."

"Now I have a bonnet, just like Sam and 'Rissa and Maggie." She grew silent a moment, as if thinking hard. "I wish I could give something to her. Sam asked when her birfday was, but she didn't know 'cause she was an orphan. But she ceb-elrates it on May Day. Will she still be here then, Pa?"

He had no idea how to answer without causing his baby girl more heartache, but Lynn didn't seem to need his reply. "'Rissa drew her a picture. Can you think of something I could give her for her birfday, Pa?"

He decided not to point out that Alison might not be there come spring. Looking into Lynn's pleading eyes, he made another decision. "I think I know something she would like to have now. You can give it to her tomorrow, once I go into town."

"What, Pa? What?" The excitement of the surprise brought the shine back to her face.

"Tomorrow." He wiped away her tears and kissed her nose. "For now—to bed."

She giggled at his low growl, kissed his cheek, then climbed off his lap.

He watched his youngest go. The children were bound to be heartbroken, even if Alison agreed to stay in town. If she left Hope for good, Rafe didn't want to think of the toll it would exact on their young hearts.

Chapter Twenty-Four

....

The following morning Rafe behaved in a peculiar manner. Alison had learned to expect his brooding silence and quicksilver changes in attitude; yet this morning seemed different. Several times she caught him staring, but once she made eye contact, he looked away.

If only she could know what ran through his mind. Did he remember last night and her bold question, almost begging him to declare an affection he refused to acknowledge and more than likely didn't feel? Yet every time her musings took her down that path, she remembered his passionate kisses. They had not come from a man who didn't feel.

Once Rafe and the older children left for town, Alison cleared away the breakfast dishes. Baby Lynn followed her around like a little shadow at her heels, and Alison stopped cleaning to look at her. Her niece smiled.

"Pa said to give you this."

Alison stared in shock; the child held out Amy's journal.

"You're sure your pa told you to give this to me?" Alison barely prevented herself from grabbing it. "He *told* you that?"

She nodded emphatically. "He said you'd like it. And when he left I should give it to you."

It confused her that Rafe didn't give it to her himself. Of course, he'd again chosen to keep his distance. Yet even his rebuff didn't taint her joy to receive the cherished book.

Impatient now to delve into this last cherished link to her sister, she sent Clarissa and Lynn to play outside and took a seat in the rocker. The boards covering the window had been flung wide, making it easy to keep an eye on the girls while at the same time giving her light to read. It still felt strange to see the empty space where the pianoforte once sat, but she felt grateful that Rafe had been able to relinquish at least one part of the past. Perhaps within Amy's journal she could find a clue to help her understand the man who had stolen her heart.

The first pages were filled with their journey. With interest she read about the daily struggles and conquests in traveling with a wagon train and Amy's cautious anticipation when she realized she carried their first child.

> *I think Rafe suspects what I'm almost certain to be true, but I don't wish to tell him until I know for sure. He is ever attentive to me, as always, but this past week has been more so. I tell him that he shouldn't fuss but secretly must admit, I enjoy his loving attentions. How fortunate I am to have found such a man for a husband! All the women on the train tell me so, but I don't need their continual reminders to acknowledge that I am blessed. In the evenings, beneath the starry sky, he plays his violin for me. Surely the angels must weep for joy to hear such glorious music fill the quiet heavens....*

Amy went on to write of her love for her husband, embellishing a few entries with accounts of intimate moments, discreet but filled with delight. Alison felt an odd mix of happiness, to know that Amy had been so blissfully content, along with envy, to realize such joys with Rafe could never be her own to experience. She remembered the kiss they'd shared—could never forget it—and her blood tingled warm throughout her being.

Alison closed the book, deciding to spread the precious entries out instead of reading them all at once. Seeing that the sun had dipped lower, she started the meal.

That evening, Rafe again ignored her, excusing himself from the table to tend to chores in the barn. She refused to allow his detachment to unsettle her, anticipating the hour she could read more of her sister's journal. When the time came to retire to her bedroom, Alison turned up the lamp and eagerly opened the book.

What a remarkable place this Kansas is. Stark yet beautiful in its simplicity and wildness. Here, there isn't a neighbor for miles. It is both a little frightening to be so alone yet exhilarating to feel, however falsely, as if we possess every blade of grass and portion of sky in sight.

Alison would love it here; she often complains about how crowded and noisy the streets of Boston are. Perhaps one day, should the railway come through, as many are saying will happen, she could visit, if she loses her animosity toward Rafe. Oh, what a happy day that would be! I shall not cease praying for it.

"Oh, Amy, if you only knew." Yet she couldn't say aloud, even alone, how the bitterness had at last given way to forgiveness, friendship, and, on her part, love.

Throughout the rest of the week, she took advantage of moments of leisure as an excuse to delve into more of Amy's musings. With Rafe's return to silence and preference for solitude except where his children were concerned, Alison gratefully basked in her sister's private thoughts, at times making Alison feel as if Amy were right there with her.

On the evening before the harvest festival, she stoked the fire to a low flame and opened the journal one last time. Rafe and the children had long retired for the night, and she had the room to herself—with the exception of the sleek tabby, which seemed to prefer snoozing in warm laps to chasing mice in a cold barn.

Sadly she read of Amy's ailments and fears, also lamenting that her sister kept them to herself. It seemed she would have told her husband!

With profound shock Alison read Amy's wishes for Alison and Rafe to meet and find a life together.

She almost dropped the book.

The graceful flow of letters became clouded as her eyes welled with tears. She could scarcely believe the words and read them again. Then she read them a third time.

It was all there. She didn't dream it.

Amy had also desired what Alison wanted and considered pointless to pursue. Had *he* read and understood Amy's last wishes? He must have—he told her he'd read the journal. And he now allowed Alison to read it, despite knowing what Amy had written! The burden of guilt to love her deceased sister's husband, no matter how absurd it had been to bear such shame, crumbled away from her heart, allowing a glimmer of hope to peek through.

Amy had *wanted* this!

But Rafe did not.

Her euphoria deflated as she recalled his return to brooding silence since she had received the book. Likely he meant his attitude as a message to Alison, not to let her hopes escalate because anything more than friendship between them remained out of the question. But these past several days, he had behaved little like a friend either!

Solemnly, she closed the journal, determined not to let Rafe Munroe hurt her again.

She slept fitfully and woke in a miserable state. As the family prepared to attend the celebration, she forced a gaiety she didn't feel, not wanting the children to see her distress.

Sam responded with enthusiasm in receiving Alison's gift of Amy's altered dress. In the sprigged green frock, her niece looked every bit a young lady, receiving both admiration and teasing from her siblings. Rafe looked at his eldest daughter with disbelief.

"My little girl went and grew up behind my back." His voice came gruff with emotion.

He glanced at Alison and gave what passed for a nod of gratitude before he abruptly turned away to ready the wagon.

"Is something wrong with Pa?" Maggie asked. "He's been acting strange for days."

So the children had also noticed his return to aloofness with regard to Alison.

"Your father will be all right," Alison assured with false cheer. "If a matter is troubling him, the festive atmosphere is sure to take it away."

"He's prob'ly frozen clear through, like me," Tucker announced. "It was cold enough in the barn last night to freeze the whiskers off a kitten."

His words made Alison realize she couldn't put off her decision any longer. She had to leave the cabin. Come Monday, she would.

All during the drive into town, Rafe stared ahead without a word to Alison. She wished he would speak to her and stop treating her as a stranger.

A cold bite nipped the wind, and she wrapped her shawl more firmly around her. The children were talkative, excited about the day, save for Sam, who bit her nails and looked as though she might jump out of the moving wagon and race back home. Alison offered an encouraging smile before again shifting her focus ahead. She had helped Sam the best she could. She hoped it would be enough.

The day had dawned sunny and bright, if cold. People flocked in droves along the main street where a stage and podium had been erected. A man, sturdy in physique and well-dressed, stood atop the small stage, a trio of townspeople surrounding him. Alison's assumption that he was the mayor proved correct when minutes later he faced the crowd and gave an effusive smile, spreading his arms wide.

"Welcome, fellow citizens of Hope. I'm pleased so many of you could attend our fine festival." He thanked the townspeople for their support, acknowledging those who'd made a contribution to the cause, and after a lengthy discourse, he dismissed everyone to enjoy the day. As the crowd dispersed, Alison spotted Ivy and moved toward her in enthusiastic greeting. Caleb gave her a warm hug, his smile brilliant, clearly the doting new father as he stood close to Ivy, who held their babe swaddled in a blanket. Alison congratulated them both.

"I need to discuss something with Rafe. Excuse me, ladies."

Alison nodded then turned her smile on Ivy once he'd gone. "I'm so happy for you." She looked at the tiny face within the soft eiderdown. "He's beautiful." Her voice came dreamy.

"Would you like to hold him?"

Alison quickly withdrew her finger from his petal-soft cheek. "Oh, no. I couldn't. I've never held a baby."

"No time like the present to start. You might need the practice some day."

"I doubt that."

"Oh?"

Alison didn't elaborate, her stomach giving an anxious flip as Ivy carefully held the child out to her. Not knowing what else to do, Alison lifted her arms to receive the precious bundle. Her first thought was how very light little Abraham felt; her second, when he opened his big blue eyes, oh so serious and sweet, and stared directly at her, was that she would give every material possession she had to have a priceless child like this of her own.

"He's perfect," she whispered.

"Hello, Mrs. Shaughnessy." Ivy's greeting brought Alison's attention to a silver-haired woman with wire-rimmed spectacles. "Have you two met? This is Miss Alison Stripling."

"Oh, you're the young woman who'll be staying at my boardinghouse?" the newcomer noted with polite enthusiasm. "The room is ready for you, dear, thanks to Mr. Munroe's skill with a hammer. You have only to let me know when you wish to move in."

"Thank you."

"What a lovely hat you have," Mrs. Shaughnessy said with appreciation.

"You like it?" Alison asked in surprise.

"Oh yes, my dear. Such a pretty thing. Did you make it? I heard you were in the millinery business."

"Yes. You might say it's a passion of mine."

Warming to the woman, she conversed with her awhile longer. Mrs. Shaughnessy cooed over the baby before excusing herself to meet a friend.

"So you're staying in Hope?" Ivy turned eagerly toward Alison once Mrs. Shaughnessy left.

"I don't know. Regardless, I'll need to move out Monday."

"So soon?" Ivy looked at her in surprise. "Do Rafe and the children know?"

"I'll tell them after we return from the festival."

"But you haven't decided where you'll go?"

"No, and that's unusual for me," she confessed. "I've often jumped into situations without thinking things through. Now I'm doing the opposite."

"Perhaps deep in your heart you don't want to go. And I know this sounds horribly selfish, but I hope you'll stay in Hope. Whatever you decide, Caleb would be happy to help you move. We discussed it, and with Rafe busy in these carpentry projects of his, Caleb would like to offer a hand."

Alison accepted with gratitude. She hated good-byes and felt it would be far less taxing on her emotions if she left when Rafe wasn't home. It would be bad enough leaving the children. Even if she did remain in Hope, it wouldn't be the same. She could no longer share in their daily trials and triumphs.

"Are you all right?" Ivy looked concerned. "You look upset."

"I'm fine." She handed the baby back, managing a smile.

The day passed in a flurry of activity and endless introductions, until Alison felt she must have met every citizen. Many of the ladies brought baked goods to share, and sweet cider had been provided to wet throats, which quickly went dry from conversation. Ivy shared an amused look with Alison as they both recalled the awful cider experience at the cabin. A spirit of easy camaraderie permeated the atmosphere, and she felt that perhaps she *could* make this her home.

If only the situation between her and Rafe wasn't so unsettling. She wished he would look at her and resume their acquaintance. But she supposed that was hoping for too much. Anything he felt might be a betrayal to Amy's memory he would never consider. She knew his feelings the first day she arrived, had resigned herself to them, so why did the sting of his rejection make her heart ache as strongly as if he'd just snubbed her?

The time came for Sam's speech, and Alison noticed how pale her face was. She put her hands on her niece's stiff shoulders, bending to see eye to eye with her.

"Remember what I told you this morning, Sam."

"That I'm to think of them as little children who once had to stand in front of grown-ups, and many at one time or another had to speak in front of adults and their peers—and they're still alive to tell about it, so I'll be fine too?"

Alison laughed. "Yes, exactly. Your speech is wonderful. I have every confidence that you'll excel and give a fine presentation."

Sam nodded and moved to take the stand. Her schoolteacher took the podium first, introducing Sam as her top student to the crowds that remained. Many people had gravitated to other areas of the street, talking in groups, or had returned to their homes, and Alison assumed Sam felt thankful for the diminished crowd.

Sam gave a stiff little curtsy, much to Alison's surprise and pleasure that her niece had received something beneficial from the etiquette lessons. "Dear fellow citizens of Hope..."

Slight nods and smiles of approval from a few of the men and women ensured that Sam had already won their hearts.

"Hope is more than the town in which we live; it's the daily fabric of our lives. On this day we give thanks to the Lord for the harvest. Some citizens have been more fortunate than others, who didn't see the bounty of their crops, but we support one another as a community and look forward to next year, planting our seed and tilling the land, secure in the faith that God will see us through any storm we might face...."

Alison listened with pride as Sam delivered her speech as if she'd been born to the podium. She touched on the founding fathers of Hope, and cited the booming growth of their town in the almost two decades since that time, closing with her own message of hope.

"My uncle Caleb, some of you might know him. He's standing over there." Sam pointed him out, and Alison felt a defeated smile lift her lips at the girl's lapse in manners. A few snickers gravitated through the crowd as Caleb doffed his hat with a charming bow. Even Rafe, standing beside him, grinned.

"He says there'll always be hope in Kansas. Lately I've come to realize what that means. Once my mother went to live with the angels, I feared nothing would be right again. And then my aunt Alison came to town...."

Her face warming to what must be crimson, Alison listened in wide-eyed shock while Sam continued the impromptu and unre-hearsed addition to her speech.

"She's taught us so much. She helped me with this speech, and she taught our family to hope again. And to laugh. Pa resumed play-ing his violin, and there's music in the cabin almost every night. If it weren't for Aunt Alison, things wouldn't be as good as they are now. My brothers are learning manners, us girls are learning to be ladies, and Pa's smiling again."

Amused titters spread throughout the area. Rafe met Alison's gaze across the crowd. He was far from smiling. In his expression she read his distress.

"It's to my aunt I wish to dedicate this speech in gratitude for all she's done." Sam curtsied again. "Thank you."

Rafe swiftly broke eye contact with Alison, turning his head away.

And in that moment Alison made her decision.

She bent to kiss Baby Lynn's cheek. "Stay with your sisters and be a good girl." She tugged the bonnet more firmly around her curly head and softly ordered Clarissa and Maggie to watch the child. Smiling over her tears, she hugged each of them.

"Is something wrong, Auntie Alison?" Clarissa asked.

"I need to talk to your aunt Ivy," she explained, unable to say more.

She found her friend standing apart from the crowd in a spot out of the wind. "Is your offer to help me move available today?"

Ivy regarded her with surprise. "You want to leave now?"

"It's best for all involved. But I don't want Rafe to know. Can you talk to Caleb without him being the wiser?"

"Yes—I need to get Abraham home anyhow. But, Alison, are you sure you want to do this?"

"It's cruel to go on allowing the children to hope for something that will never happen." She couldn't add the rest—that she herself could no longer bear Rafe's continual disregard. This was no decision she had rushed to make; it was a truth she had avoided for weeks. She was not their ma. She would never be anyone's ma. She would never be Rafe's wife.

Ivy's eyes clouded. "You're leaving us, aren't you?"

Alison nodded and Ivy reached out to hug her. "I hope you truly know what you're doing and don't come to regret this," she whispered in her ear before letting her go.

Ivy left to talk to Caleb, while Alison worked not to give in to the tears that had been building since Rafe again snubbed her. To her relief, soon she sat in Caleb and Ivy's wagon on the way to Rafe's cabin. Once there, she packed her things. She needed to hurry but felt she should at least compose a farewell note. Now and then dashing away a stubborn tear that clouded her vision, she scratched out a brief but loving missive to the children, also thanking Rafe for his courtesy as her host. "I'm ready," she said quietly to Caleb as he came for her trunk. He hadn't smiled once since he'd driven her from town, and she felt his disapproval as thick as the shawl around her shoulders, though thankfully he only nodded in reply.

Once at the boardinghouse, Caleb went to the door first to make sure Mrs. Shaughnessy had returned from the celebration. Alison held her breath, darting nervous glances around the area, sure Rafe or one of the children might suddenly appear and spot her.

Ivy hugged her, holding the baby with one arm. "I don't like this, not one bit. I had hoped that we might share our days and grow old together with our families."

Alison hugged her tightly and kissed her cheek. "You've become very dear to me. But this is something I have to do. Please understand. I promise to write, and you must fill me in on everything concerning the children."

"Of course."

At the doorstep, her farewell to Caleb came brief but just as emotional. He hugged her, making her promise to consider carefully her next step and not rush into anything.

"Believe me, Caleb, I have considered. My future isn't in Hope as I once thought."

He looked troubled by her admission and clasped her hand in both of his one last time. "Then I wish you well and pray that God's blessings abound in your life. Never forget that when we flounder with questions, the Lord has the answers."

"I won't forget."

Once her friends left, it was all Alison could do not to break down in an emotional display of grief and maintain a calm she didn't feel. Mrs. Shaunghnessy studied her in concern.

"Are you all right, dear?"

"Yes, thank you."

"I'm sorry to see you leave us so soon and me just getting to know you, but of course you may have the room for the night. It's the first one on the left at the bend of the stairs."

"If you'll tell me how much I owe, I'd like to pay now. Also, I'll need someone to take my trunk to the station in the morning."

"Oh, I couldn't take a dime. Please, since you'll be here only this one night, stay as my guest. My nephew can take your trunk to the station."

"Thank you so much. You're very kind."

Alison felt emotion again tighten her throat at yet another example of the benevolence she'd found in Hope. To curb another onset of tears, she pulled the hat pin from her hat and held her creation out to the woman. "Please, take this as a gift to show my gratitude."

"Oh!" Mrs. Shaughnessy eyed the hat with a mixture of anticipation and reluctance. "I couldn't take your pretty hat."

"Please. I insist. I can always make another."

It didn't take a second offer for the woman to happily accept. Though gratified that someone at last respected the fruits of her hard labor, Alison almost sadly laughed at her final sight of the poor scorned hat with its proud feather, which in a peculiar way had spurred her decision for coming to Hope.

Turning away before she humiliated herself in a torrent of tears, she hastened to her room.

Chapter Twenty-Five

....

Rafe gravely stared at the downcast faces of his children, struggling with what to say. His gaze again lowered to Alison's gentle words of farewell.

"We have to respect her decision," he said at last. "We can't change that."

"But why did she leave without saying good-bye?" Maggie sniffed and swiped away the moisture on her cheeks with her palm.

"Sometimes good-bye is too hard to say. Maybe she wanted to spare your feelings."

He suddenly thought of Amy's journal, realizing that his wife had done the same. But her omission hadn't spared his feelings, and Alison's unexplained departure certainly hadn't given his family less grief.

Sam held Baby Lynn, who hadn't stopped crying since Rafe learned Alison left the celebration. Worried, he had herded his children into the wagon and returned to the cabin, expecting to find her there. She'd been absent, but his brother soon arrived and told them what she'd also stated in the letter—that she would be returning to Boston tomorrow. To Rafe's shocked confusion, Caleb said very little to him in parting. His brother had never minced words before, but he'd only shaken his hand solemnly, his eyes serious.

"You got what you wanted. I hope it truly makes you happy." His words had been sincere, but Rafe didn't feel the relief that should have been his.

"It's my fault," Sam said sullenly, breaking into his thoughts. "I shouldn't have added that to my speech. I scared her away."

"No." Rafe held out his arm to her and she went to him. He hugged her, feeling her tremble with the sorrow she tried so hard to contain. "Your speech was wonderful. She said so in the letter. This was a decision she's been struggling with for some time."

"But why'd she decide to leave so suddenly if my words didn't push her there?" Sam insisted.

That was a question Rafe also wanted answered.

"She did what she thought best for everyone concerned."

"Now she won't get the present I've been making her for Christmas," Maggie said sadly. "I was sewing flowers on a handkerchief I made from a scrap of muslin. I was going to put her initials on too."

"We can send it to her through the post." Again his feeble comfort didn't erase the misery from their faces. He sighed. "We should all turn in early. It's been a long day."

After a chorus of dejected good nights and halfhearted hugs, the children trudged up to the loft. For the first time in months, Rafe entered his bedroom. Shortly after Amy died, he'd been unable to enter the room they shared and had slept by the hearth. When he resumed sleeping there, everything in the room reminded him of her—but now as he looked around, he could only think of Alison.

Amy's journal lay on a small crate used for a table, and sitting beside that was the bottle of healing balm he'd given Alison for her hands. He recalled the disaster of her first wash day added to all the other little disasters, as she worked to excel in skills like cooking, while purposely giving her worst in other things, to help him in his plan.

The bed was made, the blanket spread over it as if it had never been occupied, but the pillow bore traces of her scent—a fragrant aroma of cloves and lemongrass he assumed she'd used in some sort of oil to perfume her hair or skin. He spotted a long strand of hair on the casing, hair dark as midnight with a moonlit sheen, and grunted in self-mockery. Now he was waxing poetic, likely from reading Amy's prose.

And why was he thinking about Alison?

He shouldn't but couldn't help himself. She might have been absent from his home, but her presence lingered.

In frustration, he moved into the main room. The cinders glowed and he stoked them to life again. Idly he stared into the flames, recalling Alison's spunk and spirit and the warmth of her smile that felt like a balm to his soul. He stared toward the stove, imagining the last sight of her he'd had there: pulling a pan of cornbread from the oven, her expression tense as she eyed it in uncertainty, hoping she'd at last achieved perfection. Her dark eyes had caught his staring at her, and she'd given a little shrug.

"At least it's not burnt at the edges this time."

He had looked away at her light, forced words, unable to stare at her without wanting to take her in his arms and reassure her. Hold her. Kiss her...

He shook his head, trying to free it of such thoughts.

She wanted distance. So did he. It was for the best...wasn't it?

He looked around the quiet cabin, but the emptiness gave no peace. The room felt hollow, recent memories of her mocking him. He could imagine her in every corner he looked, just as he'd last seen her there. Smiling, laughing, shaking her finger at the boys in reprimand for teasing their sisters, baking, cleaning, humming, singing, offering encouragement and comfort and everything a mother should be to his children. Offering, without words, every-thing a man could want in a wife. He told himself for months that he never again wanted to marry, feeling pressured from all sides. First by Caleb, then his children, and finally, silently, by Alison.

No one pushed him to take a wife anymore, having clearly given up the cause. Ironically, where before he'd run from the idea, now, with no one to persuade him any longer, *now* he couldn't stop think-ing about it. Did he know what he really wanted? Had the truth been staring him in the face all along and he'd been too dim-witted to see?

He stood before the hearth, leaning with one hand on the man-tel, and stared at the low, crackling flames, losing all track of time. Memories of Amy and Alison blended in a strange whirl, causing him to recall Amy's last journal entry: *"If only Rafe could meet Ali-son and they could find a life together, this would be my ultimate wish. Yet with her in Boston and Rafe in Kansas, I fear such a hope is unattainable...."*

How bizarre that Amy's wish for Alison to come to Hope *had* come to pass. Or was it...? What if it was all part of a bigger plan than even his children could have conceived?

A tread on the stairs made him swing his gaze toward the sound. It took a moment for his sleep-deprived mind to register the sight of his eldest, still dressed in his day clothes. "Andy? What are you doing up at this hour?"

Andy eyed him in wary concern. "It's dawn, Pa. A new day."

"Is it?" Rafe looked toward the boarded window where chinks of gray light formed a square. "So it is...."

"You all right, Pa?"

Rafe continued to stare at the square of light. An unexplainable flicker of hope caught inside his heart and built to a steady all-out blaze. "Fine, Andy. Just fine. Couldn't be better."

He snatched up his coat and hat just as Sam came downstairs.

"Pa? Where are you heading off to so early?" She also looked confused. "Don't you want breakfast?"

"Haven't got the time."

He opened the door and looked back at his two oldest children, who'd both tried so hard to keep the family going when he'd been unable to manage the effort. They may not always have made the wisest choices, but then again, neither had he. His children—all of them—deserved the best he could give.

"I've got a train to catch."

"A train?" A glimmer of expectation warmed Sam's voice.

He smiled. "I'm going to go get your aunt Alison and bring her back home where she belongs."

He stepped outdoors, hearing their whoops and hollers followed by Sam's urgent summons to the other children to wake up, but he didn't linger. He had to hurry if he wanted to catch the morning train to Boston.

* * * * *

Alison sank to the bench seat by the window. How different her mood had been the last time she'd boarded a train. Then, she'd been filled with such hope...but any of that emotion would be left behind in the town of the same name.

She had the seat to herself and felt grateful that no onlookers would notice the stray tear that occasionally slid down her cheek and she whisked away. She felt relieved to be on a train, headed toward her destination—and heartbroken to leave this little area of Kansas she'd come to think of as home. No matter that she'd been bred in high society, here she finally felt as if she fit in and didn't stand out among the crowd for a history she couldn't help or change. Yes, she'd made mistakes, but so had everyone who'd become a pioneer in this wild land, and that made her like them, not different. Not separate from her peers, as had been her lot in Boston.

"Mind if I sit here?" A pleasant voice cut into her thoughts, and she looked up at the newcomer. Short and plump with hair in tight sausage curls, a woman likely in her forties smiled at her in greeting.

Alison whisked away another tear, giving a smile. "Please do."

Her train companion tsked in concern. "Your first time away from home?"

"What?" Her mind distracted, it took a moment to comprehend the question. "Oh, no. Boston is where I live." Strange how peculiar the words felt. Once it had seemed like home, but now...

"And where is your husband, dear? Is he traveling with you? I hope I haven't taken his seat."

"My husband?" Alison blinked. The traveling gloves that covered her hands concealed her lack of a wedding ring. "Oh, I'm not married."

"A fellow waiting in Boston, then?"

"No. There's no one."

"A sweet and pretty thing like you?" The woman shook her graying head of curls. "That's mighty hard to believe. Well, I'm a widow myself. Going on five years now. I'm traveling to Massachusetts to live with my daughter and her new husband. I'm Matilda Hubbard, by the way, and you are?"

"Alison Stripling."

"I'm pleased to make your acquaintance, Miss Stripling. I do hope the travel won't be tedious. It's my first time to travel cross-country by train. My dear Alfred and I, God rest his soul, came to

Kansas by wagon near thirty years ago, when nary a building was in sight...." She continued to tell Alison about her life in a cheerful manner, strongly reminiscent of Aunt Eliza. Thankful to have pleasant company to distract her mind from somber reminiscing, Alison listened while passengers filled the train and the time to depart drew near.

As Matilda spoke, her eyes darted to the window every now and then. She ended her discourse on the wonderful traits of her new son-in-law, her gaze finally coming to and remaining fixed on the window.

"It appears you left someone waiting," she said with an amused smile. "And he seems intent on gaining your attention."

Her stomach giving a little flip, Alison turned to look...and stared in disbelief.

Head and shoulders above the rest, Rafe stood on the platform, his eyes keen on her.

"Alison—come out here!"

Stunned to see him where he shouldn't be, she blinked, barely hearing his command. At the frantic expression on his face, alarm made her go cold. Had something happened to one of the children?

Quickly she stood. "Excuse me, please."

"Of course, dear. I do hope everything's all right."

So did Alison. For what possible purpose could Rafe meet her train unless he brought bad news?

She hurried to the exit, nodding in reply to the steward's warning that they would be leaving shortly. Rafe met her as she stepped onto the platform and grasped her upper arm, practically pulling her from the train.

"Rafe! Whatever's gotten into you?"

"You're not going anywhere."

"Excuse me?" She blinked in confusion. They moved out of the way of others, but he didn't release his hold. "Has one of the children had an accident? Is someone ill?"

"The children are fine. In body. Their hearts, on the other hand, are aching something fierce."

She knew he referred to her swift departure and felt ashamed to have hurt them. He seemed nervous, desperate, unlike his usual aloof self. He didn't smile, but he wasn't somber either. She had no idea how to describe his behavior, except to call it bizarre.

"Well, then, why did you come?"

His stormy blue eyes held hers. "We need to come up with another plan. A fifth one."

Her mouth dropped open at his absurd words. "A fifth one?"

He gave a stiff nod. "A better plan."

"Better..."

His solemn response ruffled her calm, causing her reply to come stiffly.

Did he truly have no concept of the toll he exacted upon her shattered heart by his inane words, by his unasked-for presence here? Alison detested good-byes and had hoped to never see his face again.... No, that wasn't exactly true, but the future she wanted she couldn't have, and she didn't want to prolong the inevitable.

"We don't need another plan. You achieved your purpose to send me packing. Now I have a train to catch. Excuse me."

Her irritation mounting, she broke away from him but only took a few steps when he grabbed her arm again and whirled her around. She gaped at his uncharacteristic behavior. His eyes burned into hers, intense.

"That was a bad plan. It had no chance of working."

She shook her head. "Whatever do you—"

"We need a plan for you to stay."

Her heart gave a jolt as if it might burst from her chest. "Why?"

"The children need you. They need a ma."

"I—I don't understand." She had begun to but shied away from hoping too much. "This is a complete turnabout from your earlier perspective of the situa—"

The shrill sound of the train whistle signaling departure interrupted her and he hurriedly said, "I've had time to consider."

"Consider what?"

He glanced toward the train. "We need to get your trunk off before it leaves."

At his high-handed attitude, she again broke away from him and crossed her arms over her chest. "You'll have to do a good sight better than that, Rafe Munroe, if you don't want me getting back on that train."

A glimmer of admiration lit his eyes though he still looked as if his nerves were frazzled.

"Alison Stripling, you are one stubborn woman." To her shock, he closed the distance she'd put between them and lifted his hands to her shoulders, clasping them in a firm but gentle manner. "*I* need you."

"To wash and cook for you?" She forced the words out of a suddenly dry throat.

"To be my wife."

A lifetime of lessons in proper decorum had no effect as her mouth dropped completely open and she gaped at him like a fish.

Surely she must be in the midst of one of her dreams. He awkwardly fell to one knee and took her hand in both of his. A few onlookers gathered but her mind felt about as clear as corn mush and she could only stare at Rafe.

"I've been a downright fool, Alison. You're as fine a woman as they come. Any man would be lucky to have you. Would you do me that honor?"

She couldn't force her mind to cooperate with her tongue. Was it only less than five minutes ago she'd been sitting inside a train, preparing to leave Hope?

His thumb stroked her hand through her glove, sending little shock waves coursing along her spine. "You taught me what it means to hope again, hope I never thought I'd have."

Tenderness touched his face and eyes, making them shine with an emotion she'd never seen before. Dare she call it love?

Her hands trembling, she brought her other one to cover his. "I do care deeply for you, Rafe. I—I have for some time. But as much as I loved my sister, I can't be a stand-in for Amy." She tried to form her whirling thoughts into logical words. "I'm not asking you to forget her or the memories you shared. That would be cruel as well as impossible. I just—it's only that—well, I need more." Her face warmed, and she lowered her voice. "I don't want to be merely a housemaid and substitute mother. I need some show of lasting affection, and as you can't give me that, I don't see how this new plan of yours can work...."

She'd barely uttered the last words when he shot to his feet. He towered over her, making her feel weak next to his strength. His eyes were glazed over with an expression that rendered her breathless.

"Lasting affection? I'm telling you that I love you, Alison Stripling. And I was blind not to see it before!"

She had no chance to breathe an answer as his large hands moved to cradle her head and his mouth came down firmly on hers. She inhaled a startled breath at the sudden coolness of his lips and the feel of his hands on her skin, all of which quickly warmed, as did their kiss. With no other thought but Rafe, Alison wound her arms around his neck.

The sudden amused clearing of a man's throat brought them to startled awareness of their surroundings. Rafe pulled away with a muffled apology and glanced at the stationmaster who'd drawn near. The man's jowls shook with contained laughter. Alison's face went flame-hot at the realization of their public demonstration of affection, but she couldn't contain the bubble of laughter that exploded from her throat to experience such happiness she'd never thought to have.

Rafe smiled at her, his expression oddly both mischievous and sheepish, reminding her of an older version of his children. Suddenly his eyes went wide. "Your trunk!"

Alison noticed with shock that the train was moving. "I left my carpetbag onboard too!"

"Not to worry, folks," the stationmaster reassured. "I'll send a wire ahead for them to deliver your things back here on the next train."

"Thank you." Alison felt confident that Matilda would keep an eye on her bag.

"Seems to me you still owe your fellah an answer."

Shyly she glanced down at the platform then up at Rafe. In all her days, she'd never envisioned a proposal such as this one, with half the passengers looking on and...a proposal...

A *proposal!*

Her foggy mind suddenly made sense of why Rafe had come.

"Did you just ask me to marry you?" she breathed in a daze, still not sure she'd heard correctly and it wasn't all a dream.

Rafe's brows lifted in clear disbelief, as if he couldn't figure her out.

The stationmaster chuckled. "Well, I'll just leave you to talk things over." He tipped his hat to her and, whistling a merry tune, walked away.

"Did you?" she insisted again, worried now she'd only imagined it.

"I did." His fingers lifted to trace her cheek, and she realized then that she was crying. "It took my heart time to realize what my mind's known all along but was buried too deep to understand." His voice came low and gentle. "I love you, Alison, and if you need me to tell you that every day until we're in our dotage, I'll do it. I *want* to marry you—today, if Caleb can manage it. What do you say? Or—maybe it's too much to ask after all that's happened? And you did say once you didn't want a man with a passel of kids—"

Noting the sudden anxiety clouding his eyes, she wanted to kiss him into silence but settled for smiling softly at him instead, not wishing to give the bystanders more to talk about.

"Rafe, I would be honored to be your wife. It's all I've wanted. To make a home with you. To be a mother to your children." *And to give you more*, she added silently, too cautious with this astounding turn in their relationship to voice the rest. "I love you too."

"Then you'll marry me? Today," he urged, his eyes now shining with all she had hoped to see there. "We can go back home and collect the children and be married before noon."

"Yes." She nodded, choking down little sobs of joy.

"Yes?" he repeated, putting his hands to her shoulders, as if to make sure.

"Yes, Rafe, I'll marry you, whenever you wish—"

Her words were cut off as he hugged her close and kissed her again, lifting her off the platform.

* * * * *

Before the noon hour arrived, they stood in Caleb and Ivy's small parlor with the children gathered around. Alison felt as if she dwelt in the clouds.

"Do you have a ring?" Caleb asked Rafe.

"A ring." Rafe looked stricken. "I plumb forgot about a ring."

Alison also grew worried. "Will our vows still be acceptable under the eyes of God?"

"Oh, definitely," Caleb assured with a smile. "The ring is only symbolic of your pledge."

"Here." Ivy hurried forward with a few inches of white yarn dangling from her fingertips. Alison recognized it as a fringe of the blanket she'd made for Abraham. "Will this do?"

"Don't see why not." Caleb nodded and Rafe took the strand, tying it around Alison's naked finger. His eyes lifted to hers once he'd made the knot. "I promise that one day a circle of gold will replace that string."

Her heart too full of joy to care either way, she told him so. "All I'll ever need I now have."

They continued staring into each other's eyes as Caleb recited the ceremony. After exchanging vows, Rafe kissed her a third time that day, setting her mind, heart, and body in a whirl. Alison decided she could quickly become dependent on such delightful treatment.

The children rushed forward to embrace them, the youngest girls giggling.

"Does this mean I can call you Ma?" Baby Lynn's eyes shone big with hope.

Alison shared an amused glance with Rafe, who gave a little nod of approval. She cupped the child's curly head. "I would be most honored."

"Yay!" Baby Lynn hugged her close.

"You know the best thing about Pa marrying Aunt Alison?" Tucker put in. "We got her back with us—*and* we don't have to sleep in the barn no more!"

Everyone laughed, and Alison's face flushed with warmth when she thought of sharing a bed with Rafe. He gently smiled at her, easing the nervous fluttering in her midsection at the thought of what that meant, of what he would teach her that meant. The love she thought never to see in his eyes filled her heart to overflowing, and she eagerly anticipated their future together.

Ivy invited them to lunch and the others moved away, leaving Rafe and Alison alone.

"When did you know you loved me?" she whispered.

"It became clear after I lost you. I knew I had to do everything I could to win you back. But you began finding your way into my heart the night of the storm, when you were so gentle and encouraging and full of faith. Maybe before that, when I saw you in that hat with the ridiculous feather blowing every which way." At his evident teasing, she laughed. He drew his brows together as if just realizing she wore another. "Where is that hat?"

"I gave it away."

"I'll miss it."

"I'll make another."

He chuckled. "You, my dear Alison, are a woman of considerable talents. Even your skills in the kitchen are improving. That is, when it doesn't involve corn bread."

"Hmph." She smiled in mock effrontery. "I promise you, my dear darling Rafe, that before the year is through I *will* make a decent batch and not burn it."

"Oh, I have no doubt. I think you can do anything you set your mind to."

"Perhaps so. I got you to fall in love with me, didn't I?"

He grinned. "That wasn't exactly hard to do. It just took more time than it should have to realize."

They chuckled low at their banter, Alison's heart light with happiness for the future she'd always wanted. With a man, *this man*, and a family to call her own. Was this day, this moment, truly real? Rafe drew her into a warm embrace, assuring her it must be.

And to think, she owed the commencement of her dreams to the mix-up of one silly hat and the mischief of five dear children. But the ending result was perfect, and God's grace had again paved a way through the storm.

Surely no citizen of Hope could be more blessed.

Epilogue

....

Fourteen months later

"What do you think's in the box, Ma?" Lynn clasped her hands under her chin, thrilled with the prospect of receiving a parcel by post.

"Hush, now." Rafe swung her up on his shoulder, and she gave an excited squeal.

Alison leveled a look his way. "I just put the baby down for a nap."

"Sorry." Despite that he carried a lively tot, Rafe bent to kiss her temple, and Alison smiled in forgiveness. True, little Gabriel, named for Rafe's grandfather, had been up half the night with colic, but she couldn't stay angry with her husband for long. The crops had been good, and her family was together, safe and happy. This was a perfect Christmas.

As Alison watched Rafe set Lynn down, her mind took a journey through the last year.

For a short time, when she carried little Gabriel, Rafe's old fears of the past collided with those of the present, tormenting him, and he'd been afraid he would lose her as he'd lost Amy. He had returned to gloominess, becoming withdrawn. But she'd been patient, assuring him she was strong and healthy and would never keep anything important secret from him. Over those months, the bond between them strengthened as they shared their qualms, also sharing in memories of Amy. Alison didn't mind him speaking of his life with her sister, since she knew she now had his love as well, and she enjoyed telling both Rafe and the children stories from their childhood.

"When Amy and I were children, Aunt Eliza would send a parcel at Christmastime just like this one. Though we preferred it when they would visit. She smelled so nice, and Uncle Bernard carried hard candies in his pocket he would give to us."

"I like the way you smell, Ma." Maggie put a hand to her shoulder. Still a tomboy, she had begun to display a few signs of becoming a little lady.

"Hurry, Pa! I'm gonna expire if I don't find out what's inside that box!"

Alison held back a laugh at Tucker's use of new vocabulary. "Give your pa a minute to catch his breath." Both boys had learned they didn't detest reading; the adventurous classics Alison shared with them had piqued their interest and improved their minds.

Andy looked every bit as eager but remained more sedate than his siblings. Almost a man, his interests had gravitated toward planning his own future, and Alison had more than a sneaking suspicion that the pretty brown-haired girl who sat in the third row at church played a big part in Andy's plans. She'd also been instrumental in getting him to realize that good grammar wasn't so bad after all, and his attitude about being ignorant had swiftly—gone to the river.

The sweet sound of a soft bleating cry melted Alison's heart as it always did, and she began to rise from the table.

"I'll get him," Samantha offered. Alison watched her move to the cradle Rafe had crafted, thinking what a fine mother she would make one day. And that day wasn't long in coming. The rejection of her boyish nickname had been the first sign she wanted to be thought of as a young lady.

Alison felt a dose of bittersweet nostalgia to realize how swiftly the children were growing up. She was proud to see how far they'd come from the mischief-makers who'd once plotted to find their pa a wife.

On second thought, she silently applauded their meddling.

Turning her attention to the crate Rafe pried open, she withdrew parcels each labeled with the recipient's name. For Alison, she found a beautiful sampler that read, "To Have Hope Is to Live Each Day to Its Fullest Measure." Beneath those words, Aunt Eliza had stitched a Bible verse: *"Therefore my heart is glad, and my glory rejoiceth: my flesh also shall rest in hope"* (Psalm 16:9).

Rafe stared in shock once he unwrapped a fine leather violin case lined in velvet. He looked up at Alison, moisture rimming his eyes. "You told her about my battered one?"

Alison nodded with a smile. He deserved the very best.

The children exulted over their gifts. Sam received a journal; Clarissa, a musical box with a ballerina; and for Maggie there was a book on animals. Lynn received a doll with a china face, and each of the boys smiled to get an ivory-handled pocketknife. Alison shook her head in wonder as each extravagant gift was uncovered. Finally, she unwrapped a soft woolen baby bunting for little Gabriel, sure to keep him warm through the winter.

"Play for us, Pa!" Clarissa begged. In the past year she'd grown taller and more slender, her love of the dance never fading. Aunt Eliza had invited her to Boston, writing to Alison that she would gladly provide lessons for the child. Rafe and Alison had discussed it long into the night and decided to accept her aunt's generous offer once Clarissa was twelve, which as rapidly as the years passed, wouldn't be long in coming.

"I'm too tuckered out tonight, honey. Maybe tomorrow."

With a secretive smile Alison went into their bedroom to pull her flute from her trunk. Within two months of marrying Rafe, she had discovered she was with child and often felt too weary to play, besides the fact she'd been too enamored of her husband's beautiful music on the violin to make her own. Music making had become a tradition in their household. Even Maggie had taken an interest in learning to play her father's violin. Samantha excelled in playing the pianoforte and now played every Sunday in Caleb's church. Even Little Lynn, no longer called "Baby," had begged Andy to show her how to play his harmonica.

Alison returned to the main room. "Well, it simply wouldn't do not to have music. This is a time for celebration!"

She curbed a laugh at the horrified looks on the children's faces. Even her own dear Rafe's eyes went a little wide with alarm.

"We—um, don't have to have music," Maggie put in hastily.

"I thought I might try to play my harmonica."

"Oh?" Alison looked at Andy in concern. "That cut on your lip still looks painful."

"If he wouldn't stop mooning over Abigail, he wouldn't have run smack-dab into that door and split his lip," Tucker said in disgust.

"We could sing," Clarissa offered hopefully.

The baby began to fuss and Samantha jiggled him in her arms. "I think he needs you."

If Alison didn't recognize her comment for the excuse it was, she would have complied.

With a smile she shook her head. "What he needs is a lullaby. I just fed and changed him. Now hush, children. It's high time I did my part to provide a night of music for this family."

"But—"

"You heard your ma," Rafe put in a bit sternly. Bless his dear heart, he also looked as if the prospect of her making music didn't bring pleasure. But who could blame him after her horrendous display? Regardless, he supported her and she loved him for it.

"Yes, Pa," a few of the children meekly responded.

Alison pulled the flute from its case. "I once told you this instrument could have been made for the angels, it can sound so heavenly. On this night, when we celebrate our Lord's birth, it seems the perfect way to give thanks."

She lifted the flute to her lips and began playing a gentle melody with as much skill as she possessed. It had been awhile since she held a flute, and it took her a few stanzas to achieve the sound she wished to create—but the stunned expressions of her beloved family satisfied her that now they knew the truth, and by their smiles they approved.

"You sure had us fooled!" Andy exclaimed when she finished the song.

"You can play?" Clarissa's eyes were wide.

"You really *can* play!" Samantha laughed in delight. "I remember when Ma used to sing that song, and you played it so beautifully."

"What's it called?" Lynn asked.

"'Silent Night.'"

"We sure don't get much of that around here," Tucker observed.

"Oh, hush," Samantha said to him.

"What? What did I say?"

Rafe stared at Alison, shaking his head a little in amazement. He took her hand, pulling her down to sit beside him. The children returned to occupying themselves with their presents, absorbed in their activities, and paid no attention to them.

"Again, you amaze me," Rafe said in frank admiration, lifting her hand to press his lips to her palm then lowering it to hold in his lap. "Most men hope to find great love once in a lifetime. I'm highly fortunate because I've known such love twice."

At his whispered declaration, her heart sang, and she laid her free hand against his jaw. "I love you with all that I am, Rafe Munroe, for all of my lifetime."

He smiled, his eyes glowing with tenderness. "Where did you learn to play like that? We should start performing duets."

The idea of them making beautiful melodies together appealed. "I've always been fond of music, and after hearing a flutist at a social gathering, I was entranced. My aunt saw to it that I had lessons. I'm horribly out of practice, but while I feel up to it, I'd like to play when I can—"

"While you feel up to it?" Rafe caught her little slip, and she felt her face warm. Alarm filled his eyes. "Alison, are you ill?"

At his troubled whisper, she hurried to assure him. "No, my love, I'm in perfect health. As a matter of fact…" She hadn't wanted to tell him like this, but it seemed a perfect opportunity and she wished to erase the fearful concern that clouded his eyes. "I think I should practice with lullabies. I'll need to play them for some time to come."

He shook his head in confusion, and she giggled at his bewildered expression. She would think that after having sired eight children—make that nine—he would understand what she didn't say.

She covered his hand with hers. "It would seem that your last plan—to become a real family—is working exceedingly well. Not only are the children happy, healthy, and improving in manners, I believe they'll have a new brother or sister come summer."

A little thrill went through her at the manner in which his eyes widened and his mouth parted. She lightly kissed that mouth and pulled back to nod in affirmation.

"Yes, my darling. I'm with child."

For the longest moment, Rafe didn't speak. When he did respond, he did so in a manner that made Alison go warm all over, by leaning toward her and again pressing his lips to hers in a long, slow kiss, as if he'd forgotten the children were in the room.

"Did you hear?" Maggie, who'd been paying more attention than Alison realized, hailed her siblings. "Ma's going to have another baby!"

"Really?" Sam straightened from putting little Gabriel in his cradle.

"Can we have a girl this time?" Clarissa asked hopefully.

"Make it another boy," Tucker insisted. "There's too many girls in this family."

"Says who?" Maggie's fists went to her hips.

"Me, that's who. Fair's fair, and we need to even things out around here."

"Well, it doesn't work like that." Alison quickly intercepted a brewing argument.

"How does it work, Ma?" Lynn wanted to know. "How do babies get here?"

Alison's face burned hot and Rafe's shoulders shook against hers as he stifled a laugh. She sent a sober, quelling look his way, lifting her brows.

"Would you care to explain, darling?"

"That's a discussion best saved for when they're older. Say in their thirties," he added under his breath.

Alison let out the laugh that had been building and sought for a suitable way to appease their curiosity. "Whatever child God sends us will be the baby He most wants us to love as part of our family. All of you love little Gabriel, don't you?"

"Oh, yes," a chorus of girlish voices gave their approval.

"'Course I do," Tucker said. "He's a boy, ain't he?"

"Oh, you!" Maggie slapped his arm. "You're incorrigible!"

"Watch it—I know what that word means now."

"Enough." Rafe shook his head in weary surrender, though his tone brooked no refusal. "Your ma wasn't finished talking."

Alison squeezed his hand. "I can promise that as much as you love Gabriel, you'll love this new baby when it comes, whether it be a brother or a sister."

Rafe gave her an approving smile for how she handled the awkward situation.

"How does it know when it's time to come?" Clarissa asked.

"God knows the perfect time." Alison smiled.

"Just like He knew when the perfect time was for Jesus to come?"

"Yes. He had that planned from the start."

"Will you tell us the Christmas story again?" Maggie pleaded. "And the part about the angel Gabriel telling Jesus's ma about him too!"

"Of course."

"Did God tell you about the new baby brother or sister?" Lynn wanted to know.

"Well, in a sense." Besides her queasy stomach and lack of appetite, there were other signs, but she would never share any of that with the children.

"Enough questions." Rafe rescued her. "The most important thing for you to know is that every baby born to this family will be loved and cared for."

Lynn walked up to them. "Like you love and care for us?"

"Exactly, Sweet Pea." Rafe picked up their baby girl and set her on his lap.

"Will you play your music for us again?" Clarissa asked. "The flute sounds pretty. I like it best."

"One more song," she agreed, "then the story, and then to bed."

At the chorus of mild groans, Rafe sent them a sharp look. "You don't each want a lump of coal in your stockings, do you?"

"No, Pa," Tucker replied.

Maggie shook her head. "We'll be good."

"Like little angels," Clarissa added.

Angels? No. Alison shared an amused look with Rafe. Their children were far from being angelic, though a good deal of their mischief had diminished the past year. But as children had a tendency to do, they still found a way of stirring up trouble. And yet Alison wouldn't trade one challenging day as their ma for all her earlier meaningless years before coming to Kansas.

The children gathered near, around the low fire crackling in the hearth. She smiled and squeezed Rafe's hand, her heart brimming over with love for her family. Silently she thanked the Lord above that, in His wisdom to give them all the best possible future, He had allowed one hope-filled letter to fall into her hands.

About the Author

....

 PAMELA GRIFFIN is an award-winning author of more than fifty books to date. Three of her romances have been named Book of the Year by the American Christian Fiction Writers organization, and she has won several other readers' choice contests. Once a professional reviewer, twice a paid critiquer, Pamela will always be a writer, which is both a passion and a ministry close to her heart.

Pamela lives with her family in central Texas, where the weather never stays sane for long. Her parents and two sons have given her a great deal of encouragement and support in all areas of her life, including her writing, but it is to God she gives the glory for where she is today.

Want a peek into local American life—past and present?
The *Love Finds You*™ series published by Summerside Press
features real towns and combines travel, romance,
and faith in one irresistible package!

The novels in the series—uniquely titled after American towns with romantic or intriguing names—inspire romance and fun. Each fictional story draws on the compelling history or the unique character of a real place. Stories center on romances kindled in small towns, old loves lost and found again on the high plains, and new loves discovered at exciting vacation getaways. Summerside Press plans to publish at least one novel set in each of the fifty states. Be sure to catch them all!

Now Available

Love Finds You in Miracle, Kentucky
by Andrea Boeshaar
ISBN: 978-1-934770-37-5

Love Finds You in Snowball, Arkansas
by Sandra D. Bricker
ISBN: 978-1-934770-45-0

Love Finds You in Romeo, Colorado
by Gwen Ford Faulkenberry
ISBN: 978-1-934770-46-7

Love Finds You in Valentine, Nebraska
by Irene Brand
ISBN: 978-1-934770-38-2

Love Finds You in Humble, Texas
by Anita Higman
ISBN: 978-1-934770-61-0

Love Finds You in Last Chance, California by Miralee Ferrell
ISBN: 978-1-934770-39-9

Love Finds You in Maiden, North Carolina
by Tamela Hancock Murray
ISBN: 978-1-934770-65-8

Love Finds You in Paradise, Pennsylvania
by Loree Lough
ISBN: 978-1-934770-66-5

Love Finds You in Treasure Island, Florida
by Debby Mayne
ISBN: 978-1-934770-80-1

Love Finds You in Liberty, Indiana
by Melanie Dobson
ISBN: 978-1-934770-74-0

Love Finds You in Revenge, Ohio
by Lisa Harris
ISBN: 978-1-934770-81-8

Love Finds You in Poetry, Texas
by Janice Hanna
ISBN: 978-1-935416-16-6

Love Finds You in Sisters, Oregon
by Melody Carlson
ISBN: 978-1-935416-18-0

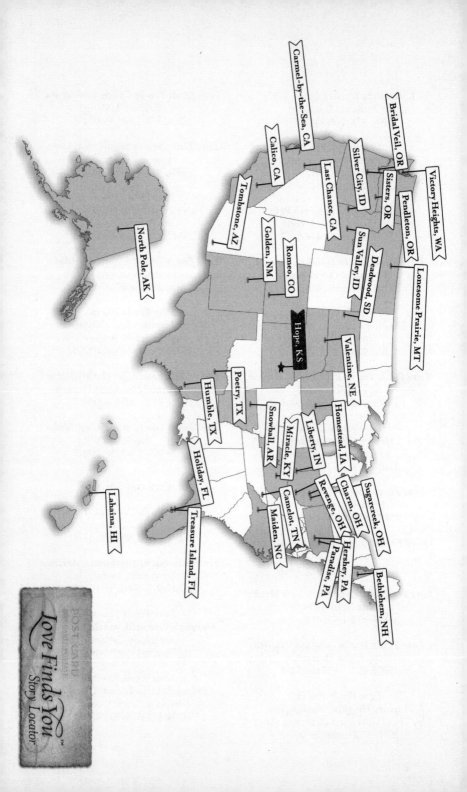